The Forgotten Curse

The Oracle's Odyssey

Book 1

S. T. Hobbs

Book and Cover design by germancreative
Map design by BMR Williams
ISBN: 979-8-9857217-6-8
First Edition: May 2023
10 9 8 7 6 5 4 3 2 1

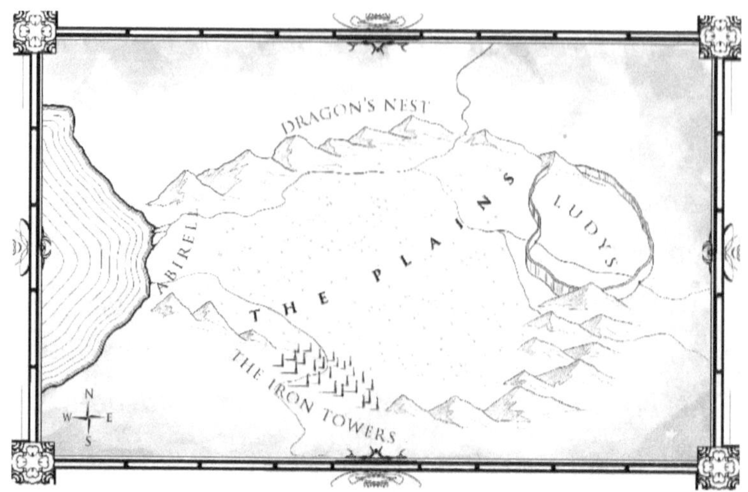
DRAGON'S NEST
ABIREL
THE PLAINS
LUDYS
THE IRON TOWERS
N
W
E
S

Table of Contents

PROLOGUE

IT ALWAYS ENDS IN FIRE.

In smoke.

In ash and cinders.

In death.

No matter how many times it plays out. No matter how many roads I take to get to it. The end never changes. And it always ends in fire.

CHAPTER 1

MY BODY BOUNCED AND jostled in rhythm with my captor's jog. Each jolt drove his shoulder into my gut and knocked my face against his back as he carried me, slung over him like a sack of grain or an animal carcass. I tried not to dwell too much on that comparison.

With my hands bound behind me and a thick, not entirely clean cloth tied through my mouth, there was little I could do to change my present circumstances. I was quite certain that the man burdened with carrying me could feel the wild cadence of my heart as it thumped against my ribs but there wasn't much I could do about that either. It does no good telling your heart you're not terrified when every other part of your body and mind says you are.

From my position upside down, there was little I could see aside from the tall grass closing in around my captor and I as we rushed through. It stood higher than a man's head. Each blade was thick and sharp, biting into the bare, exposed skin of my arms as the grass sprung back into place after being so rudely pushed aside.

Although I could not catch sight of them - thanks to my position, the darkness of night, and the grass that acted like a wispy curtain between us - I could hear others running alongside us. Their feet pounded into the ground, breaking the serenity that usually hung over the plains at night. Their heavy breathing shattered the stillness.

A pain, deep in the very center of my head, began to swell and I groaned into my gag. Of all the inconvenient times to come, this had to be the worst. A conversation between the man who carried me and the one running beside us distracted me briefly from that wedge of pain that threatened to slice my head in two.

"You're sure he's the right one?"

"If you ask me again..." I tried not to jerk in surprise at the sound of that voice. It was a girl's, not a man's. And not just any girl's. I knew this one. She was about my age or a year or two older at most.

"Alright, alright. No need for that, Rensi."

I didn't know her by that name. Or by any name, for that matter. She'd just wandered into our tribe's village a few days before. I'd seen her then, her light brown hair loose and tangled, dirt smudged all over her thin face. She looked every bit the destitute survivor she said she was. She'd spun a sorrowful tale that day when she arrived, convincing everyone, myself included, that she was the only survivor of another traveling village and that she had no other place to go. A story that, apparently, wasn't quite accurate.

"And he's really an oracle?"

As if in response to that word, the pain inside my head exploded, driving away every thought and sense, tearing reality into dust. In its place was the vision - the same one I'd had for years. A walled city. A mountain spewing fire. Voices screaming. A thunderous roar shaking the ground. Heat sizzling the air, scorching everything in its path. Fire. Fire. And more fire. Pouring from the sides of the mountain onto the walled city in liquid rivers of molten rock and flame, spreading into the vast plains beyond. Devouring and consuming until there was nothing left but black, charred earth. And then came the silence. Unlike anything I'd ever heard. The silence of an entire world robbed of breath and life. Not even a wisp of wind stirring that silence.

The end.

No voice ever spoke those words and yet they were as integral a part of the vision as the inferno that rushed over the world. No voice needed to utter those words. They simply were. The end. The end of our world. The end of our lives. The end of everything.

A shudder tore through me, ending the vision's hold but not the pain in my head. The pain was part of what brought me back, niggling its way through the haze that always lingered after a vision ceased. I'd grown to hate that pain over the fourteen years of my life almost as much as I hated the visions themselves. It clung to me for hours, sometimes days, sapping what strength the vision hadn't already taken from me. Because the visions always took my strength. Almost as if stealing my strength was what gave them their own life.

By the time I'd fought my way through the pain enough to be aware once more of my surroundings, I was no longer hanging upside down over some man's shoulder, flopping like a dying fish. Stars blinked their silvery lights above my head. Firm, lumpy ground dug into my back. And cold water crashed over my face.

I came up spluttering only to fall back down on the ground again. The gag in my mouth prevented the torrent of words I wanted to yell at whoever had the brilliant idea of half drowning me.

"Oh, good. He's awake." Rensi's voice was loud in the quiet of the night.

"Anyone would be after that."

I recognized the voice of the man who'd carried me. He'd been the one to order my silence when they'd first roused me from sleep to take me.

Forcing my eyes to open again despite the droplets of water that still clung to my face, I stared up to find both bending over me, peering down at me as if I were some rare curiosity they'd uncovered. I suppose, in a sense, that I was. I tried to glare, to push some anger into my gaze to overpower the overwhelming fear that clutched my insides just then. I can only imagine that the result was less than what I hoped for because the man whose face dominated my view broke into a broad grin and Rensi laughed outright.

"You saw something, didn't you? What did you see?" Rensi asked when her fit of laughter at my expense came to an end. She seemed to forget the gag that currently prevented anything but garbled sounds from escaping my mouth. Besides, I hardly desired to share such information with the people who'd swept into our village and dragged me out of it as a captive.

"Enough, Ren. Leave us."

This was a new voice, one that carried the authority of a chieftain. I wondered what periapt he carried. No chieftain ruled without one. It was the source of their power, their authority over their people. The tokens were said to have come from the dragons - great reptilian beasts that used to soar above the world and nest in the high mountains that cradled the plains and supposedly left behind a number of relics that lent power to those who carried them. Since no one had seen such a creature in over five hundred years, the story was little more than a myth. Still, the periapts came from somewhere and there was no denying the power they contained.

There was a shifting of bodies around me as Rensi ducked away, a pout forming on her lips before she was out of sight. Another took her place in standing over me, staring down as I lay bound and helpless on the hard earth. The darkness that still surrounded us made it difficult to see much of their faces and when a torch was handed to one of them, its bright light blinded me further. They, on the other hand, were free to study me at leisure. That knowledge made me squirm, trying to shift away from the dancing flames. The effort did me little good.

"Is he the one?"

"So she says, Drakkus."

"And none followed you here?"

"None."

Something wilted inside of me at their words. Escaping as I was now, tied hand and foot, was impossible. The only faint hope I had allowed myself during the interminable run to this spot was that someone in my village had seen what had happened and roused the others to the chase. I should have known that was not the case. The two who'd slipped inside the yurt I called home had done so without a sound. Their surprise was complete. And now, so was their escape.

The noise that slipped past my gag was unintended and sounded terribly like a frightened whimper. Not the sort of noise I wanted my captors to hear from me, but it was out, and it drew their attention fully back to me.

"You understand what we're saying, don't you?" Drakkus said.

His face was still concealed from me behind the bright light of the torch, and I was still gagged and incapable of uttering any comprehensible speech, but I did manage to nod my head. The action reminded me of the remains of the headache that still held onto me. It was easy to forget the pain in the flood of fear that filled me.

The torch was pulled away and a man stepped past its light, giving me my first good view of my captors. From my vantage point of lying flat on the ground, he was a giant of a man. A brown beard was braided like a rope halfway down his thick chest. Colored strips of leather were woven into the braid. Above that beard, only a portion of his face was visible. Although his skin had the same leathery quality of all the men I knew, there were wrinkles that softened it around his brown eyes, implying by their presence that he was quick to smile or laugh. Try as I might, and I really did try hard, I could see nothing cruel or malicious in his gaze.

Before I was finished with my inspection of him, he reached behind my head and loosened the knot that held my gag in place. The cloth pulled away with his hand and for the first time in several hours, my mouth was free. I did the most sensible and courageous thing I could think of.

I screamed.

Whether there was anyone near enough to care and respond to my scream for help, I didn't know. But that lack of knowledge was not a deterrent.

A booted heel driven into my stomach, however, was. It turned my yell for help into a silent gasp of pain. Unwanted tears stung the corners of my eyes, and I blinked up to find the same man who had released my gag looking down at me, his head cocked to one side and, judging by the way the wrinkles around one eye scrunched up, smiling in a way that made me realize just what a terrible choice I'd just made was.

"That was," he said, pausing as if to put together the right words, "not smart."

That was probably the kindest thing he could say. There were a host of other words that paraded through my mind that he might have used - foolish, idiotic, useless. Painful. The last word came to me as the full force of the foot stomping on my stomach came over me. I rolled to my side, curling my knees up to my chest in a futile effort to protect against the pain that was already swelling through my center. A fit of coughing shook my entire body as breath finally returned to my lungs.

"Let's not do it again," he continued, ignoring my coughing. I recognized his voice now. The man was Drakkus and by the weight of his words it was easy to guess that he was the chieftain. "There's no one around to hear you anyway but if you insist on making a ruckus like that, I'll put the gag back in just to spare our ears. Understand, boy?"

I lay there, still and silent, working too hard to get my breath back to answer him.

"We've no plans to harm you," Drakkus said.

The most I could manage was another nod to show him I understood his words and even that was a feeble effort due to the pain that still held onto my head. It must have sufficed, though, because the man pushed himself back up onto his feet after untying the leather bands that held my legs together.

Blood rushed tingling through my newly freed limbs, setting off a million needles of pain just beneath my skin. I hadn't realized before how numb my legs had grown in the hours since I was taken.

"Get up. We've a long way to go before the sun rises."

Hands tugged at my arms, dragging me upwards. The world righted itself in front of my eyes but the ground beneath my feet had all the steadfastness of the sea's surface. My legs tried to escape their use by folding up beneath me at the slightest hint of my weight. If it had not been for the hands still holding me, I would have been puddled on the ground within an instant.

My new position and the added light of another two torches allowed me for the first time to see where we were. We had, at some point while I was lost in the throes of my vision, left the tall grass behind us. A river flowed only a little way in front of us, its gentle gurgling a soothing sound to my racing heart. Rocks and grass competed for space on the riverbank, neither winning but both succeeding in creating what was probably a very pretty stretch of river land. Aside from the man standing behind me, holding me up, and Drakkus and Rensi, there were about four or five other men in the group.

Much to my dismay, the river was where the group now headed. I balked at the water's edge.

"I can't swim," I said to anyone who cared to listen.

Drakkus answered me, "You won't need to, boy. Don't make trouble for us now."

Hands shoved me forward and cold water closed around my leg as I took my first step in. It soaked through the leather of my pants and boots and chilled my skin. I gritted my teeth against the cold touch of water through the leather and the added weight the water gave my boots. My mother would have scolded me for traipsing through water with my only pair of boots on.

With guiding hands on my shoulders and my hands still tied behind me, I had no choice but to go along even as each sloshing step I took carried me farther and farther from my home and family and everything that was familiar. A hollow ache settled in my chest and threatened to choke me. I lowered my head to hide the terror that pounded through me.

CHAPTER 2

DRAKKUS SET A RUTHLESS PACE.

My feet were sodden as we continued our trek through the river, staying near enough to its banks that the water only came up to my knees. Even so, each step was harder than the one before. The throbbing in my head prevented me from ever being truly steady on my own feet. The ceaseless weight and pull of the water against me burned through what little strength I had left and the first streaks of gray dawn had not yet made their appearance when my legs trembled threateningly beneath me.

For the last several hours, none of the group had spoken. I jumped a little, then, when Rensi broke the silence with a whispered question in my ear.

"You really did see something back there, didn't you? What's it like having visions?"

Against the quiet backdrop of the river at night, her whisper was harsh and jarring, tearing my focus away from my own exhaustion and fear for just a moment. I mustered enough courage to glare at her briefly before lowering my head once more, not deigning to answer her questions. I wasn't planning on speaking to any of them at all if I could help it. Especially not her.

"You are an oracle, aren't you?" she asked. "What's your name?"

"Enough, Ren," Drakkus said without so much as glancing back at us.

I heard her huff and glanced sideways at her. Her lips were drawn into a pout again, and she crossed her arms over her chest. Remembering the face full of cold water I'd received at her hands, it's no wonder the temptation to stumble a little came over me just then. It wasn't much, just a trip that bumped my shoulder into the back of hers and sent her sprawling face first into the equally cold river water. She landed with a loud splash and came back up spluttering.

"You did that on purpose," Rensi said, as soon as she'd spit out enough water to say anything at all. "Father, he shoved me on purpose."

To my horror, Drakkus was the one she directed her last words at. The man was no longer plowing through the water ahead of us but had stopped and turned to face us. Arms that looked thick enough to snap me in two lay folded across his chest and for one petrifying moment I thought he might do just that. I stood, paralyzed except for my chest that rose and fell rapidly with each panicked breath I took. The moment passed when Drakkus shrugged.

"Stay away from him," he said to Rensi. He turned to me and I felt blood drain from my face as I bit down hard on my own lip. "That makes two mistakes you've made tonight. If I were you, boy, I'd stop before I made a third."

"I didn't mean to," I whispered. "I'm too tired."

The last part, at least, was true. My eyes were blurring with their need for sleep, my limbs quivering from the demands I'd put on them this night. Drakkus looked me up and down, his beard shifting slightly around his mouth as he pulled his lips into a tight line.

"Carry him," he said at last.

I found my world spinning as a man swept me off the ground and slung me over his shoulder. Once again, I was upside down and the only thing I could clearly see was the broad back of my captor.

~ ~ ~

The morning was still a pale, distant promise in the eastern sky when we left the river behind us. I was once more on my own two feet by then, plodding wearily along and silently hoping that Drakkus would not drag me much farther. I knew I ought to have been trying to think of ways to escape, to make my way back home, but a dense, sleepy fog settled over my mind and coherent thoughts scattered before I could latch onto any of them. I tried to imagine what my family was doing just then, if they had discovered my absence yet or not. I tried to imagine Father's reaction to the news of my capture. He'd send men after me. My oldest brother, Jarris, would likely be among those sent.

My head snapped up at the sound of nearby voices. The grass here was only knee high so it was easy to see the round, horse skin yurts of the village up ahead. A line of shaggy, thick boned horses was tethered out in front of the yurts. Few bothered to lift their heads at our approach, too busy chewing down the soft green grass that grew this close to the water. A handful of snorts and soft nickers greeted us as we passed them and entered the village itself.

My own village moved often enough that I recognized at once the preparations that were being made. Men moved between the yurts, taking them down and packing their possessions up inside the horse skins. Three great wagons stood on the far side of the encampment, already harnessed to teams of horses and laden with bundles.

In the very center of the camp, a massive fire burned brightly. And from the great black cauldron that hung over it came the most delicious, mouthwatering aroma I'd ever smelled. Drakkus led us straight to it and, for the first time since I'd been swept away from home, my feet were eager to follow.

"We're only stopping long enough to eat. Then we must press on," Drakkus said as he loosened the bonds that held my wrists and pushed me down onto a log near the fire.

I gritted my teeth against the ache that ripped through my shoulders as I let my arms drop to my sides. Great red welts marked my wrists where the leather thongs had dug in and rubbed, and in one or two places the skin was raw and bloodied. None of that prevented me from taking the steaming bowl that was offered to me. Horse meat and potatoes was a daily fare out here on the plains and I was starving. The first bite was in my mouth before I could stop myself. It seared my tongue and made my eyes water. Red heat flushed my face and Rensi, seated across the fire from me, pointed and laughed. She laughed so hard her own face turned red as she kicked one foot in the air and almost tipped backward off her seat. I wished she would.

Drakkus shared none of his daughter's mirth. After waiting for me to swallow that first, too hot bite, he leaned forward, resting his elbows on his knees and said, "Before I drag you another step, let's have a name, shall we?"

I tried to glare at him, but it was difficult to do with my watering eyes.

He shook his head. "None of that, now. You know my name, it's only fair I know yours."

"Korris," I mumbled at last, not wanting to argue a question of fairness at the moment.

"Korris, is it? Not much of a name for the first oracle born in over three hundred years."

All my resolve melted away then. I swallowed hard before speaking, trying to dislodge the lump that had taken up residence in my throat. "What do you want from me? To tell you your future? Will you take me home again if I do that?"

Drakkus frowned at my questions. "This isn't the first time you've been through this, is it?"

Shaking my head, I tested the temperature of my food again and found it cool enough to eat. I shoved a bite into my mouth before I could say another word. I didn't feel much like describing the other four times I'd found myself dragged away from home and at the mercy of other tribes. Those misadventures had all come to an end the same way - I told them whatever visions I could make up about them, since I had nowhere near the control over what I foresaw that everyone thought I did, and they returned me home before my father had a chance to retaliate. There was one great difference between those times and this, though. My other kidnappers had never taken me so far away. They'd always been too anxious to hear what the future held for them.

"I will take you home," Drakkus said, each word slow and measured, "but not until after our ritual is finished."

"Ritual?" The word sent a shiver down my back and a chill through my veins. I stared at Drakkus' face, trying desperately to read some measure of his intentions there but finding nothing.

"Enough. Eat." Drakkus stood, his demeanor shifting abruptly. "We leave soon."

"Not before you introduce us." A woman stepped across the open ground to stand beside Drakkus. She was almost as tall as he was but moved with the same graceful prowess of the great cats that stalked the plains, the ones who made only as much noise as they wanted when they moved and no more. Her hair was plaited and coiled high on top of her head, leather strips died green and yellow woven all the way through. They were identical to the leather strips in Drakkus' beard. She stared down at me, a half-smile breaking up the otherwise stern lines of her face. "So, this little one is the rumored oracle?"

I bristled at her reference to my size. It was hardly my fault that I'd spent most of my childhood unwell and so had missed the growth spurts that were ordinary for every other child. If anything, that could be blamed on my supposed gift of foresight.

"What is your name, little one?"

Staring down at the ground, I tightened my jaw, refusing to even acknowledge that she'd spoken to me.

"You can either give me a name or I shall be forced to resort to calling you Little One."

"Korris," I said at last.

She laughed and the sound of it was much like Rensi's laugh. "Very well, Korris, I think we shall get along just fine, won't we? You may call me Rayka."

Before I could decide how to respond to this woman who acted as if I wasn't their prisoner and they weren't my captors, Drakkus clapped his hands together. The sound echoed through the now bare encampment and sent everyone moving towards the line of horses and the three wagons. His hand fell on my shoulder, guiding me to one of the horses at the front of the line.

The horse already bore one rider - a boy who appeared to be around my age, although considerably bigger than I was. His face was so like Rayka's that Drakkus' next words came as no surprise.

"You ride with my son, Otho."

Otho looked about as excited at the arrangement as I felt. He looked down from atop his horse, disdain drawing his lips into a sneer. It was the sort of look one might give an insect right before they squash it. Drakkus gave neither of us time to question his command. His meaty hands closed around my waist and hoisted me up behind Otho. Pulling a familiar leather thong out of his pocket, he bade me wrap my arms around Otho and then tied them together at the wrists once more.

Riding double on a horse is never fun. Riding double with a complete stranger, even less so. But riding double with someone who makes no effort to hide how little they think of you is downright miserable. Pressed against Otho's back thanks to my bound hands, I could not even see what was in front of us as the tribe's caravan began moving. The saddle, barely big enough for Otho, pinched my thighs with every step the horse took. And Otho pinched my arm every time I tried to shift.

Despite that, we hadn't gone far at all before my exhaustion took over. Secured as I was, there was no danger of me falling off, at least not without pulling Otho down with me and I didn't mind that prospect enough to try to avoid it. Nor was there much Otho could do to keep me awake once my eyes began to fall shut. Either he realized this and stopped tormenting my arms or I was too deeply asleep to feel or care.

~ ~ ~

The glow of the setting sun burned against my shut eyes, slowly drawing me out of the heavy sleep I'd enjoyed for the last several hours. A lack of movement from the horse finished the job and I forced my eyes open. My face was smashed against Otho's back, a thin trickle of drool discoloring his leather jerkin. Any other time, I might have been embarrassed to have fallen so heavily asleep as to drool. However, it served Otho right and I couldn't say honestly that it didn't bring a small smile to my face. By the look in his eyes as Drakkus pulled me down a few moments later, Otho didn't quite find the same level of amusement in the situation as I did.

Drakkus did not appear to notice anything amiss between the two of us. He held the now loose leather thong in his hands and crouched down until he was eye level with me.

"You've no chance of making it back to your home if you run," he said.

I nodded my understanding.

"So, it would be a fool thing to try it."

I nodded again.

"We're close to no other villages. The rest are all moving south, following the herds."

"Why aren't you?" The words leaped out of my mouth before I could stop them. No chieftain would lead his people away from the migrating herds of deer and horses. They were our greatest source of food and clothing in the plains.

Drakkus smiled a little in a tired sort of way. "That's not for you to worry about. What I need from you is your word that you'll not try to take off on me. I've given you mine that I'll take you home just as soon as we're done with you."

Fantasies of stealing one of the horses and galloping off into the sunset dissipated into cold reality. Drakkus was right. Many hours of hard riding separated me from any hope of help and with each passing hour that distance grew. Every other tribe in the plains would be steadily moving south as winter approached. Still, childish dreams die hard.

"What if I don't want to promise that?"

"Then I'll be forced to tie you up like a prisoner."

"Isn't that what I am?" I said, scowling at the ground.

"Of course not. You're our guest - so long as you behave yourself."

I smothered the response I wanted to say and instead made one final plea. "You're sure you don't just want me to tell you your future and then you can take me home again? Then my father won't come after me."

"Father?" Drakkus tilted his head to one side and stroked his braided beard. "Rensi said you lived alone with an old woman."

I bit down on my lip hard enough to hurt. He didn't know. Rensi didn't know. I couldn't help the little thrill of exaltation that ran through me just then. Of course, Rensi didn't know. The few days she'd spent spying on our village just happened to be days when I'd been recovering from a particularly nasty bout of visions. My father hated seeing me when I was so sick and tired and always packed me off to our elder's yurt until I was recovered. That was the only place Rensi would have seen me.

My face must have betrayed my elation at having unintentionally outsmarted Rensi. Drakkus studied me hard, his eyes narrowing in a way that wasn't pleasant.

"Just who is your father, Kor?"

"Korris," I corrected under my breath. It was bad enough these people had snatched me away from my life. I didn't want them butchering my name on top of that. "He's no one important. But he'll want me back. He's rather fond of having the first oracle born in over three hundred years as his son."

Suspicion tightened Drakkus' lips into a thin, hard line but he nodded, pressing me no further on the matter. Whether he guessed the truth or not, it was impossible to tell.

"Do I have your promise, Kor?"

"It's Korris," I mumbled. "I won't run. As long as you keep your word, I'll keep mine."

CHAPTER 3

"WHAT DID YOU SEE?" Rensi scooted closer on the log we shared; her hands clasped together so tightly that her fingers were turning white.

A fire burned in front of me, and Rensi and I were joined by several others who gathered around its warmth. I glanced up at them long enough to know that they were three of the men who'd accompanied Rensi on the night of my capture. All three wore the same yellow and green strips of leather either braided into their beards or into their hair, marking them as part of Drakkus' tribe. Although they watched me, it wasn't in a way that made me think they were guarding me. More out of curiosity – the same curiosity that made Rensi ask her questions.

My own hands were busy gripping my pounding head. I had made it a whole two days with my hosts before succumbing to a vision. I'd felt it coming for hours in the knot of pain deep in the center of my head before it tore through me, ripping reality away and replacing it with the future. At least it wasn't the vision of fire and destruction and doom that I'd had ever since I was four or five. Although, it was no less morbid and far more personal.

"Was it something about us? Did you see anyone you knew in it?"

"I won't make you answer her, but since it's no secret that you have the gift of foresight, there doesn't seem to be much point in ignoring her questions," Drakkus said from where he sat a few feet away, observing me carefully. If he had been anyone but the man responsible for holding me hostage against my will, I might have mistaken his expression for concern. Clearly, they hadn't realized the heavy physical toll each vision took from me.

"Come on, Kor, just tell me," Rensi said.

"Korris," I corrected automatically. Lifting my head out of my hands, I turned to face her. "It was about you."

Rensi's eyes fairly danced with delight. She clapped her hands together. It was hard to believe, watching her, that she was at least as old as I was. "What was it? Did I do something important? Something heroic?"

I nodded, keeping my eyes on her face.

"Tell me."

"You were," I paused, running my tongue over my lips to give myself time to think, "you were running. And there was a cat, a monstrous cat, all black with golden eyes - unlike any cat I've ever seen. It was as tall as a man, its paws bigger than your head. It was hunting you." I leaned toward her, lowering my voice as I continued, "And you were running as fast as you could to get away from it, but you couldn't. It got closer and closer and closer. And then it was right behind you and it opened its giant mouth," I spread my hands apart in front of her face, "and *BAM*." I brought them together again. Rensi squealed and jumped back. "It gobbled you up in just one single bite. And you were never seen again."

Rensi smacked my chest, pushing me away from her as those gathered around us fell into laughter. Even Drakkus was chuckling, shaking his head. And that was exactly what I wanted. As long as they were laughing about some made up tale they wouldn't be asking me about what I really foresaw. I sat back, watching them, trying to come up with a smile of my own. It was difficult to do when my real vision had my insides in knots.

I had to get away.

My promise to Drakkus meant nothing in light of what I'd witnessed. I had to get back to my family. My mind whirled with ideas - half-baked plots to escape that I tossed aside almost as quickly as they came to me. The pain in my head made thinking tedious and tiresome. I couldn't wait until whatever ritual Drakkus wanted me for. I couldn't wait patiently for someone else to deliver me home safely.

Because I'd just seen my family's deaths.

Even without the hold of a vision, the scene replayed itself in my mind. Mounted warriors sweeping down from the southern mountains crushing all before them in an avalanche of crimson and black. The tribes of the plains decimated. And unlike any other vision I'd had, this one had taken the time to show me how each and every member of my family fell to the sword and spear. My father, my mother, my two older brothers, even my younger sister. I'd seen their faces in their last moments - all their pain, all their terror, all their despair. I'd watched the life fade out of each of their eyes.

As the laughter petered out around me, I clenched my jaw and kept my eyes lowered, avoiding any more attention.

"I still say he's not real," Otho said after the moment of humor had passed. "If he is, then he'd tell us what he just saw and not some made up story."

So much for avoiding attention. Every eye shifted to me and I could sense the unspoken expectation that hovered in the air around us. My fingers curled into fists that I pressed into my lap. Heat flared in my chest and my breath came hard. I hated this. I hated being something different. I hated that it made everyone think they had a right to pick and pry me apart as if I were nothing more than my supposed gift.

"What do you say, Kor? Care to prove my son wrong?"

"It's Korris. And Rensi can prove him wrong. She's the one who spied on me for days."

Drakkus smiled but it was thinner than usual, a hint of frustration lurking in his brown eyes. I stared down at my feet again. I ought to give them something, I knew. Something to make them believe me. But also something to distract them, to convince them that I was willingly playing along with whatever game Drakkus was playing.

"I foresaw my sister's birth before my mother was even with child," I said. "And I foresaw the starving winter."

A hush fell over those gathered around. There wasn't a tribe in the plains that had not felt the effects of the starving winter - a winter two years ago that was so brutal, so long, that it wiped out not only half of the people who lived in the plains but also great numbers of the herds that we followed and hunted. I had only barely survived that winter myself.

"But what did you see just now? Or the other night when we took you?" Rensi asked, her eyes wide with curiosity.

"These visions, they leave you in pain?" Rayka asked quietly before I was forced to come up with an answer to Rensi's questions. Her eyes were intent on me, reading the things I would not put into words, reading me.

"Yes. Some. Mostly just my head."

"Then we are poor hosts to make you humor us under such conditions."

Rayka rose from her seat beside Drakkus and circled the fire to come to my side. I allowed her to help me up and guide me away from the fire and towards the bedrolls that were already unpacked and laid out. Since we stayed no more than one night in the same place, the yurts had remained packed away in the wagons.

"You must think very badly of us, Korris," Rayka said when we were beyond their hearing.

I hung my head, unwilling to say just how badly I thought of them.

"It's alright. I cannot blame you. I cannot imagine having Otho or Rensi taken from me as we have taken you from your family. It is not right." For one moment, I thought she might offer to help me escape. My hopes were cruelly dashed in the next. "But it is necessary. I promise you it is. Drakkus has... There is no other way, child. You will see your family again, though. I will make Drakkus keep his word to you. Help us and I will see it done."

"What is it, exactly, that he needs me for? He doesn't ask me to tell him his future like everyone else does. What is it he wants?"

Rayka stared off into the darkness, chewing on her lip. When she spoke again, she did not turn to face me but continued to gaze at the vast nothingness of the plains that surrounded us. "That's because Drakkus doesn't need you to tell him his future. He needs you to change it."

"I can't do that," I said, raising my voice and then dropping back to a whisper when I remembered the others sitting not that far from us. "I can't even control what I see, when I see it. How am I supposed to change anything?"

"There is a ritual..."

"So he said. But what is it?"

Rayka closed her eyes and drew in a heavy breath. "It does no one any good to tell you now. Just know that Drakkus means you no harm. You must trust him."

As if I could trust the man currently hauling me north across the plains into the approaching teeth of winter. As if I could trust the man who stole me away from everyone I loved. As if I could trust the man who would keep me from my family even as they faced a brutal death.

I turned away from Rayka then and stumbled to a bedroll, hot tears burning in my eyes as I thought of the last expression I'd witnessed on my little sister, Ahashi's, face right before a spear impaled her. Ahashi, who would pick wildflowers and tuck them under my pillow when I was too weak to get up, who could light up any space with her smile. She was stupefied with terror in that final moment as a horseman in crimson and black, his face concealed by his helm, rode her down and buried his spear in her small chest. As if she were nothing but vermin to be exterminated and tossed aside.

Curled up on the cold, hard ground, I pulled the thick animal fur blanket over my head so that no one could see my face as I tried to empty my mind of the images I'd just seen. I needed them gone if I was to think of an escape. And I needed my headache to disappear. As it was, it had only grown worse since the vision passed and that usually meant that there were more coming. More than one that close together could leave me incapacitated for days. I idly wondered if Drakkus had any idea just how much trouble I could be in such a state.

I doubted it.

~ ~ ~

Fire.

Blood.

Smoke.

Ash.

Death.

A spasm ran through me as the vision loosened its hold on my mind. Already it was a murky memory, punctuated only by a handful of words. A mountain of fire. A sea of blood. A cloud of smoke. A rain of ash. And everywhere the smell of death.

I sighed as I opened my eyes to a night that shared no likeness with the pictures that filled my mind. Clouds meandered across the sky blotting out chunks of stars at a time. A soft wind brushed against my cheek, sending a chill over me. Winter was coming. The air tasted of rain and cold. And I needed to get south to my family before it arrived.

With a twist of my head, I could see Otho lying to the right of me. Rensi was on my left. Both were wrapped tightly in their furs and their breathing was deep and even. Beyond them, although I could not see without sitting up, I knew Drakkus and Rayka were similarly asleep. The other family groups in the tribe were far enough away that I didn't worry about waking them if I tried to rise. It was just the four around me that I had to be careful around.

Propping myself up on my elbow was as much as I could manage. Pain shot through my head and made it spin with just that tiny movement. My body felt as heavy and drained as if I'd spent the last two hours running instead of sleeping, each muscle aching as I tried to move.

I needed to rest. I needed to rebuild my strength. Two visions in less than a day was more than I could manage.

But I needed to get to my family. If I could just catch up to them before they reached the southern mountains, then maybe, just maybe, I could warn them and prevent the awful fates I'd witnessed. I wasn't sure if futures could be changed, but for them I would try. I would do everything in my power to alter their fate.

Gritting my teeth against the pain and exhaustion that tugged me down, I crept out from under the warmth of the furs and stole across the ground to the tethered horses. The dying embers of the evening's fires glowed, giving off just enough light for me to see where I was going. Most of the horses were dozing on their feet, too sleepy eyed to pay me much attention as I came up to them. They were passive creatures, every one of them, used to the slow monotony of traveling the plains from one end to the other time and again, in no real hurry to be anywhere. I singled out Otho's horse as the best candidate for an escape only because I'd spent the last three days riding him and hoped that would make him docile and obedient for me.

He stood quietly as I settled the saddle on his back and pulled the girth as tight as I could manage. It probably wasn't anywhere near tight enough, but my arms were shaking after just doing that and I had to somehow still pull myself up onto his back.

I was so engrossed in untangling the bridle that I didn't hear the soft crunch of dried grass being trodden down behind me.

A heavy hand came down on my shoulder.

I yelped.

"So, this is how much your word means?"

A tremor ran through me as I spun around and faced Drakkus. Any kindness I might have seen in his eyes before was gone now, replaced with cold anger.

It was terrifying.

CHAPTER 4

ORANGE EMBERS FLARED TO life as Rensi poked at the dying fire with a stick. I stared and stared at the sparks that flew up and away, dancing out of sight as they took to the wind. How I wished I could do the same.

The weight of Drakkus' hand on my wrist held me in place. I'd fought him dragging me over here and a swollen, bloody lip was all it had gotten me. He hadn't even tried to hit me. I'd just collided with his hand in my desperate struggle.

No one gathered would meet my eyes. Otho stood just at the edge of the fire's light, arms crossed over his chest, glaring at the dirt beneath his feet. Though he clearly shared his father's anger at my behavior, I wasn't sure why. He hadn't seemed that thrilled to have me around in the first place. Rensi paid the fire more attention than anything else. I turned to Rayka, but she was watching her husband, a tight frown on her face. They might have all still been asleep if I hadn't made so much noise being dragged back.

"You don't understand," I said, twisting around to see Drakkus' face. "I saw them die. I saw all of them die and I have to get back to them. I have to warn them before they reach the mountains."

Drakkus winced at my words and the sigh he released was heavy with regret. "I'm sorry, Kor..."

"Please, just let me go. You can take me again after I warn them. I'll do whatever it is you want then; you won't even have to force me." I was begging shamelessly but I didn't care. I'd seen the leather and metal band with its strange and ancient engravings in Drakkus' hand. And I knew what Drakkus planned on doing next. "Please, Drakkus. I can't just let them die."

He wavered. I know he did. I could see it in his eyes, in the way his shoulders slumped forward just a fraction. I could feel his resolve weakening in his loosening hold on my wrist. Then his hand fell away altogether, and I knew I'd won. A long, quivering breath escaped me at the realization. Now all that remained was for me to ride south as fast as a horse could carry me and then...

"I'm sorry, Korris," Drakkus said again. His voice was different this time. He had the weight of his chieftain's periapt behind it. In one hand he still held the tethering band, in his other was a knife with an alabaster blade unlike any knife I'd ever seen. So that was his periapt. The source of his authority.

I took a step back from him but the fire was behind me and Rayka and Otho and Rensi. I was sure none of them would help me. My breath was snatched away in horror as Drakkus pricked his own finger with the tip of the blade and smeared the drop of blood that welled out of the wound onto the engravings of the band, murmuring words too softly for me to catch. Another step back and I was practically standing in the fire, shaking my head in a mute and final plea.

He dropped the dagger, snatched my right arm in his hand and closed the band around my wrist before I could fully comprehend what had just happened.

The weight of it was sudden; instant and startling. I let out a cry of shock as it slammed into me, binding me to Drakkus in a way that was subconscious but complete.

The tethering.

Something I'd only ever heard about but never seen done. That was the greatest power periapts yielded to the chieftains who carried them. The ability to bind a person to them. An invisible cord that kept them close and obedient to their will. The strength of the tethering lay solely in the strength of the periapt. Some chieftains had only enough strength to tether a single person to them. Some could compel the tethered one. The strongest chieftains, the warrior chieftains, were said to be able to bind their entire tribes to them, turning them into formidable armies. It was said to stem from the dragons' most innate nature - the desire to hoard all things to themselves.

Not knowing the full strength of Drakkus' periapt, I had no way of knowing exactly what this tethering entailed, whether he could command and control me through it. All I did know was that even the most basic, weakest tethering would prevent me from leaving his side until he released it.

I choked off another cry as the full weight of it sank into me.

My family would die.

My gift was pointless. Useless to save them.

They would die and it was all the fault of the man standing in front of me. A man who, despite what he'd just done to me, looked as if he were the one betrayed.

Drakkus said nothing but his face twisted up as if something inside him hurt and his hand rested on my shoulder in a gesture that I'm sure was meant to be consoling and perhaps a little apologetic.

It didn't matter.

A hot, bitter flame of hatred burned inside me. It stole away all reason and left me empty except for the scorching need to lash out. I shoved his hand away from me; shoved him away, my fists puny against his broad chest. He stepped back more because he wanted to than because I was strong enough to move him.

Clutching the bound wrist with my other hand, I stumbled away. Away from the warmth of the fire and the prying eyes that were feasting on my distress. The darkness swallowed me up, but none gave chase. They knew they didn't need to. The tether let me wander as far as a distant rise in the ground before I felt its painful tug through the band, a heat inside my arm as if it were too close a fire. I sat there - at the very edge of my invisible boundary.

My skin rose up in a million little bumps as the night chill settled over me. I shivered as I drew my knees up to my chest and hugged my arms around me. Trying to push away the despair that hung over me was like trying to claw my own skin off. It wouldn't go away. If anything, it got worse. Coupled with my aching head, a weariness that would take days to recuperate from, and the uncomfortable presence of the tethering band, I think I could have sat there forever if I'd been allowed. I lacked the will to get myself up, surely.

A hand rested on my shoulder, and I flinched, startled that someone had crept up behind me without my knowing it.

"Drakkus should not have done this to you," Rayka said.

They were empty words. Hollow against the weight of the band on my wrist. If he ought not to have put it on me, she ought not to have stayed silent while he did.

She lowered herself onto the ground beside me. Her arm draped over my shoulder and with the slightest pressure she pulled me towards her. I resisted at first, resenting her almost as much as I resented Drakkus. But loneliness was as powerful as my anger, and I wanted the comfort even if it could change nothing about my circumstances. I rested my head against her shoulder, reminded of my own mother.

"This thing you've seen, you know it happens this winter? There is no chance, perhaps, that it is later?"

"I don't know. It's not as if each vision comes with a day and time on it."

"Then this is a most cruel thing we are demanding of you and for that I will always be sorry."

I wasn't sure what was worse just then – the tether Drakkus had put on me or her belated and useless pity.

I lifted my wrist up to her like a dog holding up their wounded paw, begging for help in that single gesture. "Undo it. Please. Whatever it is you need me to do, I'll do it, just as soon as I warn them."

Rayka sucked in a breath, and I knew her next words would do nothing more than disappoint. "I cannot undo it, Korris, although I promise you, I want to. Only Drakkus or one who shares his blood can sever the tether."

"Then they will die. They'll all die, and it will be all your fault." I pulled away from her then and turned so that my back was to her.

Her attempt to comfort me was over. At some point, I noticed her absence and knew she'd returned to the encampment. I didn't budge from my spot. Nor could I sleep despite my fatigue. The hours of a night had never passed more slowly nor had dawn ever seemed such a bleak and lonely thing.

I sat there, staring toward the south, toward my family. Only once more in that long night was there any interruption to my dark thoughts. That was when I heard a horse and rider galloping away from us, its outline barely visible in the darkness. If I hadn't been so wrapped up in my own misery, I might have wondered who it was and where they were fleeing to.

~ ~ ~

Otho came to fetch me in the morning before the sun was even halfway above the eastern horizon. I was still sitting there, my knees drawn up to my chest, hugging myself as if that was enough comfort to drive away the fear and horror.

"Father says you must come and eat before we leave," he said, standing behind me.

So Drakkus' periapt either wasn't strong enough to compel my obedience through the tether or he thought it better not to use it to its full power.

"Didn't you hear me?"

I kept my eyes on the distant south, ignoring Otho's voice.

"I said, you have to come back with me. It's what Father wants," Otho said, his voice raising a pitch and ending in a squeak.

Once more, I ignored him. Out of the corner of my eye, I saw his hands clench into fists and his face grow red.

"If he wants me to come, he can get me himself," I said. I'd hoped to sound just as furious as I felt, but I'd started shivering sometime during the night and my teeth chattered as I spoke, sadly diminishing the effect I wanted.

Otho snorted. "You're just making it harder than it needs to be, you know."

His hands shot forward faster than I could think and shoved me face first into the dirt. It took me only a moment to roll onto my back and face him. He stood over me, his hands on his hips, and I knew there was something more he wanted to say.

"Did you see that I was going to do that before it happened? You didn't. Just like you didn't see that Father would catch you again before you even made it out of our camp. Or that we were going to steal you away in the night. My father's pinning everything on you and I don't think you're even real."

Not bothering to sit up, I just laid my head back and shut my eyes. "Everything," I muttered to myself. My family. My tribe. He was risking all that. For what? What was so important? What was it that could not even wait until I'd had a chance to warn my family of the danger that lay in the south?

"You think he really wants to drag you along like this? You think he really wants to be moving north instead of south? He hates what he has to do and the worst of it is, you're probably not even the one he needs. You can't even see enough of the future to keep yourself out of trouble."

Just to shut him up, I pushed myself up off the ground. My legs wobbled beneath me, and it was nothing more than determination that prevented me from collapsing once more to the ground. The aftermath of both visions so close together was worse than I'd convinced myself. But it was better to walk away now, better to ignore him, better to not tell him that for all the futures I could see there was one I never saw and that was my own.

I was blind to it.

Chapter 5

FROST NIPPED THE AIR, coating the dried grass in a fine layer that sparkled in the bright morning sunlight. Each day, the northern mountains drew closer. What had just been dark smudges against the horizon just two days before was now a sharp, jagged edge that broke the skyline. Even so, I doubted we'd reach them before the first snow fell.

From my seat at the very edge of the encampment, I watched the others prepare the day's first meal and gather up their few belongings that had been unpacked for the night. Aside from Drakkus and his family, I'd spoken to exactly none of the other members of the tribe. They avoided me as much as I avoided them, ignoring my presence as if I was nothing. Although one or two of the men who had helped capture me would sit around the fire each evening with Drakkus and his family, they made no effort to speak to me.

At that moment, I was avoiding even Drakkus and his family. I had been since that night almost a week before when Drakkus tethered me to him.

The crackle and hiss of dry grass and brush burning was tempting. It was cold sitting so far away from the camp's fires. But rather than indulge myself in their warmth, I hugged my arms around myself and blew hot air onto my fingers.

"Come sit by the fire, Korris," Rayka called out to me when she noticed me. She was standing by the largest fire, stirring the steaming contents of their cauldron. When I didn't move or even acknowledge her words, she shook her head and said something to Rensi that sent Rensi darting off to the wagons.

To take my mind off the cold and off of everything else that plagued it, I tried once more to find a weakness in the band on my wrist. It was too snug to slip over my hand, although I had rubbed the heel of my hand raw with trying. There was no visible seam to show where it closed. No clasp or lock that could be undone. I twisted it around and around. The metal woven into it was unlike the heavy iron that was used to form weapons and tools. It was a deep, reddish color and thin, delicate even. Woven in and out of the leather band, it formed an intricate pattern that surely meant something to Drakkus but was indiscernible to me.

Footsteps pounded up to me and I looked up. And frowned. Rensi was jogging toward me, her hair loose and flying behind her, her arms full of something soft and furry. She dumped it at my feet.

"Mother says since you won't come sit by the fire, you might as well bundle up so you don't die of cold."

I looked from her to the fur coat she'd thrown in front of me. My bare arms craved the warmth it promised and, almost as if to convince me to accept, a shiver ran through my body just then.

Rensi bit her lip and tossed a glance over her shoulder at the camp. Dropping to her knees in front of me, she said, "I am sorry about your family, Kor. If I'd known..."

"You what? Wouldn't have told your father about me?"

She didn't need to answer because we both already knew the truth. Drakkus and his entire family were in agreement on the necessity of me being with them. Her eyes darted to the band on my wrist. "He's never done that to anyone before."

"Is that somehow supposed to make me feel better?"

"No. I just... I didn't think he'd actually ever use it. He hates using the periapt. He says a real leader shouldn't have some ancient token doing all the work for him."

"Except when it's most convenient for him." I shifted away from her. "You can take the coat back. I don't want it."

Rensi was chewing on her lip still as she stood up. She didn't take the coat and I wished she had. It would have removed the temptation to accept it. I wasn't accepting anything from these people who thought their token care of me made up for what they were doing.

No one needed to collect me when it was time to go. I'd learned that the second morning after being tethered. They simply began moving away. I could either join them and spare myself the pain or wait until they'd moved far enough away that the invisible tether seared my arm and dragged me after them. Since my headache had only just vanished, I chose the least painful course. I lingered at the edge of the camp until they were mounting up. Then, and only then, did I drag myself over and face the prospect of putting even more distance between myself and my family.

Otho was already on his horse, the beast stamping a hoof and snorting its impatience with our slow start. But before I could pull myself up behind Otho, Drakkus nudged his own horse in between us.

"You're riding with me today."

It was the first he'd spoken to me since that night and my mouth dropped open in stunned confusion before I could catch myself. I clamped it shut again.

"And you will wear this," Rayka said, coming up beside me. In her hand was the coat Rensi had tried to give me. She must have retrieved it from where I'd left it lying on the ground. "You'll die of cold if you persist like this. You've nothing to be gained by this stubbornness."

I can't really explain why, in that moment, her words snapped something inside of me. It had been growing for days - a tension built entirely out of fear and anger and despair.

I snatched the coat from her hands and threw it straight into the fire that was only a few feet away. A gasp escaped Rayka's lips as she stared first at the now burning coat and then at me. She looked hurt, offended, as if the gift of a coat was more than sufficient to make up for my captivity.

"I don't want your coat," I said, or rather, I yelled. Although, at that moment, I didn't realize my voice was raised. "I don't want anything from you. I want to go home, and you won't let me. I want to save my family, and you..."

"That's enough, Kor," Drakkus said, ending my flood of words almost before they really started. There was so much more I wanted to say, but my mouth clamped shut and instead I glared up at Drakkus. "Our agreement still stands. When we are through, I will return you to your home and family."

"My dead family."

Drakkus winced at my words and for a moment I could almost believe that he truly did hate what he was doing. I could almost convince myself that he wasn't as cruel as the band on my wrist proclaimed him. That he really didn't mean for any harm to come to me.

Until I remembered that night and the vision and how I was nothing but a tool in whatever scheme he had planned and how my family's lives meant nothing to him. And that he was going to force me to ride with him today.

He held out his hand, waiting to pull me onto his horse with him. Chest heaving with all the anger I couldn't unleash on him, I didn't budge. He might have had me tethered to him and forced to go along, but that didn't mean I had to willingly cooperate with his every wish.

"Kor, just get on the horse."

I set my jaw, folded my arms across my chest and took a deliberate step back.

Exasperation flitted across his face. His hand slid down to the hilt of the dagger I now knew was his periapt and a moment later the searing pain that usually came if I tried to wander too far from his camp spread through my arm. My face twisted with the pain, but I stood my ground.

"Drakkus, stop. You said you wouldn't," Rayka said from somewhere behind me, her voice satisfyingly horrified.

"Come here, Korris."

This time my feet obeyed against my will, treacherously carrying me toward the man I hated more with every passing moment. I was powerless to stop my own body and with horror I recognized why. He *could* compel through the periapt. Which meant I was even more of a slave to him than I'd thought. The thought made my insides twist. My thoughts scrambled, trying to think of which periapt could be his and just how much more he could do with it.

When I'd reached his horse's side, he leaned over and took me by the arm, pulling me up in front of him on the saddle. It was only when I was seated there, his arms imprisoning me on either side as he picked up his reins, that the pain in my arm dissipated. The hollowness that replaced it was almost worse - like he'd reached inside my soul and taken some piece of me out of it.

"I would prefer not to do that again, Kor."

If that was his attempt to make it better, to make me less furious, then it was futile. If he hoped to guarantee my cooperation through such force, it was in vain. The only thing that helped my mood was seeing the way Rayka looked at Drakkus from where she sat on her own horse. Her disapproval was evident in the tight-lipped frown that lengthened her face, and I was thankful that she, at least, was appalled at what Drakkus had done.

"I'd prefer to not be here," I mumbled.

"Yes, you've made your thoughts quite clear on that matter."

He allowed us to ride in silence for some time, which, although I refused to admit it, I appreciated. It gave me time to recollect the tattered remnants of my thoughts and put them back together, to regain whatever piece of me had been chipped away by that encounter, before facing whatever caused him to want me to ride with him.

~ ~ ~

“What do you know about the last oracle?”

Drakkus’ voice roused me from the sleepy monotony of our horse’s movement. I stiffened, realizing just how close I’d come to falling asleep in the arms of the man I hated more than anyone else. The sun was now high overhead, but its warmth was too distant to be felt. A tiny part of me regretted tossing the fur coat into the fire. I doubted very much I’d be given another opportunity to bundle up against the deepening cold. And every day we traveled took us farther into that cold.

“I asked you a question.”

I shrugged; the motion difficult when pressed against Drakkus’ chest. He sighed and I watched as his left hand relinquished its hold on the reins to his right. He was reaching for his periapt, I knew. As much as I dreaded the pain that would come from it, I kept my mouth shut. Tensing against him, I waited.

No pain ever came, though. Nor did any compelling command to answer his question. Drakkus rubbed his free hand over his face.

“I’m not going to hurt you to get you to answer me,” Drakkus said, clearly understanding why I’d suddenly gone rigid against him. “This conversation is solely for your benefit, not mine.”

"So, you'll only hurt me when it benefits you."

"I didn't say that, did I?"

"Didn't need to," I muttered too quietly for him to hear as I leaned forward to pat the horse's neck. It was really just an excuse to distance myself from him, even if it was only by a few inches.

"Do you know anything at all about the last oracle?" Drakkus tried again.

"He died."

"The last oracle was a woman. And yes, she died. Over three hundred years ago."

Marking the beginning of the Silence - the space of three hundred years without the gift of foresight, leaving humanity blind to their future, to their ends, to their fates. I was the end of the Silence. Or so said my father and our tribe's elder. That was the extent of my knowledge regarding past oracles.

"When did you first have a vision?"

I considered returning to my silence and refusing to answer him, but there was a bit of curiosity that I'd lived with for years and it was difficult to ignore in the face of possible answers. Drakkus knew something about oracles that I did not. That my father did not. I hated being clueless about my own gift.

"Like I said, Kor, this is..."

"I was four, or maybe five. I don't remember exactly."

"Ten years, then. That's how long we've had an oracle," Drakkus said, but quietly as if he was talking to himself now and not me. "Your village hid you well. Rumors around you are not nearly so old."

Because my village took that long to believe that I was anything other than half-mad. If it hadn't been for my father, I'd probably have been thrown out of the village as a weakness they could not tolerate, not worth the extra trouble I caused with my bouts of debilitating headaches. Left to die like others who were maimed or crippled or otherwise deemed useless.

It wasn't until the starving winter. It wasn't until every word I'd spoken about that winter came true. They'd started believing me then. Sometimes, that was worse than when they thought I was a raving madman. They put so much weight, so much trust in my words.

"You cannot go south again," Drakkus said, interrupting my wandering thoughts and sending a jolt through me.

"But my family..."

"Either they will survive this winter, or they will not. It is beyond your power to change that, and I have done all in my power to change it. The rest is up to your family."

"It wouldn't have been if you'd let me go," I said, my voice rising a pitch. I glanced around, wondering if anyone else had noticed. It was then that I realized that Drakkus had guided his horse out well in front of the rest of the tribe, giving us enough distance that there was no risk of our conversation being overheard.

"You can't change the future, Kor, even if you know it."

"But that's what you want me to do. Rayka told me. She said you didn't need to know your future; you needed me to change it." The breath Drakkus sucked in was full of frustration and I braced myself for some outward display of that anger. It never came and I plunged on, happy to spew out some of the anger I'd bottled up. "You don't even care what happens to my family. Otho, Rensi, and Rayka keep saying you hate what you have to do but I don't think you even care. All you care about is how you can use me."

"That is not true," he said. "Just because I did not allow you to run off to your family does not mean I don't care. They will be warned, but not by you."

I tried to twist around enough in the saddle to get a look at his face. "Who will warn them?"

"If you hadn't run off that night, you would have known that I sent one of my men." Drakkus paused a moment, letting his words sink into me, but not giving me enough time to answer him. "You cannot go south ever again, Korris. You need to understand that. The queen of the Iron Towers will not tolerate any gifted in her lands. But she hates the gift of foresight above all others."

"I've gone south every winter of my life and no harm has ever come to me."

"Yes, but that was before anyone knew who you were."

"No one really knows now. The only reason you know is because Rensi spied on us."

"How do you think I knew to send Ren? You're wrong, Kor, people know about you. And that means you are no longer safe."

Laughter bubbled up inside of me, absurd and unhelpful in the moment. My captor telling me I wasn't safe? What sense did that make? What sense did any of this make?

"You don't believe me?"

"Oh, I believe you. This," I held my wrist up so that he could see the band he'd put on it, "proves you're right. I'm not safe. Especially from people who don't care what happens to anyone aside from themselves."

"I'm not your enemy."

"Then let me go." I twisted around again. "You said yourself, I can't change the future. I can't help you."

"Rayka wasn't wrong when she said that. But she also wasn't entirely right. I don't want you to change the future. I need you to undo the past."

"I can't do that," I said again. "And I don't really want to."

Before we could get into a discussion about my wants, Drakkus shifted the conversation back to the past again. "Do you know how the last oracle died?"

I was surrendering to the urge of obstinacy once more. Drakkus must have sensed it in the rigid line of my back as I straightened and pulled away from him. He certainly understood it in my lengthening silence.

"Fentra was killed. Murdered, some stories say. Stabbed to death on some mountainside history's forgotten."

Shocked out of my determination to remain quiet, I uttered one word, "Why?"

I felt Drakkus' shoulders lift and then fall in a shrug. But he knew. I knew he did. He wouldn't have brought up this story now if he didn't know, if there hadn't been something about it that he wanted to tell me.

"There are more stories surrounding her last moments than there are years in between her life and now. But there is one thing every story agrees on. She needed to die."

Ice gripped my heart at his words. It spread through my chest and made each breath harder than the last. It crept over my skin and made me want to jump from his horse and run despite the pain I knew it would cause me.

"You're taking me somewhere to kill me?"

CHAPTER 6

"CAN KOR COME WITH US?" Rensi asked Drakkus, not bothering to ask me if I wanted to go. Nor had she said, at least in my hearing, where it was that she was going.

Drakkus looked me over, his eyes searching my face. I shuffled my feet in the dust, unwilling to meet his gaze. Unwilling to read his face. He hadn't answered my final question. He hadn't denied it. Instead, he had sighed and shifted our conversation abruptly to the topic of what I saw in my visions. And I...

I'd stopped listening to him. Stopped answering him.

"He may, but only if he wants to."

My mouth dropped open at the words. I didn't want any of this. And I certainly didn't want him pretending to care about my wants now.

"Come on, Kor," Rensi said, her voice distant and ringing in my head.

There was an ache there, one I'd been trying to ignore. The sort of ache that heralded the coming of a vision. It was getting worse and there was a heat running through my veins keeping it company. A heat that felt like my blood was boiling and yet none of that heat was shared with the rest of my body. The skin of my bare arms was bluish with the cold, a series of shivers convulsing me every few minutes when my mind remembered that it ought to protest the cold.

Drakkus was still watching me, his eyes still searching me but now he was no longer alone. Rayka stood beside him, her lips pursed. I was sure if I lingered, she would speak. Probably about the coat I'd burned. Perhaps about how useless my stubborn resistance to her care was. Or maybe she would turn on Drakkus and chastise him for his use of the tether and for causing me pain. I might not mind that, but I would definitely mind any of the other things she could talk about.

That decided me. I didn't know where Rensi and Otho were going but it had to be better than staying with Drakkus and Rayka. Wrapping my arms around myself in an effort to block out some of the cold, I followed Rensi through the patches of dried grass.

She moved quickly, inheriting her mother's grace and prowess. With a few more years, she would probably also equal her mother in height. But for now she was all arms and legs that, though they moved gracefully enough, were uncertain of their place when she wasn't moving. I followed her sure footsteps, each one easily seen in the flattened, broken grass. Even now I didn't bother to ask where we were going or why. Partly because it was easy to see where we were headed. A small wood lay a stone's throw from our encampment and Otho was already waiting near the edge of it, bouncing on the balls of his feet as we approached.

"Why'd you bring him?" Otho asked Rensi when we reached him.

In his hand he held a short spear. In his other hand, a short bow. Several arrows stood up in a pouch hanging from his waist. It was easy then to guess their purpose. Hunting was the livelihood of every tribe in the plains, but I wasn't sure what was left to hunt with winter so close.

"Because I wanted to, and Father said I could."

My head was truly beginning to throb, robbing me of the will to say anything on my own behalf. When they started into the woods, I followed without thinking.

"He won't be able to go with us very far," Otho said.

I pushed the pain away far enough to realize what he was talking about. After so many days with it on, the subtle weight of the band and its tethering went mostly unnoticed. But he was right. I wouldn't be able to follow along very far at all.

Rensi didn't seem concerned. She stopped where she was and crouched, dried leaves crunching beneath her as she pressed the palm of her hand against the earth. Otho stopped walking and stood beside her, both unsurprised and unimpressed by whatever she was doing. If my head hadn't been hurting so very badly, I might have been curious. Instead, I was thinking that the carpet of dried leaves and twigs and moss looked like the perfect place to lay down and rest my head.

"Do you feel any?" Otho asked.

Rensi nodded and stood. "Not far."

"Feel any what?" I said, trying to force the presence of my headache away, trying to pretend there wasn't fire scalding my insides at that moment.

The smile on Rensi's face wavered before my eyes. Her mouth moved, but her words never reached me. The gold and red and orange of the leaf coated ground blurred into smears of color that came closer and closer to my eyes. Then the gold and orange and red turned to flames. Hot flames that flickered and grew. Devouring flames that left blackened ash behind. The same vision. The same fire. The same walled city. The same screaming. The only difference was the voice. I'd never heard a voice before. I'd heard many; many screaming, crying, wordless voices. But never *a* voice. A single, coherent, speaking voice. Words I could understand. I'd never understood anything that was said in a vision. I could see. I could hear. Sometimes I could even feel. But never understand.

"Free me," the voice said. It was deep, and high. Soft and loud. A resonating whisper, burrowed in a recess of my mind I hadn't known existed. Ancient and ageless.

The fire around me grew, swelling, to a thunderous roar. I ran from it until I could no longer run. Then I crawled from it, from the voice in my head. This time I could feel the flames, catching on my hand, running down my arm, consuming my flesh, melting it from bones.

The screaming returned, no longer confined to my mind but now flooding my ears, filling what I knew to be reality. Overwhelming the veil between now and later.

Reality.

Present.

What really was, what was really happening.

Time stopped spinning, stopped tugging me into its distant stream. But the screaming continued. So did the burning in my arm.

"Kor, stop moving." Otho's voice reached me from beyond the screaming, from beyond the ragged remains of the future that clung like a drowning man to driftwood at the fringes of my mind. "Just stop moving. You're making it worse."

The words barely filtered through the mindless haze that the pain caused. It wasn't until his hand fell heavy and solid on my shoulder that I realized I was crawling, clawing my way across the leaf covered ground, desperate to escape a fire that burned somewhere in the future. That burned inside of me.

His hand was ice against my skin, quenching the fire that ran beneath it but only in that small spot. It sent a shudder through me. He succeeded in stopping my desperate efforts to escape the burning. And, strangely, that eased some of the burning pain that raced up and down my arm.

"What is wrong with you?"

I tried to speak, to form words with lips that refused to cooperate. Whatever senseless gibberish fell from my mouth, it must have been enough to convince Otho that what was wrong with me was nothing I could control or stop. His hand didn't leave my shoulder, gripping it as if he were afraid I'd evaporate before his eyes. But he didn't press me further for explanations I was in no condition to give.

My ears were ringing. Buzzing with sounds both present and future. I lay, panting, my face pressed against the cold, crisp leaves. Dirt and twigs and bits of dried leaf clung to my sweat slickened cheek. I wasn't moving anymore. Time wasn't moving anymore. Otho stood over me and I imagined Rensi was close. I was gasping, each breath hitching, an ache in my lungs and throat that came from overuse. There was no scorched earth. No flames licking their greedy way up my arm.

Just the woods. The songs of the birds and the chittering of the squirrels picked up exactly where I'd left them off.

New sounds filtered in. Footsteps crunching the dry leaves, approaching faster than a walk but slower than a sprint. And with their approach, the last pain fled my arm and I stared at it as it lay flopped on the ground before my eyes, half expecting to see the terrible, charred remains of my own limb. But it was whole and undamaged, the skin still blue with the cold, still bearing the tethering band.

"What happened?" Drakkus said, dropping to his knees at my side.

His voice sounded too loud, too close. I wanted to cover my ears but my arms had ceased to do my bidding.

"I don't know. We stopped for Ren to track and he just laid down. Said he didn't want to go further." That was news to me. I couldn't remember saying anything, although I did remember trying to speak. "We left him for just a few minutes and by the time we came back he was gone. Ren tracked him, but then he started screaming and it was easy to find him. He was running away from us."

Amazing how much of the present one misses when they're lost in the future. My knowledge of what happened was severely limited to a certain fiery mountain and a walled city I'd never seen and a voice in my head that I'd never heard.

Otho's account of the last few minutes was quite different from mine. If, indeed, it was only a few minutes. The exhaustion that crept over me made me think that more time had passed than that.

I was no longer on my stomach with my face pressed against the ground but I didn't remember rolling myself over. Squinting against the sunlight that poured easily through the mostly barren trees, my eyes burned and I was sure if I could see myself in a looking glass I would have found them shot through with red. Everything burned, actually. As if the fire from the vision had just become trapped inside me rather than returning to where it belonged in the future.

Drakkus, Otho, and Rensi were all staring down at me. Their expressions ranged wildly for just three people. Drakkus managed to cram concern, frustration, guilt, and resignation all onto his face, making it quite uncomfortable to stare at.

Rensi was just a mixture of worry and curiosity.

Even Otho succeeded in conjuring up some fleeting anxiety on my behalf. Very fleeting. It was gone almost before I noticed its presence, replaced with irritation. Why he was irritated, I couldn't guess. He wasn't the one whose entire body now ached with phantom pains of events yet to take place.

Suddenly hating the spectacle I was giving them, I pushed an elbow up beneath me and tried to rise. Tried. Because the motion set off a dizziness that made everything blur together and made me wonder what was up and what was down.

Strong hands closed around my shoulders, pulling me up and holding me steady. I'd shut my eyes again in the desperate hope that it might still the spinning trees but even with them shut I knew it was Drakkus that held me up. I was regaining enough of my senses to know I didn't want his help even if I couldn't quite recall why in that moment. Pulling away from his grasp, my legs decided they were no longer capable of bearing my weight. My side met the ground with a crunch.

It was in that moment, much to my humiliation, that I realized the dampness on my face was not entirely sweat but also tears.

I'd cried.

At some point during my vision or coming out of it. Probably when it felt as if my arm was burning off.

I forced myself up again, willing my legs to remember their purpose. Drakkus sighed in resignation and watched me stagger the first two steps by myself.

That was as far as I got before I started to topple again, my legs trembling beneath me. A tree was conveniently close by for me to clutch but I could hardly use the tree to make it back to camp.

"Just let me help you, Korris," Drakkus said.

I couldn't have stopped him this time. Part of me no longer wanted to. Something was wrong with me. Something about the vision was wrong, about the way it fed into me, making me part of it and not just a witness to it. There was something wrong with the weakness it had left behind in me, the heat inside of me. With his hands on my shoulders, we started forward again.

Chapter 7

MY MIND DRIFTED. THERE was nothing better for it to do. Even the task of putting one foot in front of the other had been taken from me long before we exited the woods. Drakkus allowed me to collapse twice and refuse further assistance; the third time he'd scooped me up in his arms as if I weighed no more than a cat's cub and I couldn't work up the voice or energy to protest.

So, instead, I let my mind drift. That was a dangerous thing. I'd thought it would wander back to the flames, to the voice in the dark, to the destruction that marked the end of the world. It didn't.

It didn't visit any part of the future. Instead, it took me traipsing back into the past. All the way back it went, to days that were little more than a golden haze of pleasantry in my memory. There was comfort in those days, days when I was with my family, protected by them, loved by them. There was an ache in them, too. There was pain in remembering what was and what would likely never be again if my vision of them proved correct. Images of my life floated past my closed eyes, melding gentle warmth with the fire in my veins, turning the throbbing in my head to a distant annoyance.

There was the memory of sitting at my father's knee as the sun went down, Jarris and Missel crowded close with me, listening to the stories my father would tell. He told amazing stories of the days when dragons had flown above us. He told silly stories that had us laughing until our sides ached. Sometimes, he told us sad stories, but I tried not to remember those ones.

There were memories of my mother I visited too. Helping her scrub the great iron pots with sand and water after a meal. Helping her gather berries, usually with little Ahashi following every step of the way. Ahashi and I would eat more berries than we'd collect, but Mother never seemed to mind.

I liked the past. There was nothing I could do about it, nothing to dread about it, no wild plans to change it. It just was. It had already happened. The past was an anchor, of sorts. One I latched onto that day with a fervency born from the strangeness and terror of the future. In a way, nothing bad could linger in the past. When I looked back on any day of my childhood, even the ones that should have been tinged with sorrow or anger or disappointment, there was a brightness to it. I lost myself to that brightness, to that warmth.

Until voices dragged me back into the present.

"What have you done to him now?" That was Rayka's voice, strangely shrill in my ears, making the ringing from earlier return with force, drawing the ache back to the surface.

"Nothing. He's had a vision, I think. And he tried to run past the tether," Drakkus answered her.

"Lay him here. There's more wrong with him than a vision." I felt my body sinking, weightless, to the ground. My helplessness ought to have frightened me, but I think I'd left all my fear behind in that wood, facing the vision and the pain that followed. "Why would he try to run past it?"

The ground was softer than I remembered it being. Warm and soft. It closed around me and for a moment I wondered if this was what it felt like when one is buried after death. I could have fallen into a deep sleep there if it weren't for the voices that kept speaking above me and a pain in my head that was gaining strength again.

"Probably because he's decided that I'm planning on killing him."

"Why would he think that?"

"I told him a bit about Fentra."

"Ah. But you told him you would not, didn't you?"

It's amazing how much more talkative they were when they thought I was beyond comprehending. I almost was. They were almost right. The sleepiness that stole over me now was like a fog, shutting my mind down.

"Why waste breath on words he wouldn't believe anyway? He's made up his mind about it and only proof will change it. I've already promised to take him home when he's through. If he doesn't believe that, he'll not believe anything else I say."

"There has to be a better way. It's just wrong, what we're doing to him."

Listening to Rayka give voice to my own grievance was always satisfying. It was almost enough to rouse me. Almost. The pull of the soft ground was just too tempting. There was something soft and heavy laying over me now, too. Warmth seeped into my skin, joining the heat that already coursed through my veins. It had been such a long time since I'd been warm.

"We're out of time, Rayka. This is it, our one chance to break the curse. I can't take months or weeks or even days trying to convince him to play his part. It happens now or it doesn't happen."

Something icy rested against my forehead. A hand, I realized belatedly.

"I still think there's a better way," Rayka said, her voice lower this time, quieter. She spoke those words to herself, not to Drakkus.

I wasn't sure if he'd walked away after laying me on the ground but Rayka's full attention was turned on me now. I felt her fingers glide over my forehead and down my cheek. They sent a chill through me and I shivered despite the warmth of the earth that wrapped around me.

"You should not have been so stubborn, Korris. You've gone and made yourself ill with the cold," she said, her words chastising but her tone gentle.

Words tried to escape my lips but they were little more than a puff of air, carried away before they could be heard or understood.

"No, don't try to speak, child. Whatever's wrong with you, it's more than a fever and more than just a vision. Perhaps it's the two together bent on taking you down."

That made sense - in a distant, abstract way. Everything was distant and abstract just then. And the ground was so soft and warm.

So soft.

So warm.

~ ~ ~

Those same voices that had kept me awake returned, leaking into troubled, restless dreams. I lacked even the desire to open my eyes to find them. They were near, I knew. And from the sound of their voices, we were no longer out in the open air of the plains but in an enclosed, tight space. That was the extent of my sensory exploration into my surroundings. I was too weary, too sore, too feverish to care more.

"We're out of time waiting. If we don't reach it by the solstice, this is all pointless."

I was annoyed that they insisted on speaking so close to me, disturbing me. There was more annoyance in Drakkus' voice though. I suppose my illness could be counted as good luck if it upset Drakkus' plans. If I could have managed it then, I would have smiled.

"Perhaps if we would just..."

"We have no choice, Rayka. You know that as well as I do. We're out of time. It happens on the solstice, or everything is lost."

All of a sudden, it was work to keep my eyes shut. I wasn't supposed to be hearing this and I could no longer take any pleasure in it. There was something inside me like a little lump of coal, always burning but sometimes, like now, flaring up. The anger I'd felt, not from when Drakkus first took me but from when he tethered me, leaped to life despite my lingering frailty.

"Like you've made me lose everything?" My own voice surprised me, sounding strange in my ears. There was little strength to it, but much conviction. I opened my eyes to find them both sitting there, watching me, somehow not taken aback by my being awake and hearing them.

"I've taken nothing from you yet, Kor, that you had not already lost," he answered me wearily.

Yet.

I heard the unspoken threat. And I puzzled over it. Just like I puzzled over the last bit. He'd taken my family from me, taken my home from me. Taken me from me with his wretched tether and compulsion. I still wasn't convinced that he didn't plan on taking my life from me when this was all over, despite his words to Rayka just then.

For a moment, the three of us just stared at one another - I at Drakkus, Drakkus at me, and Rayka splitting her gaze between the two of us. She shook her head.

Drakkus was the first to make a move. He rose so quickly it made my head spin watching him and then he leaned down, put a hand on my arm and pulled me up as well. My head really did spin then.

"Drakkus, he shouldn't..."

"He'll ride with me. He can rest as he needs to in the saddle, but we cannot waste another day here."

Rayka, to my dismay, argued my case no further. Although she chewed on her lip in that way of hers that I now knew meant she was troubled, she moved around the yurt that had apparently been pitched in my honor. A coat was in her hands when she approached again, but she did not offer it to me like the last one. Instead, while Drakkus held me up and held me still, she put it on me herself. I knew I ought to shrug it off just to prove a point but...

"Don't even think about it," Rayka said, her eyes narrowed, reading my thoughts almost as well as my own mother had been able to. "You could have died from that fever and all just because you're too stubborn to take a good thing when it's handed to you."

I let my head hang at that and gave up thoughts of losing the coat somewhere along the way. It was warm. And comfortable, even if it was made for someone Otho's size and not mine. Now that I was wrapped in its protective warmth, I didn't think I possessed the willpower capable of throwing it off again.

Guided outside the yurt by Drakkus' supporting hands, my eyes blinked at the brightness of sunlight glaring off the snow. It had snowed. White, powdery stuff that coated the ground and glittered with a dazzling intensity in the sun. I'd never stepped in snow. The closest I'd ever been to even seeing it was staring up at the snow and ice capped peaks of the mountains that ringed the northern side of the plains basin. We'd always spent our winters in the warm shadows of the southern mountains.

It crunched beneath the weight of my boots, giving a little before packing firm. Wisps of wind sent swirls of the white stuff skating just above the ground. The entire world around me was transformed by winter's attire. And it was beautiful, in a cold, aching, blinding sort of way. I wondered why we ran from it every year. I mean, on the surface I knew. The herds moved south and the herds were our food. But it seemed a shame to abandon such a magnificent season every year.

"Quite a sight, isn't it?" Rensi said.

I jumped a little in Drakkus' grasp. I hadn't realized she was standing so close. Memories of the woods and what happened there rose to the surface and made me reluctant to say anything at all. They'd seen me cry, they'd seen me scream with pain that wasn't mine and pain that was. They believed I was trying to run away. They'd seen me at my weakest. That grated against all my pride.

A familiar pout formed on Rensi's lips when it became clear that I wasn't going to answer her. Of course, as bundled up as she was against the cold, it was hard to make much of her face out and I could only see she was pouting by the way it pulled the corners of her eyes down and wrinkled her eyebrows together.

"I didn't mean for you to try to run then. Or for you to be hurt. I just thought you'd like to do something other than sit and worry."

So, they all still thought I'd tried to run intentionally. I wondered what I'd done to make them think I was so insane. If I hadn't fought the tether in the two weeks it had been on me, why do it now? It wasn't something you could escape by pulling against it with all your might. I knew that.

"I didn't run," I muttered, unwilling to let the matter rest.

The way Rensi's eyebrows lifted told me she disbelieved me.

"You were running," Otho said, coming up just then, leading his father's horse. "Until you couldn't run anymore. And then you were crawling. As if that was going to help you get away."

"I didn't run," I said again.

Not another word was said about the matter, not because they had nothing to say but because Drakkus released his hold on me to mount his horse and I sank straight down into the cold, wet snow.

"Help him stand, Otho."

The blood that rushed to my face then had very little to do with the cold or my recent bout of fever and far more to do with my wounded pride. I should at least be able to stand on my own.

Between Otho and Drakkus, I found myself settled on the tall, broad back of Drakkus' horse. It was a good thing the animal was as patient and steady as it was. I was hardly a skilled rider in the very best of health; I was abysmal now.

CHAPTER 8

DRAKKUS WANTED TO SPEAK. I could tell by the way he kept drawing in a breath. By the way he held it then let it go with a shake of his head. The horse beneath us swayed from side to side in the rolling, meandering walk that it could maintain all day.

Drakkus wanted to speak, but I didn't want to listen or answer the questions I was almost certain he wished to ask. Mostly, I just wanted to rest and that was difficult to do on the back of a moving horse, pressed against a man I hated, with the sun and snow mingling to make a blinding glare that shone red through my closed eyelids. I tried to hold myself rigid, as far from him as I could get, but my joints and head ached.

Drakkus wanted to speak, but as time passed, I understood that he wasn't going to break the silence until

I did. And as soon as I knew that, a desperate longing to know what it was that he wanted to say filled me. I fought it off just as I fought off the urge to let myself slump against him and fall asleep.

Patience frayed inside me.

I gave in to the urge to rest first, releasing the tension that held my body. Sleep was not long in following nor was it long in staying. The sun's travels across the sky showed that only two or three hours had passed when I awoke again. Still, it was enough to push some life back into me.

In silence, we continued, until the last vestige of my patience had worn away. I cleared my throat once or twice while I tried to think of what I should say.

"How long was I... you know?" That wasn't a dangerous question.

"A week. You were sick for a week."

"Oh." I'd expected a day or two. No wonder he was annoyed. A week lost on the move could throw the very best plans into chaos. The words, "I'm sorry," rose to my lips but I bit them off before they could escape. He didn't deserve an apology. And I didn't owe him one.

"Are you often sick like that after a vision?"

"All the time." Which was a little bit of a lie but one I didn't feel the least bit guilty for. Drakkus would have to rethink his plans if I feigned such illness at every turn.

"But you've had at least three since we took you before this last one, and suffered nothing more than a headache and fatigue."

I wasn't sure how to argue that. He'd seen through my lie and I wasn't ready to admit that I'd tried deception.

I slept again, until the sun was low in the sky, changing the snow from its dazzling white to a fiery orange. Another long silence ensued even after I was awake but I didn't feel the same burden to break this one. Drakkus guided his horse slightly away from the others, drawing us to the side where anything we said would be between just the two of us. The mountains we'd been moving toward for weeks now overshadowed us, less than an hour's ride away.

"Why were you running from the tether?" Drakkus asked. It was the first time he'd spoken openly of the tether and he said the word quietly, as if he were ashamed of it.

"I wasn't running from it."

"Otho and Rensi both say you were, and my children aren't prone to lie."

"I wasn't running from it," I insisted again, my voice quieter than before. I shut my eyes, remembering those minutes or hours in the woods. I still had no idea how much time passed from the start of the vision to when Otho caught up to me. The events of the vision may not have been real yet, but the pain had been. The pain in my arm had been more than real.

"Then what were you running from?" Drakkus pulled the horse to a stop.

"I...," the words bottled up inside me, refusing to be spoken to this man. I wasn't sure I could explain even to my own father and mother. There had been something so wrong, so different about that last vision. It frightened me more than any vision had a right to. And the worst of it was, I couldn't say what, exactly, about it set me so on edge. There was the voice, yes. But two little words shouldn't have reduced me to a screaming, crying child running from unseen monsters.

"What did you see, Kor?"

The horse stamped a hoof against the ground and snorted. Its head dropped suddenly to grab at a mouthful of grass, nearly unseating me. Drakkus dismounted and pulled me down after him. Although my legs wobbled a little, I found I could stand on my own. In the distance beyond him, I could see that the others were stopped as well, building fires and setting up a camp. The flames that leaped to life caused a shiver to crawl up my back.

"Fire," I said, facing him and meeting his eyes for once. I wished I could push those images into his mind like they were burned into mine for no other reason than that I wanted someone else to be forced to bear the same burden of knowledge that I carried. "So much fire. And death."

He waited, saying nothing, although a shadow flitted across his face.

"A mountain burning, running down into a walled city..."

"A walled city? Wedged between two mountains? With ivory walls?"

"Yes," I said. I frowned a little, thinking back to the city. It was wedged between two mountains, blocking any passage between the towering landmarks with the great walls that encompassed the city. I'd never seen it except in my visions but..., "You know it?"

"Ludys. Gate city to the Outlands. I know it. Go on." It was unusually terse for him.

Another shiver had run through me at the mention of the Outlands. If Ludys stood between us and the Outlands, then the implications of my vision were so much worse. The Outlands were full of the monsters' mothers warned their children of at night to encourage their good behavior. They were death and ruin. A part of the world that had broken open and let in all the foulest creatures night and pain and horror could conjure.

The mountains that ringed the plains were our barrier against the horrors that dwelled on the other side, gifts from the Fates some said. There were only four places where the mountains failed in their task.

Four gateways.

Four weaknesses.

One to the south in the lands of the Iron Towers. That was the only one I'd seen in person and it was protected night and day by the best warriors the queen could summon. Another lay in the north, a gap in the mountains guarded by the mountain dwellers who made their homes in the old dragon caves. They had aptly named their settlement Dragon's Nest. A third lay in the west where the mountains gave way to the sea and this was kept by the sea city of Abirell. Ludys was the eastern gateway.

"Go on, Kor," Drakkus said again, drawing me out of my own revelations and back to our conversation. "What else did you see?"

"The fire, it burned everything in its path. The city, the plains, everything. There was nothing left but the ashes. And," I stopped. The voice was new. The words it spoke were new. I wasn't sure if I was ready to share that part yet.

"And?"

"It was different this time."

"You've seen it before?"

I nodded, kicking at the snow until I'd worn away enough for the brown grass to show through. Drakkus' horse appreciated the effort, huffing its gratitude as it stuck its nose into the spot and started tearing up the grass.

"How many times?"

I shrugged. I'd already shared too much. Before Drakkus had taken me, there were only three people I'd ever shared my visions with. My father and mother, and our elder. All the people who'd whisked me out of our encampment in the dead of night had gotten whatever story I could make up, never the truth. Drakkus now had the truth. I could only imagine how that would feature in his plans for me.

Drakkus lowered himself so that we were eye to eye, his knee in the snow. It was the first time I'd really had as much a chance to study him as he had me. Lines of worry showed up easily on his weathered skin. There were three of them right in the middle of his forehead. Shadows darkened the lids beneath his eyes. Weariness and concern made his eyes dull.

"You said this time was different," he said the words slowly, carefully, gauging their effect on my face. "How was it different?"

If I was home, I would have confided in Mother. I would have drawn her into some corner where it was just the two of us and told her everything, seeking a comfort I was fast outgrowing. Here, though, there was no one I trusted enough to tell and no one whose comfort I would stoop to accept.

Drakkus wasn't going to let the matter rest until I'd given him something, though. I could see that in the hard set of his face. He plainly meant to wait me out if I chose to be stubborn about it. I tossed around the idea of lying but dismissed it rather quickly. Drakkus would see through it.

And so, I tried something different. Swallowing hard, I said, "I don't really want to tell you."

He let out a heavy breath through his nose and looked past me, out into the plains where dusk was playing tricks with the dying light of the sun. I watched as his left hand dropped to the dagger at his side, coming to rest lightly on its hilt. His thoughts were out of reach for me, hidden behind dark eyes that stared at nothing.

"Are you going to hurt me to get your answer?"

My words made him shift his gaze back to my face, a troubled frown adding another line or two across his brow. He didn't answer right away. I think it was because he himself didn't know his answer. He wanted what I had to say, I could see it on his face. He was disappointed that I chose not to disclose anything further. And the fact that his hand had wandered to the periapt revealed his temptation to use it.

He wanted what I had to say, and I stood there, watching him battle his own desire, and growing more fearful with every silent moment that passed. If he used it, if he woke that pain that I'd felt back in the woods, I would speak. I knew I would. I was, after all, only fourteen and that pain had been like no other I'd ever felt. My courage faltered just at the thought of it, and it made my heart race with sick anticipation.

He lifted his hand from the dagger, and I let out a shuddering breath. "I'm not going to hurt you to get you to answer me, Kor," he repeated the same words he'd said earlier, although there was a strain in his tone that hadn't existed before. "No matter how much I want that answer."

And I believed him.

It didn't make sense to believe him, but I did. Perhaps because I'd watched him wrestle with his answer before he gave it. Perhaps because he removed his hand from the periapt. Perhaps just because I was so weak and tired still from my illness and loneliness was dogging my steps, wearing down my distrust. I didn't know why, but I did believe him. And I knew that, if he'd answered me at once, without a thought, I would not have.

For another moment swollen with tension, his eyes left my face and went instead to the band on my wrist. Wild hope sprung up inside me then, for I could see his own doubts about the tether. His own guilt. If it was strange that I believed his earlier words, it was even stranger when I believed, in that moment, that he really did hate the thing and hated that he had to use it.

I drew a soft breath and held it in, not willing to disturb the moment and destroy my chances. If he took it off, I would be gone. Running south for the family he'd forced me to give up on. Standing here, right next to his horse and separated from the others, it would be the best chance I had, and I would take it, even if it was a poor chance at best and probably doomed to failure.

He knew that, of course. I couldn't keep the hope off my face and in the end, it condemned me. He straightened and the despair that followed was like a tidal wave compared to what I'd felt before. My hope had risen high and so my disappointment had farther to fall.

He opened his mouth and started to speak. "I...," he stopped, shaking his head to rid it of whatever he meant to say. "Come, Kor," he said. "The camp is ready."

"I'm staying out here," I said, letting the full bitterness of my disappointment taint my voice. To reinforce my words, I sat down. The snow was cold and wet, seeping into my leather pants and sending a chill through me. I would regret my decision very quickly once he left me but that didn't mean I was going to change it.

"No."

Drakkus was a big enough man, and I was a small enough boy, that he didn't need to use his periapt to bring me to his camp. One hand closed around my arm, hauling me to my feet. It was forceful, but not painful. With that hand still on my arm, we walked the distance to the nearest fire and once in its warm embrace, I was loath to return to the cold. Kicking the snow away, I cleared a spot on the ground to sit on. Before I could, Rayka was there, a bundle of fur blankets in her hands.

"You're not getting sick again," she said by way of explanation as she arranged one for me to sit on, pushed me gently onto it and then wrapped the others about my shoulders.

Such care I could resent, but not refuse. Not anymore. I grabbed the sides of the blanket that draped over my shoulders and pulled it tight around me.

Rensi and Otho were both seated at the fire already. In his hands, Otho whittled one end of a thick straight stick into a sharp point with his knife and paid little attention to anything else. Rensi, however, waited until a wooden bowl of steaming stew - this time made from rabbit, potatoes, and some sort of stringy green vegetable that I wasn't familiar with - was placed in my hands and then she moved over to take a seat beside me. She pulled a corner of the blanket I was sitting on out to give herself a dry place to sit as well.

She was as hesitant as her father had been to strike up a conversation with me although it was clear from her moving over beside me that she wanted to. I ignored her, too busy filling my mouth and relishing the magic that savory, hot food could work on a mood.

"I'm glad you're feeling better," she ventured at last.

I muttered my thanks in between bites without bothering to look her way. Since the only reason she was probably glad I was feeling better was because it allowed us to move on with whatever they had planned, I didn't think I owed her any more than that.

"I was just trying to make things better for you, you know. I didn't know a vision could make you...," she let her words trail off.

"Make me what?" I shouldn't have pressed, especially since I already knew the answer. But she was the architect of my captivity, and I couldn't forgive that with just a few nice words from her. Besides, I was still reeling from the bitterness of disappointment, and it clouded my reason.

"You know," she said, shrugging.

"Make me go half-mad? Was that what you were going to say? You didn't know they could make me run and scream and cry like a child?" I hadn't known they could do that, myself, but there was no way I was sharing that with her.

She shrugged again, folding her hands in her lap and then unfolding them to lean back on them. "I guess that's about what I was going to say. Are they often like that?"

First Drakkus, now Rensi. I was tired of talking about my visions and my gift. They made my entire life shrink into that one little thing. Or not so little thing, I suppose. It did dominate a great portion of my time and energy. Either way, it didn't matter. I was done talking about it and I was definitely done talking to Rensi.

Rensi gave a loud huff and shifted her position again, this time leaning forward to hold her hands up to the fire.

"Why'd you bother to come sit by the fire if you were just going to ignore all of us?"

"It wasn't my choice," I said. I waved a hand toward Drakkus and Rayka. "They won't let me risk getting sick again. Why do you have to keep bothering me with questions? Don't you have somebody else you can pester?"

Her bright burst of laughter surprised me. She tossed her arms out, nearly smacking me in the face with one flailing hand, gesturing to the rest of the camp. "Yes, so many people. I'd love to sit around a fire and listen to grown men talk about troubled times, and dark days, and ill fortune."

Her words dug into me, stirring an ember of uneasiness that I'd neglected since I was first brought here. I lifted my head and truly took notice of the people beyond our campfire. I'd had little interest in learning anything about this tribe when they captured me and that interest had stayed small. Now, however, I studied the groups that huddled around the two or three other fires.

They were all men.

Aside from Rayka, Rensi, and Otho there were no other women and children.

This was no ordinary tribe and I'd been a fool not to see it before.

CHAPTER 9

NIGHTHAWKS PUNCTURED THE silence of the night with their cries. An occasional shriek or squeal, the swoop of wings told of the night hunt that took place around us. I envied those hawks their freedom as I lay awake in my bedroll with Rensi and Otho on either side of me. I envied the weightlessness of their lives, the way they lived purely through their instincts and senses, bound to no man, slave to no gift. Their wild calls sang across the wind, pulling my thoughts with them.

I tugged my blanket up a little higher, nestled into the warmth a little deeper, and turned my mind to escape. Since Drakkus had tethered me, I'd tried to steer far from such thoughts, since they were hopeless and useless. But now I wasn't so sure. I'd thought escape impossible but since Rensi's efforts earlier that night to befriend me, my mind was beginning to explore a new idea.

Rayka could be blamed, really, for putting the thought in my head. She was, after all, the one who told me a secret of the tethering that I had not known when I'd begged her to remove it. Only Drakkus could remove it. Only Drakkus or one who shared his blood. Rensi could undo the tether. Otho could too, I suppose. I didn't think my chances of getting on his good side would be quite as easy as Rensi's.

Beside me, one of them was snoring softly. I suppressed a ridiculous urge to laugh when I realized that it was Rensi. That would hardly help.

Restless because I'd slept so much during the day, I sat up, moving with great care to prevent waking anyone else. They slept soundly, confident in the tether to do its job of keeping me in place. And it would. I wouldn't fight it, not ever again, not knowing just how bad the pain of it could get. But I wanted space to think, and I moved away toward the glowing remains of our fire, toting my blankets with me.

Befriending Rensi didn't sound so difficult on the surface. She wasn't unfriendly. If I could only get over how much I hated what she'd done, it would be easy. I wasn't sure I could do that. Every time I thought about how she'd wandered into our village, dressed in clothes torn by some wild animal, telling everyone a sad story, worming her way into our pity and care just so that she could set eyes on me and lay the path for Drakkus to take me, the hot ember of anger that lodged in my heart burned brighter and hotter. She was the first reason why I'd never get to see my family again and I couldn't forgive that. Not now, not ever.

"You should not be up," Drakkus said from directly behind me.

I jumped with a yelp, my blankets falling away as I scrambled to my feet.

"I wasn't running. I'm just sitting here. It's not doing any harm," I answered, babbling a little because my heart was skipping wildly enough to beat itself out of my chest at his unexpected interruption.

"You should be asleep."

I took two or three deep breaths, telling myself that he had no idea what I was doing or what I was planning.

"I slept most of the day. I'm not really that tired."

"You've been sick for a week; you still need rest." His words lost some of their force when he sat down next to where I'd been sitting and motioned for me to resume my seat. Just because he'd done that, I wanted to run back to my bedroll. Sense told me not to refuse, though. "Give me the knife, Kor."

I stared at him, my eyes widening.

He was unimpressed by my mock innocence, holding out a hand palm up, waiting for me to place Otho's knife that I'd slipped away from him only about an hour earlier while he slept in it. My clenched fingers were reluctant to release the weapon into his expectant hand. I didn't even have a good plan for how I'd put it to use, I just knew that I felt a great deal better with some means of defense in my hands.

Drakkus set it aside without a word. He didn't bother to scold me for my foolishness in taking it and I had to admit I was glad of that. It hadn't been among my most brilliant ideas. But it was better than nothing and I was tired of doing nothing.

"Go on, Kor. Ask your questions. I think you'll find I answer them a bit more willingly than you do mine."

Now that he'd suggested it, the questions that had been plaguing me disappeared in a wave of obstinacy. I hunched over a little, grabbing a nearby stick and stirring up the fire. A shower of sparks flew up into the night sky and my eyes followed them. A few flames leapt to life, and I inched myself forward to feel its warmth.

"We've reached the mountains. We'll start up them tomorrow," Drakkus said, ignoring my sullen silence.

"What happens then?" I'd already forgotten my own determination to remain quiet.

"It's where we're going. It's where we need to be for the ritual."

I thought about the last oracle. I thought about the little Drakkus shared with me about her. Killed on a forgotten mountainside, killed because everyone agreed she needed to die. Perhaps that mountainside wasn't so forgotten. Perhaps Drakkus knew exactly which mountainside was involved. Perhaps this ritual was nothing more than a way to end me and ensure that no more oracles would be born. All of the sudden, there was a question I desperately wished to ask but I was rather frightened of the true answer. And so, I thought of a different one.

"What soldiers wear black and crimson?"

Drakkus turned to stare at me, a quizzical look on his face. "That's the question you want the answer to?"

"You said you'd answer me."

"I did," Drakkus said with a solemn nod. "Black and crimson are the colors of Queen Cholla's Purge."

"Queen Cholla?"

"Queen of the Iron Towers," Drakkus clarified. He was still studying me, and I turned my head away from him, denying him the opportunity to try to read my thoughts.

"What does she use them for? And why do they have such a ridiculous name?"

"I already told you Queen Cholla hates the gifted. She believes them cursed, corrupted, tainted by whatever evil dwells in the Outlands. Her Border Guard protects against all threats from the Outlands, her Purge protects the Iron Towers from all threats inside - mostly by apprehending any gifted who cross her borders. I would assume that's where their name comes from - they purge her kingdom of the tainted."

I leaned forward, cradling my chin in the palms of my hands as I set my elbows on my knees. There was something entrancing about the little flames in front of my eyes and for a long moment I didn't bother to answer because I was too busy staring at the fire, turning his words over in my mind. I shut my eyes and brought the images of the vision back.

Black and crimson soldiers sweeping down the slopes of the southern mountains, trampling and killing everyone in their path. For what? If they were her Purge, charged only with the destruction of the gifted or tainted as she called them, why wipe out the plains' tribes? She'd opened her borders to us every winter, letting us seek refuge in the warmth of her land in exchange for small payments and favors.

"Why did you want to know about them?" Drakkus asked when the silence had stretched on too long.

The band on my wrist grew heavy, its unseen tether quite suffocating in that moment. My fingers tried to slide under it and twist it around to loosen it, but it was as snug as the night he'd first put it on and I'd failed up to that point to wear any weakness into the leather and metal.

I angled my face towards his, meeting his eyes without bothering to hide the full depth of my fury, and said, "Those are the warriors that kill my family. The ones you're letting kill my family."

I was on my feet before I knew it, backing away from him before I did something that would earn me the pain of the tether. Drakkus was just as quick. He caught hold of my arm and I could go no further.

"You hate me."

The words hardly needed to be said. I had hated him from the first moment he tethered me to him. But I'd never said them and now that he had I realized hatred didn't even begin to cover what I harbored for him. Now that he said them, whatever good sense told me to remain silent, to ignore the heat rising inside me, abandoned me.

"Someday you'll pay for their deaths," I said, my voice hushed to a whisper. The coldness of it in my own ears frightened me a little, mostly because I realized as I spoke that I meant it. I meant every bit of it. If my father and my mother died, if my brothers died, if Ahashi died... I would find a way to make him suffer for it. Him and Rensi and Otho and even Rayka. Because they knew what they were doing to me, and they pretended to hate it and yet they still did it.

"You hate me," he repeated. "But there is so much more at stake than your family's lives. What we're doing could save thousands."

"But I don't care about thousands. I care about my family."

"You're an oracle, Kor. You stopped belonging to yourself and to your family from the first moment you had a vision."

The words were like a slap on my face, stinging and sharp. For a moment, my mind reeled from their effect. I twisted my arm out of his grasp. “Well, I don’t belong to you, either,” I said. It was all I could think of to say.

Drakkus reached out to grab me again but stopped when I flinched and backed away. “No, you don’t. But nothing I’m doing right now is for me.”

“I’ve decided I’m tired now.”

“Listen to me,” he said, his words arresting my retreat as if he had grabbed me. There was a sadness in his eyes that I had not noticed before and his voice softened a little as he went on, “I told you I sent someone to warn your family. That’s all that could ever have been done to save them. You know that.”

I stood there, listening to his words but barely hearing them. I hated him too much to hear what he had to say.

“Kor, I don’t want to do this. Do you really think I’d choose to take my family north into winter because I want to? There are terrible things that will happen if we don’t do this, though. Terrible things that will happen to everyone, including your family. This ritual, what I am doing, it can change that.”

“What terrible things can happen to my family if they’re already dead?”

Drakkus ran his hand over his face. “You’ve only seen that happen once. How many times have you seen the world ending?”

He'd asked me that before and I hadn't answered him. I looked up at him. And despite my best efforts to do so, I could find nothing insincere in his eyes.

"More than once," I answered.

"We can stop that from happening. We can stop the fire that burns through the plains. But I need you to do it."

All that fire, all that death. The vision I had lived with since I was four or five years old. I wanted to believe him. I wanted to believe that I could help prevent that awful end. I wanted to believe that because then I could believe there was some real purpose to my gift.

"How do you stop the end of the world?"

"That's what the ritual is for. I promised you when I took you that I meant you no harm. I still mean you no harm, Kor. But I do need you for this ritual or we are all lost."

I'd believed him before – when he said he would not hurt me to drag an answer from me. Shutting my eyes, I brought up the memory of that fiery vision. I let myself relive the destruction and death.

"You have me anyway," I said, holding up my tethered wrist, although with a little less anger than before. Despite everything he'd done to me, he truly thought he was saving the world and I couldn't be angry with that no matter how hard I tried.

I made up my mind in that moment to stop fighting him, at least until the ritual was done. Then I would fight him at every step until I was returned to my family.

But until then, I believed him.

CHAPTER 10

THERE IS A RULE AMONG the plains' people that is pounded into our consciousness from the moment we take our first steps - never venture into the mountains. Even our time spent in the Iron Towers is spent on the flat land just below the southern slopes. There is a tacit relationship between those who dwell in the plains and those who make their homes in the mountains and that is that we have nothing to do with each other. We may as well not exist to each other. So long as this arrangement is adhered to, no conflict arises between the two.

In my lifetime, the only mountain people I'd seen were the handful that came down from the Iron Towers to trade in the winter. There was a valley there that was neutral ground for any transactions that took place.

Otherwise, the mountain dwellers were as distant and unknown to me as the creatures that lurked in the Outlands. Stories abounded of how close the mountain people had grown to their neighbors in the Outlands, how similar they had become, how thin the line between man and monster had become.

I'm sure their stories about us painted the wanderers of the plains in just as poor a light.

Morning's pale light, filtered through thin gray clouds that hid the ice capped peaks from view, found me still as far south of the camp as my tether would allow me. As glad as I was that the long hours of the night were now over, I dreaded what day held, even as I planned my complete compliance.

We were to enter the mountains. We were to leave the safety of the plains, break all timeless agreements that kept our world so carefully balanced and at peace, and we were going to ascend the rocky heights that rose like cold, colossal sentinels behind my back.

Noise from the camp alerted me to the others waking. Getting to my feet and trying to stretch the stiffness that had settled deep in my bones from the cold away, I started back without waiting for anyone to come after me or for the tether to do its work.

After so many mornings of the same routine, it was startling to walk into the camp and find nothing moving the same way. Although the men who'd traveled with us and who I'd yet to say so much as a word to were up, there were no efforts being made to pack and saddle the horses. Mostly, they were just milling about. Although, even their leisurely behavior that morning had more order in it than most tribes managed to achieve.

I watched with mild, bored curiosity as the man who had carried me over his shoulder the night of my capture, broke apart from the some of the others and made his way toward Drakkus and Otho. He was the one who most often joined our campfire, although when I was around it, he never spoke.

The only thing that was the same was Rayka. She stood, her back to me, over the cauldron, stirring its steaming contents methodically. Drawn both by the warmth of the fire and by the smell of cooking food, I stole across the empty ground and found a clear spot to sit across from her. She didn't notice me at first, her gaze distant and her thoughts elsewhere. A sad smile flitted across her face when she did see me.

"You will be very tired today," she said.

I shrugged. "It doesn't matter. I'll just get dragged along anyway." Probably not the best thing to say when I was determined to be the complacent and compliant prisoner with them.

"Drakkus does not always make it easy to trust him." I agreed but said nothing. Although, after our last conversation, I trusted him a bit more than I had before. "We start up the mountains today and the horses cannot carry us there. It will not be an easy journey, but we are close to the end."

"Are we?"

She ladled some of the thick porridge into a wooden bowl and handed it to me. Bits of dried berries were mixed in with the cooked grain, sweetening it a little.

I lifted the bowl to my nose and drew in a deep breath. It smelled almost like the food my mother cooked. I savored the scent of it while waiting for it to cool enough to eat, closing my eyes so that I could imagine myself at home with my family.

Soon, I promised myself. Soon, just as soon as I finished whatever ritual it was Drakkus required of me.

"We are. Three or four days more, Korris. Then we can return you home and put all of this behind us." She said it almost as if it was herself she was trying to persuade and not me. The ladle stopped its slow, lazy circles in the porridge as she stared beyond me to the mountains. "And perhaps then you can forgive us for what we've done to you."

"Have you ever been in the mountains?" No other tribes had been, I knew. But what Drakkus had was more of a troop than a tribe.

The smile that softened her face this time was wistful. "I have."

I was about to ask her if the stories I'd heard were true when Rensi flopped onto the ground beside me, nearly upsetting the bowl of hot porridge I had in my hands.

"Watch what you're doing, Rensi," Rayka said. "Where's your brother?"

"Still arguing with Father."

Rayka frowned, a quick downward tug of her lips before she caught herself. "Watch this," she said to Rensi, leaning her ladle against the side of the cauldron. "And eat. If we don't get a start soon we might as well not start at all today."

Before Rensi could answer her, Rayka was gone, her firm footsteps carrying her away from us and toward wherever Drakkus and Otho were.

I swallowed down a bite, wincing as it burned my tongue and throat. "What are they arguing about?"

"I," Rensi's eyes flicked away, "I can't say. Father doesn't... Never mind. Why are you talking to me? You're usually all sullen and silent when I try to get you to talk to me."

I didn't have a good answer for her, not one I could share with her at least. Taking another bite, I decided it best not to answer at all. Rensi laughed, quick and sharp. It felt especially loud in the quiet of the early morning.

"There you go again." She got up and spooned out her own bowlful. "All sullen and silent."

"I'm not..."

"So, have you ever had a vision that I was in?" she asked before I could argue that there was nothing sullen about my behavior.

"No."

"That's disappointing."

"Since all of my visions seem to be about death and destruction, I'd say that not being in them is a very good thing."

"You never see anything happy?"

I would have stopped answering her questions by then if it had been any other morning. And I wanted to stop answering them now. Even with my parents or our tribe's elder, there was a limit to how much talking about my gift that I could tolerate.

I shut my eyes a moment, reminding myself that I wanted to be Rensi's friend because Rensi could undo the tether. And if Drakkus failed to keep his word, I needed her on my side.

"The happiest thing I foresaw was my sister's birth, but my mother almost died from that. Other than that, it's just...," my words trailed off.

Had Drakkus' man reached my family? Had he convinced my father that the threat was real, that the vision was truly his son's? Was it even possible for fates once foreseen to be changed?

I felt the first pulses of pain deep in the center of my head, then, and knew it would not be many hours before another vision came.

"You can tell when one is coming, can't you?"

Holding my head between my hands, I nodded.

"What was the first vision you ever had?"

I groaned my annoyance and for once Rensi seemed to get the hint. She stopped asking her questions.

~ ~ ~

"We're the only ones going?" I asked after Drakkus stated that it was time to go and only he and his family got up.

"The fewer people come, the better it is," Drakkus said. He shouldered a heavy pack, as did the others, then turned to me with a smaller one in his hands. "We carry what we need."

I shrugged it into place on my shoulders, uncomfortably conscious of the pain that was building inside my head. The vision was getting closer. Blinking and shaking my head in a futile effort to clear the pain away, I found the others all watching me.

"What?"

"You're in pain," Rayka said, carefully avoiding Drakkus' eyes. It was enough to make me wonder what he and Otho were arguing about.

"A little."

"Then we'd best get started before you require us to stop again," Drakkus said. He, too, seemed to be avoiding Rayka. "The solstice is in four days. We need to reach Yul before then."

In response, I held up my banded wrist. "Then go. You've made sure I have to follow."

Drakkus gave me a single, terse nod before turning and heading for the nearest mountain slope. If he didn't like being reminded about the tether, he shouldn't have put it on me in the first place. Rayka and then Rensi began to follow after him.

"Otho," Drakkus called over his shoulder, "help him if he needs it."

Otho gave a grunt of acknowledgement and then leaned near enough to my ear that I alone could hear his whisper, "You'd better not need it."

Gritting my teeth against the swelling pain and the first sensation of my strength draining away into the power of a vision, I said nothing but took that first step forward. Within ten steps, I had broken the first rule of my people - never venture into the mountains.

CHAPTER 11

I HAVE TO STOP," I GASPED the words out, clutching my head between my hands.

Otho's hand on my shoulder pushed me another step forward. "They're already too far ahead of us."

I squirmed away from his hand and sat down on a rock before I tumbled backward down the steep trail we'd just come up. My vision was swimming with the pain inside my head.

"We can't just stop here, Kor," Otho said, an edge of worry to his voice.

Squinting up at him, I watched as his eyes darted all around, never lingering on one thing for more than a moment. His face, normally the same tan that marked all the plains people, was a sickly white.

Before I could try to decipher why, my eyes no longer saw Otho or anything else on that mountainside as the vision transported me into the future.

It wasn't fire this time. There was no smoke hanging heavy in the air. No roaring flames. But there were screams still. Shouts. The sort of wild yells a hunting party might make when cornering a fierce prey. There was the twang and hiss of bows being drawn and arrows released. The sweet scent of blood filled the air. The sickening wet thud of spears piercing flesh cut some of the screams and shouts off.

It was a camp. There were yurts up, although not many. There was a line of horses tied out to graze. There were three great wagons. A fire in the middle, burning brightly underneath a big, black cauldron. A cauldron that Rayka was no longer stirring.

It was Drakkus' camp.

And it was Drakkus' men dying.

The invaders, mostly hidden by gray fur hoods and scarves that covered the lower halves of their faces, were working their way from one end of the camp to the other. They wielded an assortment of short hunting spears and axes. Drakkus' men fought back, but still they fell, one by one.

Time slowed down as it had when I'd witnessed my family's death.

It carried me over the scene as if I were floating across the air.

Drakkus laying in a pool of blood.

Rensi shrieking as two of the attackers pulled her away from his body.

Rayka and Otho nowhere to be seen.

And then came the stillness, when my senses began to release their hold on the future, freezing the final image before it wavered and collapsed, and I opened my eyes to the present. This vision let go easier than my last one had. Then again, it hadn't fed into me the same as the last one had, either. I was just a witness to this one, not a part of it. I could only hope that meant I was not a part of the actual event, whenever that happened.

I was moaning, I realized with a start. And shaking. Or rather, Otho was shaking me. Hard. I managed to get a hand up to shove him away but all I accomplished was shoving myself off the rock backwards.

"Why'd you do that?"

His voice was loud and made me realize that my ears were still ringing a bit. I blinked my eyes a few times and found myself staring up at the gray sky, although Otho's pale, scowling face blocked a large portion of that gray sky out.

"What happened?" Drakkus said from somewhere nearby.

"He had a vision, I guess," Otho answered.

"Why didn't you call for us to stop?"

"I thought you wanted us to stay as quiet as we could. At least Kor didn't start screaming his head off like last time."

Still swimming my way out of the after effects of the vision, I was surprised how much strength I could push into my glare. My back was arched over the pack that was still attached to it, making my position not only uncomfortable but almost impossible for me to get myself out of. Drakkus leaned down and grabbed the straps of the pack and pulled. I came up with it, sitting on the cold, wet snow, trying to piece together what I'd just seen while at the same time adjusting back to the present.

Despite the pounding that remained in my head, Drakkus only gave me a few moments to collect myself before helping me the rest of the way up. I staggered at once, my legs wobbling not only from the effects of the vision but also from the strain of climbing a mountain all day.

The pack was gone from my shoulders and I looked behind me to find Rayka handing it off to her son.

"It's enough you have to carry the burden of the future with you. I think we can manage to carry that for you for a bit," she said, glancing pointedly in Drakkus' direction.

The burden of the future was a considerable weight at that moment. I nodded my thanks to her, though, unable to get any coherent words out. Otho didn't appear pleased at his mother's decision but he didn't utter a word of complaint.

"Was this the same one you told me about?" Drakkus asked.

Dropping my eyes, I felt the blood rush from my face as I shook my head.

"What was it?" he said.

"Something else."

I could have warned him then. I could have told them what awaited them and their camp. I almost did. But I didn't. Because of my family, because of the tether that bound me to him, because of the anger I'd nurtured for the last several weeks. I stayed silent, condemning them to the same ignorance that he'd condemned my family to.

For I knew, in the most honest part of myself, that my father would have simply murdered the man who brought him my warning, thinking it nothing more than a trick to keep him out of the safety of the Iron Towers. I knew that Drakkus' efforts to save both my family and his thousands couldn't work and my family would suffer for it.

I could have warned them.

But I didn't.

~ ~ ~

Rayka roused me early, long before the sun had shown its face. I tried to pull my blanket over my head again.

Her hand on my shoulder was gentle but her voice was firm. "Korris, we have to keep moving."

A yawn threatened to pull my jaw apart but I did manage to sit up. If I was home, I reminded myself, I would be allowed to sleep as many hours as I needed. No one dared wake me after a vision, fearing my father's wrath should some harm come to me.

Rayka shook me again and this time I peeled away the warm blanket and shivered in the cold air that nipped at my cheeks and nose and hands. Not much other skin showed, thanks to the coat Rayka now forced me to wear.

Everything around us was gray. Gray rock, gray snow, gray sky. Gray and gloomy. Unlike the tree and grass covered slopes that we traveled to in the south, these northern mountains were like giant piles of rock and stone heaped upon each other. I saw no sign of dormant greenery, no sign that there was anything alive amongst all that rock. Just rock and more rock, rising up into jagged peaks and edges. The trail wove in and out of big boulders, some standing higher than our heads as we passed by them.

A few snowflakes floated on the thin mountain air, letting it carry them wherever it wanted. It was colder up here than it had been in the plains. And for a reason I did not understand, there was no fire to huddle close to that morning. No hot food to warm us from the inside out. Rayka handed me a small flat loaf of bread that had been cooked at least two days before in the ashes of a fire. I brushed the blackened ash dust off and bit into it. There was a handful of dried berries to go with it, and a piece of tough, dried horse meat. All of it was washed down with icy cold water that made me convulse in a sudden shiver as it went down my throat.

"We lost hours yesterday," Drakkus said. "Let's hope that's the only vision you'll have between here and Yul."

I looked up at him, my mouth still full of horse meat that was taking far too long to chew, and realized that all four of them were ready and waiting only on me. They must have been up, moving around, and I hadn't so much as stirred.

Drakkus had my pack this time and I wondered if he would pass it off to me as soon as I stood or if Rayka would even let him.

He didn't.

And I was careful not to mention it.

Our walking arrangements differed little from the day before except that Otho, instead of walking behind me, stayed close to my side. The strange pallor I'd noticed on him the day before lingered still – evidence of a fear that I didn't understand.

"How bad is it?" he asked after we'd spent more than an hour climbing the trail in concentrated silence. It was no easy thing to force one foot in front of the other when my head was still trying to decide whether the world around us was spinning or not.

It was so unlike him to start a conversation, that I glanced his way with a bewildered frown. "How bad is what?"

"Your visions. How bad are they? What are they like?"

If it were Rensi, I would have just ignored the questions. I still considered doing that even though they came from him but there was a bright apprehension in his eyes, a fear that I hadn't given much thought to.

Trying to steady my breathing, which was getting harder to do the higher we climbed, I screwed my face up and actually gave some thought to his questions.

"I suppose they're bad. It's not like there's another oracle for me to compare them to, though, so I don't know."

"What's it like when they come?"

The sudden bout of curiosity was almost as alarming as the color of his complexion. I threw a quick glance at the others ahead. We were trailing them by quite a bit again. There just wasn't any way for me to keep the pace Drakkus set.

"It's," my frown deepened, "it's not something I can explain."

"It's terrifying, isn't it?"

I shook my head, more from pride than honesty. It *was* terrifying.

"You ran off screaming during the one..."

"That's not normal. I haven't done that any other time."

"So, it's not usually that bad?"

I stopped walking and turned to face him. He was more than a head taller than me, and I had to tip my head back to meet his eyes.

"What is the ritual?"

His gaze skipped away from mine. "I can't tell you, Kor. I don't know it. Father says we can't know ahead of time, or it will ruin it."

I pressed my lips together, almost forgetting my decision to play along with whatever they wanted for now.

"Come on, we need to catch up," Otho said, tugging at my arm.

~ ~ ~

For so long, it had been just the five of us. Just our conversations. Just our footsteps on the rocks. I started, then, when I looked ahead and found Drakkus, Rayka, and Rensi all standing before a stranger. Otho and I hurried to catch up then, even though it left me panting for breath by the time we stopped just behind Rayka and Rensi.

"Daughter," the man said, bowing his head slightly in Rayka's direction. "You have come."

"Father," she replied with the same inclination of her head. "We have come, as we arranged."

He was an old man. The wrinkles of his face hinted that he'd seen at least sixty winters. There was no hair left on his head, but a thin silver beard shadowed his lower face. If he hadn't been stooped over a little, he would have stood equal in height to Drakkus, and the sharp lines of his face bore a strong similarity to Rayka's own. It was easy to see their likeness.

His clothes consisted almost entirely out of a variety of animal pelts, stitched together to form trousers and coat and hat. It made a patchwork of colors ranging from the red of a fox to the deep brown of a bear, a bit of gray from a wolf and tawny yellow from one of the great cats.

He held out a hand and Drakkus clasped his arm. "You have brought him?"

"As promised," Drakkus said, releasing the man's arm and turning to gesture towards me. I shrank back before I could stop myself.

Sharp, brown eyes peered out from under thick silver eyebrows at me. They didn't blink once as the old man looked me up and down, the beard above his mouth twitching as he worked his mouth back and forth. He rubbed his wrinkled hands together and made little huffing noises all the while.

"Not much to look at, is he? Nor half as big as I expected but that's better, I suppose. It will make the ritual easier."

After swallowing every protest I wanted to make, I studied the ground with the same intensity he'd turned on me. With one booted foot, I scuffed up the snow and mixed it with the brown dirt beneath.

"Lift your head, boy."

I clenched my teeth together and maintained my perusal of the ground.

"Korris," Drakkus said, a warning note in his voice.

I just had to play along a little longer. Just a little bit longer. Then all of this would be over, and I could run away home again.

Bracing myself with a deep breath, I lifted my chin.

"Korris, is it?"

"Korris," Rayka said, "this is my father, Borssa."

They didn't seem too put out when I made no response to the introduction. The gleam in Borssa's eyes told me he didn't much care how I felt about any of it. He was getting what he wanted. And I had the nagging feeling that I was what he wanted.

With that feeling, came the weight of realization that this ritual might not end with me still alive. Borssa certainly didn't look like he would stop whatever their plan was just on account of my life.

"Excellent, excellent." Borssa clapped his hands together. "Let us not waste any more time. The solstice is upon us. And all is prepared for ritual."

Chapter 12

I WASN'T GOING TO FIGHT Drakkus. That's what I told myself as uneasiness wormed its way inside me. I wasn't going to fight him because I wanted to stop the fiery end of the world as much as he did. But Borssa filled me with such reluctance that I wasn't sure I could keep my promise to myself.

The sun was sinking fast. Its dying rays washed over the mountains, painting them in a fierce orange and brilliant gold, a deep purple and a serene blue. I kept my eyes on that sunset. I kept my feet moving forward. Inside my chest, my heart was trying to beat its way out of my skin and a cold premonition lodged itself in my mind. It could be my last sunset, if my instincts were worth anything.

And if it was, it was a spectacular one.

Behind me, Otho was quiet, too lost in whatever apprehension kept the blood from his face to try resuming our earlier conversation. I was tempted to ask him what troubled him so, but I think I was too afraid of the answer.

Ahead of me, Drakkus and Borssa walked side by side. Rayka and Rensi had remained behind, tending a fire that I wasn't sure I would still be alive to enjoy later that night.

There was something unsettling in the way Borssa looked at me, in his appraisal of me. I'd seen men eye up horse carcasses in the same way - measuring exactly how much meat and skin and fur they could get from it. Borssa hadn't stopped measuring me. Even now, as we ascended, I could feel his eyes coming back to me again and again.

For the first time in my life, I wished for the deep pain in my head that warned of a coming vision. I wished for this reality to be ripped from me and replaced with the future because then I wouldn't have to face whatever it was that was coming. It had always been a relief to return to the present. No more. I was tempted to fake a vision. If I'd believed it would have fooled Drakkus, I think I would have.

My feet were heavy, dragging through the snow.

"Catch up, boys," Borssa called back to us. "The sun is setting and there's work to be done."

I moved no faster.

Actually, I stopped. So fast and so abrupt that Otho walked straight into me. He was so caught up in his own thoughts that he didn't even chastise me, just moved around me and kept going.

"Otho," I said softly, giving voice to a desperate idea that was only half formed, "you can take it off. I know you don't want to do this either. Take it off and we can go, we can run. They can't make us do this."

Otho had paused but kept his back to me as I spoke. I watched it stiffen as he understood what I was asking. Then he turned and there was such a dark fire in his eyes that I regretted asking.

"I may not want to do this, but I have to. I won't be the reason Father loses everything. Do you really think I'd go against him?"

I did. I could see beyond his indignant anger that there was a part of him that wanted nothing more than to escape whatever awaited us. Before he could succumb to the temptation, he spun around on his heel and marched forward. A slight tug in my tether told me that we'd hung back too far and I shuffled on myself.

"At least tell me if this is going to end with me dead," I whispered when I'd caught up to Otho.

He gave me a funny look. "Father promised you he'd take you home when we're through. That should be answer enough."

"He could take my dead body home and still be keeping what he promised."

"If it kills you, it will kill me too."

In that moment, there was absolutely nothing assuring about that statement. There was something wrong with Borssa and his glee, something wrong with the way he looked over his shoulder at us, licking his lips as if tasting our fear and discomfiture.

With only the sun's rim still making a stand against the night sky, we reached a plateau. In the light of day, I'm sure the view was breathtaking. Even in the darkness, it was unlike anything I'd ever seen. The world dropped out before us in unfathomable darkness with only a smattering of stars to show where earth ended and sky began.

Borssa and Drakkus stopped in front of a large, flat rock that had been swept clear of the powdery snow that covered the rest of the mountain. A clay jar sat on one side of it. A small bundle of scented sticks sat inside it, burning slowly and saturating the air over the rock with a thick incense. It made the entire scene hazy and surreal.

"Work to be done tonight. Destinies to be changed tonight," Borssa murmured to himself as he circled the rock, peering into the jar and waving a hand through the smoke that curled up from it. "Games to be played tonight. Fates to be cheated tonight." He lifted a large, gourd shaped flask to his lips and drank deeply. Then he passed it to Drakkus who passed it to Otho without a drink.

Otho took it and swallowed at least three gulps of the stuff before coming away coughing and spluttering. He held it out to me but I shook my head and stepped back. The incensed smoke was already filling my head, slowing my thoughts.

"Drink it, Korris," Drakkus said.

I snatched it from Otho's hands and put it to my lips, glaring at Drakkus all the while. Without Rayka to temper him, I didn't think Drakkus would hesitate to use his periapt on me and whatever it was I faced, I wanted to face it on my own, not compelled through some ancient relic.

The drink was bitter stuff, brewed from who knows what, and it went down hard, burning and scorching all the way down to my stomach. My eyes watered and I was coughing as bad as Otho. But then the burning faded and in its place was a numbness that spread first through my abdomen and then my chest and finally all the way into my limbs and head. My mind emptied itself of everything and left me staring stupidly at the wisps of scented smoke that continued to wrap their way around me.

"Take your clothes off," Borssa said, his voice sounding as if it were coming from the other side of the mountain. "Nothing can stand between you and the Fates. Nothing to get in the way."

I shook my head. "I don't want to," I tried to say, but I knew the words were slurred. My tongue felt swollen and dry.

Otho was already halfway out of his clothes by the time I gave up trying to protest and started fumbling with mine. His face had gone slack with the numbness the drink gave to us. All the trepidation I'd seen in him before, gone.

I ought to have been cold. Freezing, even. We were on the top of a mountain in the heart of winter with snow falling around us, but all I could feel was the lingering warmth of the drink and the deepening numbness.

I lifted eyes that could only just stay open and saw Drakkus, his image blurring into two or three before I could bring him into focus. There was such a strange look on his face. I tried to read it. He was worried, I think. Almost alarmed. And in a distant, foggy sort of way I shared that alarm.

We were kneeling, Otho and I, on the flat rock but I don't remember being told to do so. Nor do I remember walking over to it. My head was spinning, worse than it did with any vision, and every thought I tried to hold onto slid away like water between my fingers.

"Drakkus," I managed to get his name out. "Please."

I wasn't sure what I was asking. I didn't know how to put into words what I wanted just then. I only knew that I had trusted him when he said he would not harm me, and that trust was breaking fast.

Borssa's old, wrinkled face filled my vision then. There was no glee in his eyes now, only deadly seriousness as he took my right hand in his and pulled it toward Otho. I stared at my hand then, for though I could see him touching it and I wanted to pull away from that touch, I could not.

"Drakkus knows what must happen or the world is doomed. The power of sight must lie in the blood of a king or a future king or the curse of Fentra will destroy the world. The power of sight is a gift you were given and now must give." He placed my hand flat over Otho's, my palm resting over top of his. His skin was like ice against mine and I saw, through half lidded, blurred eyes, that his entire body was turning blue with the cold. "First borns alone may carry the sight. And Otho is the first born of Drakkus."

A blade of obsidian gleamed in the darkness before my eyes. I watched without feeling as Borssa plunged it into the top of my hand. It pushed between the bones and tendons of my fingers and slid all the way through into Otho's until it stuck fast in a crevice of the rock.

"Blood of the gifted meets blood of the firstborn and so we cheat the Fates and end the curse," Borssa said as he stepped back from us.

A voice in my head told me to pull away, to wrench the knife free. But whatever was in that drink had a stronger voice and it bade me stay and rest. The effort of holding my eyes open was the greatest defiance I was capable of. I stared and stared at my own bleeding hand, at Otho's bleeding hand beneath mine. His face was no longer blue but white, bathed in the cold light of the full moon that had risen behind me.

“It takes a long night to hide from the Fates,” Borssa continued his rant and I only half heard him. “Only one night a year can it be done. The longest night of winter.”

There ought to be pain, I knew. There ought to be anger. But when I tried to reach into myself to find anything, I came up empty handed.

The moon rose higher and still my blood flowed, staining the rock. I would have thought that after so long and in such cold, our blood would have ceased its flowing.

Owls commenced their night hunts around us. I heard the beat of their wings, the screech of their prey as they fled and were caught. Time marched on and I could keep no count of the hours. But still I felt nothing. I was kneeling naked and bleeding on a rock in the middle of the night, in the cold of winter and I felt nothing.

And that nothingness terrified me.

Fear flooded me, awakening a heat inside me that finally drove away the maddening numbness. The pain followed and with it my voice. A wordless cry escaped my chapped, frozen lips.

Otho’s head snapped up at the sound, his own face twisting in a grimace of newfound pain.

He looked past me, panting through the pain, and then whispered, “The sun is almost up.”

My eyes found Drakkus then.

His promise not to hurt me was empty. His words, useless. He stood still in the same spot he'd stood when the night had started. He'd watched it all and had stopped nothing.

~ ~ ~

Dull light burned through my shut eyelids, drawing me out of my stupefied sleep. There was a pain behind my eyes that told me waking would be full of regrets. There were voices in my ears, muted by distance and some sort of wall. They were too quiet for me to put together their words or even who the speakers were.

As my senses wandered back to me, I realized I was lying on a bed, well off the cold, hard ground that I was used to sleeping on. I'd only ever been on a bed once before in my life.

It had been when I was still very young and my father had arranged for me to see a healer in the Iron Towers one winter. He'd hoped for some tonic that could cure what everyone believed to be my madness. What he got was a few days free of his youngest son and a hefty debt that he'd spent all winter bargaining and working to pay off. And I was left with my madness and a vile draught that I eventually convinced my mother to toss out when it became clear it had no impact on the visions.

A heavy, musty scent lingered on the air around me and at last I lifted my eyelids and took in the sight of my surroundings. The only light that came in came from an opening in the stone wall some distance from me. I was surrounded by drab, gray rock. The only different substance in the room was a packed dirt floor. A cave. I was in a cave.

A more unwelcoming place I don't know that I'd ever seen.

The longer I was awake, the more memories fell into place. Otho and I had been held in place by the knife until the sun rose. By then the combined haze created by Borssa's drink and the incense had worn off almost entirely but cold, blood loss and shock had taken its place. No sooner had the knife been withdrawn than I collapsed in a faint.

How I'd made it to a bed, I could only guess. I must have been carried. That thought frightened me because I had no memory at all of anyone touching me or picking me up.

The sleep that had finally taken me held no restfulness. It was fraught with visions and nightmares and memories. No new visions had come but I'd seen the end of the world over and over again.

"You've been a long time in waking," a woman said and I jerked back in surprise. I hadn't noticed anyone else in the room.

Shifting my head, I found her. She was seated on a large rock that jutted up out of the dirt floor, one leg crossed gracefully over the other and her hands resting with practiced stillness on her lap. Black hair hung all undone around her shoulders, stark against the translucent paleness of her skin. Her face was thin and long, reaching a sharp point at her chin. But it was her eyes that I was drawn to over and over again. They lacked the two tones in the middle that everyone else's eyes had. Instead, the circle of her eyes was all the same inky black and larger than most so that only a little white showed around them. Her gaze was unblinking and unsettling.

"Who are you?" I asked, not quite certain I wanted the answer. Perhaps I was still dreaming. Perhaps the effects of Borssa's drink were still hanging onto my blood.

Her pale, almost colorless lips pursed in a thoughtful frown. "I am known to most as Destiny, young Korris."

"What do you want with me?" Another person interested in my gift, no doubt. I wasn't sure I could take her answer if it was that. I wasn't sure there was much left of myself to give to anyone else.

"I do not like when others tamper with my game pieces. I do not like it at all." Aside from speaking, she moved not at all. No nervous intertwining of her fingers, not even a visible rise and fall of her chest to show she breathed. If it weren't for her voice, I could have thought her a statue or a corpse. "The game must be played to its end, young Korris. It is already well begun. Destiny cannot be altered nor can a Fate be denied."

Heaviness shut my eyes then, a heaviness that sleepiness couldn't account for. I did not open them again for many hours and when I did there was no sign of the woman named Destiny. I could convince myself that her presence had just been another dream, another part of the madness that had descended on my sleep thanks to Borssa's drink.

CHAPTER 13

THERE WERE VOICES IN MY ears again.

Words that were too quiet for me to understand.

But they were coming closer. Each sentence was louder and clearer than the last and I realized they were entering the cave. Not ready to face anyone just yet, I kept my eyes shut and my breathing shallow and steady. I'd yet to sort through anything that took place on the night of the solstice, however many nights ago that was. I truly didn't know how many days or nights had passed since then.

They stopped just inside the entrance, their voices lowered but the walls and ceiling of the cave brought their words to me anyway.

"Of course, it didn't work," Rayka said. "You tampered with the game pieces of the Fates, and you thought it would work?"

Her words echoed the words of the strange woman whose presence earlier I still couldn't quite believe.

"Your father said it was the only way," Drakkus said.

"Don't put all of this on my father. You're the one who planned all this. You're the one who dragged us halfway across the plains in the winter and up these mountains. You're the one..."

"I didn't know that's how Borssa planned to break it," Drakkus said, interrupting what would probably have been a very long tirade.

"You didn't know? Because he didn't tell you or because you chose not to know?"

There was a silence after that, inflamed by a tension I could feel even lying on the bed, pretending to sleep.

"Borssa said there was a way to break the curse. He told me only that it required the oracle, my son, and the winter solstice. He told me that no harm could come from it to either Otho or Korris. That is what I knew." His voice dropped a little and I had to strain to catch his next words. "That is all I asked him to tell me."

"Then you chose your ignorance. Don't blame that on my father. I warned you he'd stop at nothing to have his hand in the game. He's been aching for years to be numbered among the greats. Why didn't you at least ask?" There was pain in her voice when she spoke those last words.

When Drakkus spoke again, I think he forgot how close they were to me and how hard they'd been trying to not be overheard. His voice was raised a little when he said, "It's done, Rayka. It's done and it didn't work so what is it you want me to do?"

Rayka sighed and I could picture her shaking her head, chewing on her lip in that troubled way of hers. "I married a king, not a thief, Drakkus. If you'll stoop far enough to try to rob a gift from another, how much better are you than your brother? He steals a crown and you steal a gift to get it back? What I want is for you to make this right. Take him south. Take him home. We've no right to keep him a moment longer. Now go. Yours hardly needs to be the first face he sees when he wakes. And stay away from Otho, too."

I kept my eyes shut; my breathing measured as a single set of footsteps padded across the dirt floor. A warm hand came to rest on my forehead as Rayka stopped beside me. Her fingers trailed down my face in a mothering caress and I could keep my eyes shut no longer.

It was a sad smile that greeted me. A sad smile and troubled eyes. There was a whole host of words behind her eyes, just waiting to be said, but she remained silent. Giving me the chance to speak first, if I wanted, giving me a choice between conversation and silence. I shifted in my bed, conscious all at once of the fact that, though I'd been well wrapped with blankets, I was still undressed from that night on the rock.

"What happened?" I asked. Although the memory of that night was there, it was in tatters, bits and pieces of it that were all torn apart by whatever happened. There were words Borssa had said that made little sense to me. And I desperately wished to make sense of it.

"How do you feel?" she asked, ignoring my own question.

"Tired. Sore." Hurt and betrayed. Angry. Violated. Deeply violated. I decided the first two words were sufficient. Rayka was already on my side. "How long have I been asleep?"

"Almost three days. But I'm not sure what good it did you, raving as you were for the better part of it."

I furrowed my brow as I stared up at her. "I talked in my sleep?"

"Talked, shouted, thrashed around. Made enough noise to rouse a corpse."

"Oh."

She lifted my right arm out from underneath the blankets and cold air on my bare skin made me shiver. My eyes followed her hands as she reached for the bandage wrapped around the palm of my own. Dried blood had stained both the front and back of it, turning it into an ugly rust brown. Rayka loosened it and pulled it away, revealing the thin, bloody line Borssa's blade had left behind.

"He cut me," I said in a quiet, stunned voice. Lying there alone, I could tell myself it was just a nightmare, that none of what happened at the top of the mountain was real. Staring at the wound left behind, there was no denying it.

"Yes, he did."

There were tears in Rayka's eyes when I looked up from my hand to her face. I wasn't sure why she was the one crying. Her hand hadn't been cut. She hadn't had to kneel naked on a cold rock in the middle of winter for an entire night.

"Why? What was it they wanted from me?"

Rayka reached above my head to a shelf cut into the rock wall that I could only see if I tipped my head all the way back. It was too much effort and I gave it up quickly. There must have been a bowl of water there for I heard her wring the water out of a cloth before she brought it down to my hand. I winced as she dabbed it against the cut.

"I'm sorry," she said softly. "For everything. I should have...," she shook her head. "I didn't know exactly what the ritual was. I should never have let Drakkus try anyway. I'm no better than he was. You have every right to hate us all."

"What was it they wanted from me?" I said again, half sitting up. I wanted that answer. I needed it. Of all the murky memories from that night, that was the hardest to make sense of. Borssa had said something about it, I just couldn't remember what.

"Don't. Lie back down, Korris. You need to rest so that we can take you home again."

"No." I pushed against her hand on my chest, sitting up all the way, forgetting that the blankets were my only covering. "What were they doing to me? He said something about giving my gift." It was coming back, all in a rush, one memory tumbling over the other. "That's what they were doing, wasn't it? They were stealing it from me? They were giving it to Otho."

Rayka didn't need to speak for me to know her answer. My memories were true.

I was shaking, my teeth chattering against each other, my breath coming heavy and fast. None of that was from the cold, though. I barely felt the cold. Drawing my knees up to my chest, I sucked in one ragged breath after another. Like the night Drakkus told me of the man he sent after my family, no matter how hard I tried to slow down and steady my breathing, it just wasn't enough. A tight band settled over my ribs, shrinking with every breath I gasped in. My lungs burned and black began to cloud my eyes again.

"Korris." Rayka's voice was distant, lost in the deafening roar of blood pounding in my head and ears. "Korris, it didn't work. The ritual didn't work. Otho has no more foresight than I or Drakkus does. The visions are still yours and yours alone. It didn't work and Drakkus is going to take you home again just as soon as you feel up to the journey. He's going to take you back to your family and you can put all of this behind you."

She was rambling, one hand rubbing small, soothing circles on my back. I clutched the blankets up in my fists and pressed them to my eyes and tried to focus on her voice. On her words.

Home.

Family.

Home.

Family.

The words slipped in and out in a steady rhythm. My home. My family. This was over. I could go home. I could return to my family. The tightness in my chest eased up a little but only enough for a horrible, choked sound to come out of my mouth.

"They're dead," I cried.

"You don't know that, Korris. You don't know that."

Because there was a yawning ache inside of me that no words of comfort could fill, I said no more. I solicited no more of her empathy and instead fell back onto the bed and curled up with my back to her.

"Korris, let me finish taking care of your hand."

"It's fine."

She said nothing more but she made no move to leave. Perhaps she thought I would relent or perhaps she was afraid of what I might do if left to myself. How long she sat there, I would never know. Sleep came and stole me away from the torment of being awake and facing the hollowness left behind by what Drakkus and Borssa had attempted to do to me.

~ ~ ~

I kept to that bed for another two days. For those two days, not another word left my mouth, although Rayka and even Rensi came in often and tried to speak to me. I turned away from them both. Drakkus came in only when he thought I was asleep and although I rarely was, I let him believe so because I wasn't at all interested in hearing his reasons or excuses or explanations or apologies. There weren't words that could make everything right again. Otho was the only one who never came, and I gathered from a whispered conversation between Rayka and Drakkus late one night that he was worse off than I was.

It was a hand on my shoulder that woke me on the third morning. I shrugged it off without a thought and rolled to face the gray rock wall. Bleak stone was a better sight than any of my captors.

"Get up, Kor," Drakkus said, the first words he'd attempted to speak to me since that night. "We start for the plains today."

The plains and whatever awaited me there. I squeezed my eyes shut, blocking out the image of Ahashi's death. If I went south, what would I find? A field of bodies? It didn't matter. I had to at least try to return to them and lying in this bed high up in the mountains wasn't doing me any good. Rest couldn't cure the fury and hatred that had taken root in the very deepest parts of me. Nothing could. Except, perhaps, revenge.

I also didn't plan on getting up while Drakkus was standing there.

"Kor, I...,"

"Don't bother," I said, breaking my days-long silence. "Just get out."

He didn't argue with me, although I'm quite sure he wanted to. He stepped away from me and said, "We'll leave as soon as you're ready."

CHAPTER 14

RAYKA FUSSED OVER ME WHEN I finally dragged myself out of the shelter of the cave and out into the open sunlight. My eyes took several moments to adjust to the brilliant light, and I rubbed at them as she straightened my coat and pulled a fur cap over my ears. She tried to grab my hand and examine the wound there, but I snatched it away from her before she got the chance.

"Keep it clean," she said as she stepped back. She smiled for my sake, I think, but it came out sad and broken looking. "I'll not be along to take care of you if you get sick from an infection."

I squinted up at her, my eyes still watering a bit from the brightness of the sun on white snow after so many days of gloom. It made it quite difficult to maintain the frosty, sullen glare I'd perfected over the last few days. "You're not coming?"

She was chewing on her lip as she shook her head. Her eyes went to Drakkus and there was a lot she said in that look, although none of it was meant for me. "Otho and I are staying with my father for the remainder of this winter. Drakkus will return you south to your family just as he promised you he would."

Just the way she said it told me that it was her idea to keep this promise now instead of waiting until the spring.

"Take these," she said, pushing a pair of mittens into my hands. "I'm not sure the Fates will bring my path across yours again, Korris, but I hope in time you will be able to forgive me for the part I've played in all this. We have wronged you most cruelly."

I dropped my gaze and stared at the mittens. She wanted me to reassure her that the day would come when I could look back on any of them with anything less than bitter hatred and I couldn't. I couldn't even pretend such a lie. Not right now, at least. Right now, it was all I could do not to flee back into the shelter of the cave where I didn't have to be reminded quite so brutally of my circumstances.

"Let's go, Kor," Drakkus called out from where he and Rensi waited.

I never thought I'd be glad to see Rensi, but I was then. The thought of trekking back down the mountains with only Drakkus at my side turned my stomach. Rensi, at least, was a distraction.

There was no pack for me to carry this time. No Otho to come up behind me and insist I keep going. No Rayka to remind the others of what my visions cost me. No dread for what awaited me in the ritual. There was only the tramp of our feet in the snow, the howling of the wind as it whipped around the mountain peaks seeking a way through, the distant chatter of birds who made their homes there, and an emptiness that ate up everything inside of me.

For a while, there were no visions, either. Considering how many times I'd relived the end of our world in the past few days, I wasn't about to complain about that.

For two days we hiked our way back down the steep, rocky trails. They were treacherous in the snow, slick in parts, and hiding rocks and stones in others. It took everything I had in me just to stay on my feet.

For two days, we camped in the dark, not daring to light a fire for fear of drawing the mountain dwellers to us. We ate our cold, hard, dry food.

And for two days, I said not one word to either of them. Rensi tried once or twice to strike up a conversation and though I could admit to being tempted to accept the diversion she offered, I maintained my stony aloofness. It was all I had left, and I clung to it with the same ferocity a wild cat held onto its kill with.

They spoke to each other at times, walking side by side ahead of me, their voices too quiet to carry their words back to me. I preferred it when they did talk to one another because then I could lose myself to my own thoughts. Although, as dark as those were, that probably wasn't a good thing. They ranged from recalling my family's final moments to wild hope that my father had stayed away from the Iron Towers, from despair to anger and back again until I didn't know where one ended and the other began.

It was on the third day, with Drakkus' camp in sight, that the pain in my head returned and I knew my reprieve was over. Drakkus and Rensi had been doing such a good job ignoring me that neither noticed when I fell further and further behind as I nursed the pain that grew. I stopped eventually, finding a nook in the rocks that rose up on either side of the trail to sit in. If it weren't for the tether on my wrist, I doubt very much that they would have noticed my absence before reaching camp.

My cry as the tether snapped and pulled, searing my arm, drew their attention back to me.

"Why did you stop?" Drakkus asked when they had retraced their steps to my side. When I didn't bother to answer, he knelt in front of me, bringing his face level with mine. "You should have said something if we were moving too fast. We would have slowed down for you."

My hands pressed to the sides of my head, I raised my eyes to his. I hoped he could see everything I couldn't say. And then, because I wasn't sure he could, I decided to try to say it anyway. "Stop pretending to care. You let him cut me. It was your idea. You let me bleed all night on that rock. You tried to steal my gift from me and give it to your son. I'm glad it didn't work. I'm glad you failed. You didn't change anything. The world still ends the same way. You didn't save your thousands any more than you saved my family."

There was a lot more I was going to say, but the words dropped off as the vision overtook my mind. In its hold, I saw the vast sea that lay in the west between a break in the ring of mountains.

The sight of the sea could only mean one thing. Abirell.

I saw Abirell, gateway of the west.

And it was full of dead and dying. A putrid stench filled the crowded streets, rising from bodies that had fallen where they stood. No one moved to bury the dead. The only ones out in the streets were those either rushing from one place to another or those whose skin was already beginning to rot with plague. There was no sound in this vision. I heard none of the wailing over loved ones' corpses that I saw. I heard none of the cries of the vultures swooping in to claim their feast among the unfortunate.

But it was weighty. It settled over me, dragging me down into its despair, drowning me in its anguish. It cracked something inside of me open, making me want to weep for the suffering and death I saw and even when the vision had fled back to its place in the future, the heaviness lingered, feeding on my own dark thoughts. I wanted to curl up and never move again. If I'd been standing near a cliff's edge, I would have been sorely tempted to throw myself from it and end it all before I met such a fate.

"Korris."

So much death. So much suffering. And for what? There was nothing, nothing to look forward to except more pain and death.

"Korris."

Easier to end it sooner rather than later. Because it would end. Be it through fire or disease or war, the end was coming for all of us and it was a terrible, terrible thing. As if the Fates were unleashing all their fury upon the last of humanity.

"Korris."

There would be no one waiting for me when I returned south. No one to say my name. No one to care whether I lived or died. I was just a game piece, a plaything of the Fates, for those granted more power than I.

"Korris."

My eyes snapped open only to find that I was looking through a blur of tears. Drakkus and Rensi were on the other side of that blur. I wanted to stop. I tried to stop. No fourteen-year-old boy wants to be seen sobbing, especially by the man he hates more than anything in the world. But there was such sadness. It flowed out of me, unstoppable as the waves of the ocean, consuming me. Tears were running freely down my cheeks, soaking the fur collar of my coat and I could do absolutely nothing about it because I couldn't rid myself of the oppressive sorrow that had accompanied my vision.

"Just leave me," I whispered, giving into it. "There's nothing left for me to go back to."

"What did you see?" Drakkus asked.

"Death. It all ends in death."

Rensi frowned from where she stood over Drakkus' shoulder. "I hate to say it, Kor, but that's how it's always ended. For everyone, everywhere."

Drakkus twisted his head around to give her a look that probably meant, "Shut up."

She shrugged. "It's true, though. We're all dying eventually. There's nothing strange about that."

I turned away from them both, bringing first one sleeve up and then the other to wipe away the tears. They were stopping now, drying up of their own will. I rubbed every trace of them away until my face was throbbing and raw. And then I rubbed some more, trying to rid myself of the taint of them, of their weakness.

Thanks to Rensi's words, my own thoughts were beginning to reassert themselves but even that wasn't enough to fully rid me of the weight that my vision pressed onto me.

"Did you see them die again? Your family, I mean," Drakkus asked when I had begun to regain control of myself. "Are theirs the deaths you saw?"

Shaking my head, I kept myself carefully turned away from them, thankful that I'd chosen to nestle myself in this crevice of rock before the vision came. I curled into it now, resting the side of my head against the cold, rough stone.

"You've only seen them die once?"

I nodded, not sure why it mattered.

"Then you don't know that there's nothing to go back to." He stood up again then hesitated. "If you want to stay here tonight instead of trying to reach the camp, we can..."

"No," I said, cutting him off. I pushed to my feet, gripping the rock beside me to maintain my fragile balance. "No."

I couldn't stand the thought of another cold night out with just them for company.

My body had different ideas of what we should do, though. I staggered a step or two, careening against the rocks as my legs refused to cooperate. The weight of the vision seemed to have settled firmly on my shoulders, driving me back to the ground, as if I were wearing that pack again, only it was full of rocks instead. Drakkus reached out a hand to steady me but my humiliation a few moments earlier fueled me now. I shoved his hand away and tried to take another step.

The ground rose up to meet my face and it would have been a painful fall if Drakkus hadn't caught me from behind, pulling me upright against his chest. Something snapped inside me then and I thrashed and flailed against him.

"Don't touch me," I cried out, throwing myself against his imprisoning arm even as my legs buckled underneath me.

"Stop fighting me, Kor. Just stop fighting and let me help you."

His words were reason, but I was wild with rage and fear. They pumped strength into me that I hadn't had a moment before and I jerked my right arm free from him, throwing it up in the air before his face. Flinging the evidence of his betrayal in front of his eyes.

"I did stop fighting you and then you let this happen," I hissed out between clenched teeth.

Drakkus released me as quickly as he'd caught me as soon as the words were out of my mouth. Somehow, I managed to stay upright, panting and leaning against a rock. I glared back at him and Rensi before stepping away from the rock and starting down the trail myself.

CHAPTER 15

EYES FOLLOWED ME WHEN I walked into the camp well ahead of Drakkus and Rensi. Questioning, curious eyes that I had a wicked desire to stab out just then. The rage that had taken over in the mountain still simmered inside me, lending me the strength I needed to pass through the circle of yurts and seat myself at the roaring fire that burned in the center of that circle.

Behind me, I could hear one or two of the men greeting Drakkus. A hush fell over the entire camp when one of the men called across the clearing between the yurts and asked, "Did it work?"

My jaw ached from how tight I'd held it for the last hour and the ache grew worse as I worked it back and forth in anticipation of Drakkus' answer. Apparently, his men did not require a verbal answer, though. Drakkus must have just shaken his head or given some other sign of his disappointing failure because a moment later the hush was replaced with a collective sigh of defeat.

"Wasn't he the right one?" This from the man who'd carried me over his shoulder the night of my capture. "Rensi said for sure that he was."

"It just didn't work," Drakkus said at last, his voice coming from close behind me. "We'll find another way."

I tensed at his words and turned but he wasn't looking at me. He was already moving on to speak with one of his men. I wished Rayka was there. Without her presence, I didn't trust Drakkus to keep his word, especially not after what he'd just said. His other way might well involve my imminent death.

"How's your hand?"

I glanced over to find Rensi lowering herself onto the ground beside me. There was worry in her eyes and I noticed she chewed on her lip the same way her mother did, only she accompanied the gesture by also twirling a strand of hair tight around one finger.

"It's just fine."

"Will you let me see it?"

We'd been through this the first night after leaving Borssa's cave. Rayka had charged Rensi with the care of my hand but she'd forgotten that I had to be a willing participant in that care and I most certainly wasn't.

"No."

"Fine. Then at least show me you can use it."

"I've been using it just fine."

Rensi snorted, a sound that was almost identical to the one Otho made when he was aggravated or disbelieving. "Despise me all you like, Kor, but I'm not an idiot. And I know you haven't been using it. Which is a little funny since it's the same hand you always used before."

Using my teeth, I tried to pull the mitten off but it stuck fast and tugged on the oozing scab beneath. I muttered my frustration under my breath and tried again. With each pull, it gave a little and hurt a lot. Rensi sat, cross legged and leaning back on her hands, watching my efforts with a raised eyebrow.

"Just fine, is it?" she said after I bit off a cry as the mitten came completely free.

I think it took half the skin off my hand with it. Thick yellow pus bubbled out of the cut that I'd been too afraid to look at since we'd left Borssa's cave. And before that, I'd refused Rayka's continued care of it out of pure obstinacy. I wasn't letting them pick and choose when they cared for me. A web of dark red and purple spread outward from the cut across skin that was shiny with swelling. Black tinged the torn edges of skin. It reeked of decay and I wrinkled my nose up as the smell hit me. I should have checked it before.

"Oh, Kor, that's," Rensi swallowed a gag of her own, "that's really awful. Why didn't you let me check it before?"

"Why do you care?"

The swelling went all the way up my fingers, making them too fat and the skin too tight to bend. I turned it over to look at the back of my hand where the knife had first gone in. It looked no better than my palm.

"It'll need burned," Drakkus said as he joined us at the fire. He had his knife out; not the alabaster periapt, but just a plain iron blade and he laid it just inside the fire.

"You're not touching it," I said, hugging the whole arm to myself.

"Don't be..."

"Give me one good reason why I'd let you touch it?"

Drakkus sighed and rubbed a hand over his face and all the way down his beard. "I'm sorry, Korris. I'm sorry for the way all of this turned out. Rayka was right, I should have asked Borssa what it was he planned on doing. But I didn't and this happened. And you are only going to make it worse if you won't let us take care of it."

I looked around at the men who had gathered. There wasn't one of them that I even knew the name of. And each one of them had a hand in my capture and captivity. Even Rensi who sat, leaning back, watching me still with her mild curiosity.

"Fine," I mumbled. If I didn't agree, he was just as likely to either use his periapt and force me or have his men hold me down. I was completely on my own now without even Rayka on my side. "You can do it."

When he pulled the red hot blade off the fire a few minutes later, I quailed at the sight of it. Nausea roiled my gut and I swallowed down the sick lump that rose in my throat.

"Do you want something to bite down on?" he asked.

I nodded, incapable of speech just then.

He dug inside one of his pockets and came up with a relatively clean scrap of cloth that he twisted up and held against my lips. I took it far more willingly than I'd taken the gag that they forced into my mouth upon my capture all those weeks ago.

"Hold his arm," Drakkus said to one of his men.

It was the man who'd carried me over his shoulder that came up to me and took hold of my arm. His hands gripped me hard, reminding me a little of when he'd tied my hands behind me that night. Instinct told me to fight the grasp and I started to before reason won out. It would be better to hold still and get it over with as quickly as possible. A second set of hands held me by the shoulders, pinning my left arm safely out of the way.

"Ready?"

Blinking fast and breathing hard already, I gave him a quick, sharp nod. I ought to have shut my eyes but instead I watched the knife descend just as I had on that rock up in the mountain. I watched it pierce the swollen, pus-filled abscess, spewing its contents across my hand. I watched as the skin sizzled and blistered against the heat.

And I screamed.

And screamed.

I was still screaming when he pulled the knife out and then ran it through a second and then a third time, each time burning away a little more of the pus, a little more of the vile infection that corrupted the wound. The cloth between my teeth did little to muffle my screams. Nor did the flow of cold water that followed the knife's ministrations. Drakkus poured generous amounts of it on both sides of the wound, washing away what the knife had failed to remove and soothing the burning at the same time.

"It's done," Drakkus said after what felt like an eternity.

I was sagging against the chest of the man who held my shoulders, shaking from the pain and powerless to acknowledge his words.

"Dress it before we eat, Ren."

Rensi nodded and pulled her pack toward her. It took her only a moment of digging through it to come up with a white strip of cloth and a clay pot with a lid tied onto it. I recognized the contents as soon as she loosened the leather thong holding the lid in place. It was the same salve her mother had first put on the wound and that I'd refused after. It had an odd smell of lemon and garlic and cinnamon. The price for just a little jar of that tincture must have been exorbitant. Rensi smeared it all over my hand, making me wince, before wrapping it up in the cloth. Then she leaned back again, her hands holding her up, and inspected her work with a satisfied smile.

Although I'd expected him to walk away again when he was finished, Drakkus remained sitting on his heels in front of me. He'd cleaned off his knife and slid it back into its scabbard but now he had the other one out - the alabaster blade that served as his periapt. I shrank away from him without meaning to.

"Give me your arm, Kor," he said, holding out his hand.

"Why?"

"Because I think it's time I take that off." He waved his free hand toward the tethering band that I'd almost forgotten about. It was tighter than it had been, thanks to the swelling that had traveled down to my wrist.

It took a moment for his words to register, a moment where I just stared uncomprehending at him. Then in a rush I understood. He was going to break the tether. He was going to set me free. I could go home then, not even waiting for him to take me.

I'd just placed my arm in his hand when Rensi sat straight up.

"Someone else is here, Father," she said, her eyes wide. "And there's a lot of them. I feel them coming."

Drakkus dropped my arm before she was even finished speaking and looked around, his eyes taking in every inch of the camp in a hasty sweep. A shout came from one of the watchmen on the outskirts of the camp. A shout that was cut off halfway through.

And that's when it came to me.

The cauldron over the fire but no Rayka tending it. Men dressed in gray furs with scarves concealing most of their faces. Drakkus' camp under attack.

I'd seen it all before. And I knew what happened next.

At least, I knew what happened to everyone else. My fate remained as much a mystery as it had always been. I was blind to it still. I hadn't even known that I would be in the camp when it came under attack.

More shouts came, mingling with the shrill whinny of the terrified horses. Drakkus was on his feet, hauling Rensi and I both up at the same time.

"Get him out of here, Ren," he said, turning to us.

Behind him, I saw the attackers. Men in gray furs, led by a man whose hood featured an entire wolf's head on it. That was all I had the chance to see before Rensi pulled me around and away from the fight. Away from her father who I knew was about to die.

Chapter 16

WHERE DO YOU HIDE IN the plains?

In the summer, you might find grass tall enough to conceal you. But in the winter? There's nothing. Not a single thing to hide behind. Nor can you run far enough to disappear from sight without being noticed.

If we could have reached the horses, we might have made it. But the horses were already absorbed into the ranks of the attackers and well out of our reach.

If we could have reached the mountains that were only a stone's throw away, we might have made it. But that was the direction in which the attack came, and there were mountain dwellers scattered still about the foot of the mountains, looking to pick off any who ran for the shelter of the rocks.

Rensi fled behind the farthest yurt and stopped, dropping to a crouch and pulling me down with her. Her other arm hugged her waist as she fought to bring her breathing back under control.

"We can't stay here," I insisted, trying to pull my arm out of a grip that had grown iron out of fear. "We have to get farther away."

"I can't just leave him," she snapped back at me.

"There's nothing you can do for him."

"There's nothing you even want to do for him."

I hung my head and said not another word. I'd known. I'd known this was coming and I'd said nothing. The worst of it was, that I knew I ought to feel some measure of guilt or remorse for my silence. But I didn't. There was nothing but the grim satisfaction of knowing that I'd had my revenge, even if it was a mountain tribe that was the tool to deliver it.

Still clutching my arm that was beginning to grow numb beneath the force of her grip, Rensi crawled to the edge of the yurt and peeked out from behind it.

She let out a sharp gasp and released my arm at last. "No," she whispered, then louder, "No."

Before I could stop her she was gone, running back the way we came, running to her father. Running to his already dead body. I inched my way to the same spot Rensi had just abandoned and peered around the side of the yurt.

Everything was exactly as I'd envisioned it. Drakkus lay in a growing pool of blood not far from the fire we'd all been sitting by. His men fought and fought well. I saw not one of them yield and ask for mercy but still they fell and those who did not die were overpowered and disarmed.

It was the pool of blood in the fresh white snow that drew my eyes again and again. I couldn't look away. It seeped slowly across the snow, staining it. Such a pretty color, really, that it was hard to believe it meant death. Rensi ruined the image it made when she stumbled through it and fell to her knees at Drakkus' side. I could hear her voice, wild with grief, as she begged him to not be dead. But if she'd looked at that crimson painting on the snow she would have known, like me, that it was too late.

Three of the mountain men broke through the last of Drakkus' men and started for Rensi. I tried to call a warning to her, even though I knew it wouldn't matter, but my throat tightened up and no sound came out. They were on her now, one of them grabbing a fistful of her loose hair, another dodging her swinging arm. She had a knife in that hand. An alabaster one. It sliced across the stomach of the man yanking her hair, adding another splash of red to the white snow.

I ought to have run. I knew that. My head knew that. But my feet refused to act upon that knowledge. My eyes refused to tear themselves away from the scene, shutting out everything, every sound, every sense, that wasn't directly in front of me.

A thick hand closed over my mouth, another wrapped around my throat. My breath was cut off in its constricting grasp. Stars danced in the darkness that filled my eyes.

"Keep him alive," a voice said and the hand on my throat was gone. "He's the one Brym wanted."

New hands closed in on my arms and hauled me back, dragging me toward the mountains. I lost sight of the center of the camp, of Rensi who didn't stand a chance against so many, of Drakkus' dead body. My feet were moving beneath me, carrying me along at the pace my new captors set. I didn't notice the distance until the pain came. And even then I was rushed along so that I didn't have a chance to resist.

Even when the pain wrenched a cry from me, it wasn't until I was stopped dead in my tracks by the invisible force of the tether that the man hauling me along realized something was wrong. He tried to pull me further up the trail but all that did was increase the pain in my arm, spreading it through the rest of my body. I couldn't budge another step even if I wanted to.

"What's wrong with him?" the man with the wolf head hood asked.

"It's the tether," I managed to get out between gritted teeth. "I can't go on."

A pair of cold blue eyes regarded me from under that dead wolf's head. It was really a disconcerting combination. His eyes left my face and found the band on my wrist. He grabbed my hand and pulled my arm away from my body. The imprisoning arms of the other man held me still so that my arm was stretched taut between them.

"Cut it off," he ordered.

In the second it took for me to understand that he was talking about the entire lower half of my arm and not just slicing through the band, a third man had hoisted his ax in the air.

"No!" I yelled, pulling free with a strength I hadn't realized was mine before. I slipped into shameless begging with the ease of desperation. "No. Rensi... the girl... she can undo it. Please, please, don't cut it off. Just have her undo it and then you can take me anywhere."

Those blue eyes studied me again and I held my breath, knowing that whatever came out of his mouth next would be final. Knowing that if it came down to it, he would not hesitate to sacrifice my limb for my capture. After all, they didn't need my arms, just my visions. He jerked his chin back in the direction of the camp. I followed the motion with my eyes and saw that Rensi was already on her way to join us, held between two men.

"That girl?"

"Yes. She can undo it. Please, just let her."

Rensi twisted and fought her captors' grip every step of the way up the trail, spitting out threats she was in no position to act on, until they came to a stop in front of us.

The blue-eyed man held my arm up in front of her. "Release it."

"What makes you think I can?" Rensi said, straightening and setting her jaw in defiance.

"He says so." Another jerk of his chin, this time in my direction.

"Please, Rensi. Or they're just going to cut it off."

"You can't cut a tethering band. Everyone knows that."

"No, my arm. They'll cut my arm off if you don't," I said, my voice shaking no matter how I tried to stop it. "Please, Ren?"

It had been my plan to convince Rensi to undo the tether before but not like this. Not just so I could be dragged off in yet another direction that didn't lead home. Not just so I could become someone else's game piece for a while. But the alternative was unthinkable.

Rensi bit down on her lip, her eyes darting, as she thought about it. I hadn't realized sparing my arm would be such a difficult choice. When Blue Eyes lifted a finger to signal the man with his ax, she relented with a small nod. Her arms were dropped and she snatched Drakkus' periapt out of the belt of the man on the right before he could stop her. Pricking her finger and squeezing a bead of blood out of the tiny wound, she stepped toward me.

I knew the moment I met her eyes that something was wrong. Rensi's gaze skimmed away from mine. She touched the blood to the engravings and smeared it, murmuring a set of words that sounded very similar to the ones Drakkus whispered when he put it on me. I blew out a long breath and waited for the band to come apart.

She stepped back, her jaw locked once more, and stared past me to Blue Eyes.

The band didn't budge.

There was no release from its subtle presence.

There was nothing.

"Rensi?"

"You can't undo it?"

"It's fixed. The tether is mine now instead of my father's. Keep me alive and keep me with him and you can take him wherever you want to go." Her eyes dared him to challenge her.

"Or we kill you, cut his arm off, and still take him wherever we want to go."

"I'm a tracker. I'm worth more to you alive than dead."

I was too stunned to say anything more. I stared down at my wrist and its band, at the fresh bandage that covered my hand. I couldn't quite bring myself to believe what she'd just done.

A grunt from Blue Eyes signaled the end of their conversation. Either she really was worth more to them alive than dead, or he was in a hurry to move on. Others had come up behind us from the camp, leading the handful of Drakkus' men that they'd managed to subdue without killing. There were around twenty and none were without wounds and the snow beneath us was quickly turning red from all the blood that was still flowing.

Blue Eyes gave a sharp whistle and men bearing chains swarmed around us. Despite the surety of my tether, I was subjected to the same restraints as all the others. Heavy iron shackles were clamped about my wrists and I was shoved along with the rest when we began to move forward.

Back up the same mountain we'd descended only an hour or two before we went. I squeezed between two others to catch up to Rensi and fell in step beside her.

"Why'd you do that?" I whispered, glancing to see if any of our captors noticed or cared. The nearest one watched us but made no effort to stop me from speaking. "You could have just severed it."

"Then they wouldn't have had a reason to keep me alive."

"Or they would have just had a really good reason to cut off my whole hand."

She looked at me without turning her head. "I'm not dying yet, Kor, and if that tether is what keeps me alive, I'm going to use it and there's nothing you can do about it."

Cruel words for someone who was just as much a prisoner now as I was. And cruel words rose up inside me in response. "I knew this was going to happen. I watched it happen before."

She turned to me then, eyes blazing with fury. "You knew? And you said nothing?"

"I saw your father die," I continued, happy to turn all my fear into ruthless anger. It gave me at least an illusion of control. "I saw them take you."

"And you said nothing?" she repeated. "You could have stopped this. You could have saved him."

"I did as much to save your family as your father did to save mine."

"That's not true. He sent someone..."

I blew out a sharp breath. "Would your father have listened to some stranger riding into his camp with that kind of warning? 'We captured your son and plan on taking him far away for our own purposes but in the meantime, he says you shouldn't go south.' Yes, I'm sure my father listened to that."

Rensi opened her mouth to speak and then closed it again, her eyebrows furrowing together in a troubled frown.

"It wasn't enough, Ren. You know it wasn't. He should have let me go."

For a long time, we silently trudged along, side by side, unwilling partners in captivity. My anger had time to die down and when I heard a quiet sniffling coming from

Rensi, the first tiny seed of remorse tried to sink its roots into me. I tore it away. She didn't deserve my sympathy. She deserved what was happening right now. She deserved to know what it felt like to be chained and dragged along against her will.

The pace was unrelenting, our captors determined to cover as much ground as possible before the sun went down. We'd left the trail Drakkus, Rensi and I had come down, veering off into another, more rugged path. It was impossible to walk shoulder to shoulder in some places, the rocks rising sharply on either side. Rensi and I were in front of the other captives, but we could hear every time one of them fell and struggled to rise. Blue Eyes and his men had little regard for the wounded, as savage as any mountain dwellers I'd heard stories about. It was easy to believe they were only a step away from the monsters that inhabited the Outlands when I heard them cut the throat of a man who could no longer keep up.

It was a relief when night robbed us of the light we needed to travel by. I sank down next to Rensi, not because I wanted to speak to her or have anything to do with her really, but she was the only one I knew even a little and even my anger couldn't deny that.

"You were right," Rensi whispered as she leaned against the rock next to me.

"What?"

"What you said earlier. You were right."

"I," I stopped because the sharp words that I wanted to say died away as I realized her admission.

"You wanted him to die, didn't you? For what he did to you?"

Put like that, I didn't much care for the sound of it. Had I wanted him to suffer for what he did to me? Yes. Had I wanted him to be as helpless to save his family as I had been to save mine? Yes. But had I wanted him to die? I wasn't sure and I wasn't sure it mattered.

Rensi took my silence for an answer.

She tipped her head back against the rock and shut her eyes, but I could see the tears that still escaped and rolled down her cheeks. I turned away, too caught up in my own dark thoughts to care anymore. I'd wanted her anger, her hurt. I hadn't wanted her understanding and acceptance. It struck a sore blow to my vengeance.

Chapter 17

"WELCOME TO DRAGON'S NEST," Blue Eyes called out with a sweeping gesture of his arm and a sneer on his face.

In the almost week it had taken us to reach this barren, rocky spot he claimed was the famed Dragon's Nest, I had yet to learn his actual name.

Stopping beside Rensi, I took in our new surroundings. It wasn't much to look at unless one had a great love for grim shades of white and gray. Where we stood was a narrow valley cutting between two cliff-like slopes that looked quite impossible to climb until I noticed the series of staircases and walkways carved out of the very wall of rock. Cave mouths peppered the cliffs on both sides and from these, faces peered out at us. The valley and the cliffs stretched on and on.

The stairs only reached the first level of those caves. From there, flimsy rope ladders that danced and whipped about hung between the layers of caves, providing access to those brave or foolish enough to put their trust in them. Higher still, rope bridges swayed, connecting one side of Dragon's Nest to the other. Considering that there was nothing but sharp, rugged rock beneath my feet, I doubted a fall from one of those bridges could be survived. The people who called this home were truly another breed.

A cutting wind blew straight through the valley, biting through my clothes that, I had to admit, were not in the best condition anymore. I was still wearing the soft leather jerkin and pants I'd been captured in with only the fur coat, hat and mittens to add any protection against the cold. My thoughts drifted to Rayka who had given me the coat and hat and mittens. I wondered if the entire winter would pass before she ventured out of the mountains and discovered what had happened to us.

I shifted from one foot to the other, uncomfortably conscious of the cold that seeped up from the ground and through the soles of my boots. My boots, which had been quite sturdy many long weeks ago, were showing signs of the many weeks of unrelenting travel I'd put them through. Bits of ice and snow sped across the wind, stinging my cheeks until I brought the crook of my arm up to shield myself.

"Look, Kor," Rensi said, her voice almost carried away by the ferocity of the wind.

I followed her gaze to what lay beyond the long, narrow valley. It was only barely visible in the nonstop swirl of snow and ice. A shadow that could not be driven away by the light of any sun.

The Outlands.

I'd never seen them before, only heard of them.

The darkness of the Outlands was like a void, sucking in all the light it could touch and destroying it. What monsters lurked inside that realm of shadow was anyone's guess. No one had ever returned alive from the Outlands. At least, none that I'd heard of.

The faces that had been peering out at us from the caves became people. They swarmed down their rope ladders and stone staircases, filling the valley up around us. There were men, women, and children among those gathered to inspect us. Each was bundled up so thickly in furs of various gray that they looked like walking, waddling mounds of blankets. Scarves shielded most of their faces, making it difficult to get a good look at any of them. Thick, fur lined boots that made me jealous of their warmth seemed the most common foot gear. A few even had wolf head hoods such as Blue Eyes.

They gathered around us, milling about as if waiting for something, murmuring amongst themselves. Copper coins and bright beads, the currency of the mountain dwellers, changed hands a few times.

"They're making bets on us," Rensi said when she noticed the same thing. "Probably on which one of us will die first."

"Oh." I couldn't think of a single other thing to say than that. If they were betting on who would be the first to die, then they'd all already lost for our numbers were far smaller now than when we started. Blue Eyes hadn't any patience with those whose wounds prevented them from keeping up and eight of the twenty men who'd been our fellow prisoners had died along the trail. Despite the part they'd played in my capture, it was difficult to watch the callous manner in which those men had been murdered. It made me almost pity them.

"Don't worry. It won't be you," she added. She'd read my silence wrong, but I didn't correct her. "You just have to tell them who you are, and they'll keep you alive."

Just like Drakkus had. Alive, to suit their own purposes and meet their own needs. For a fleeting second, I thought about what it would be like if Borssa's ritual had worked. If the transfer of my gift to Otho had been successful.

I'd die.

That's what it would be like.

The throng of observers parted like grass, drawing away to each side to form a human pathway. An expectant hush fell over them and Blue Eyes and his men moved among us quickly, shoving us into something of a line and then pushing us one by one to our knees.

I caught myself with my right hand as I went down hard and grimaced. The cut still wasn't healed. At this point, I wasn't sure it ever would. The last I'd seen it was right after Drakkus burned the infection out and Rensi put a salve and a bandage on it. For the last week, I hadn't dared unwrap that bandage.

Cold snow melted under my knees and shins, dampening the leather of my boots and pants, and working its way to my skin. If we knelt for much longer, I'd have been shivering like a leaf in the wind. I bowed my head to protect my face from the savage wind and to allow myself to draw breath without it being snatched ruthlessly away.

Rensi's elbow caught me in the side, and I looked up to find the reason for the sudden silence and our manhandling.

Draped in more furs than I'd ever seen anyone wear, a stooped, withered person approached, leaning heavily on a staff that stood well above their head. Unlike the other members of Dragon's Nest, they wore no hood. All that was left of their hair was a few white strands that hung limp and languid from their balding scalp. It wasn't until they stopped just in front of us that I realized they were a woman.

She was more ancient than any elder I'd seen, not an inch of her face free of papery wrinkles. Her shoulders were rounded over, her neck bent with the weight of age. Gray eyes that resembled the same shade as piles of filthy slush left behind at winter's end stared out at us with an intensity that defied her age. She looked us over one by one, nodding as she finished her visual assessment of each. When she reached me, her eyes narrowed, and her gaze sharpened.

With slow, tottering steps she came to stand in front of me.

"Time walker," she said, a gravelly edge to her voice. She leaned in close. Her fingers with nails like talons stretched out and caught me by the chin. Her grip tightened as she lifted my head and tilted it first to one side then the other, her fingernails digging into my cold skin. When she smiled, her face only inches from my own, the stench of her rotten breath filled my nose. What teeth she had left were yellow and gray with decay. "Time walker," she said again, taking my face between both of her withered hands. She gave a darting look to the crowd around us and raised her voice, "The time walker is mine. Feed the others to the Outlanders."

A protest rippled down the line from the others. A cry for mercy.

My face still held between her hands, I could only sense the warriors closing in on the line of us from behind, pulling the others to their feet.

"Wait," Rensi cried out from beside me. "He is tethered to me. If you keep him, you must keep me too."

The old woman released my face and tapped one long nail against her chin. "Girlie is afraid to face the

Outlanders," she announced, breaking into a laughter that cut almost as much as the wind did. Those standing nearest joined in with the raucous sound. "Girlie likes to be kept safe in the plains but doesn't like to be the one keeping the others safe." She whirled on Rensi with more speed than I'd thought possible. "Plains wanderers are trash." She spat on the ground in front of Rensi. "Good for nothing but feeding the monsters. We cut off the tether and then you go to the Outlanders."

Rensi hadn't lied when she said she wouldn't die yet. She hadn't lied when she said she'd do whatever it took, even if it meant using me. With a calmness I marveled at, she stood and spoke. "You could. You could maim your oracle and kill me. But if you do that, do you know what you risk?"

The question hung unanswered in the air. A clever thing, that question. I didn't know the answer to it and looking at the old hag in front of me, I could tell she didn't either. Her aged face twisted up with suspicion but also a little bit of wariness.

After that telling pause, Rensi went on. "You risk lies every time he tells you the future. You risk his curse upon time. Fentra's curse lives on now, even three hundred years past her death. Is that what you wish to risk?"

"You think your life matters that much to him?"

"No, I think his arm matters that much to him and for him to keep that you will need to keep me."

The glower in the old woman's eyes as she stared up at Rensi from her stooped position was enough to tell me Rensi had won. She'd have laughed the words off if Rensi hadn't. A withered hand fluttered and the warriors stepped away from Rensi and turned their attention fully on the handful of Drakkus' men who were still alive after our travels.

Fed to the Outlanders. That's what the old woman had said was to be done with them. I stared past the old woman, passed the throng of people and into the darkness of the Outlands, an idea slowly taking shape in my head. An idea put there by Rensi's defiance. No, from before that. It came from the seed of guilt that had begun to worm its way inside me. I'd wanted revenge, but I didn't want to be a murderer. Especially, I didn't want to stand here and look into the eyes of those men as they were condemned to a death worse than any I could imagine. I owed them nothing. But I didn't wish them dead. Not like that.

"Stop," I said.

My voice wasn't raised, nor did I think it carried very far but everything stopped at that one word and became silent. The warriors, their prisoners, the people gathered to gawk at the spectacle. They all froze, waiting for me to speak again.

The old woman eyed me with malice and intrigue but said nothing.

Swallowing down the queasiness that threatened my stomach, I said, "If you want my gift of foresight, you will not kill any of them."

"Is that so?" Her mouth pinched up, shifting the wrinkles on her face.

"It is."

"And if they live?"

"I am yours." The words made me sick to say but I was really hers already. This at least put some of the choice back into my hands.

Beside me, I heard Rensi gasp softly and felt her shift closer to me, her hand brushing against mine. I think my words took her by surprise, almost as much as they had me. I heard her whisper my name in question but did not dare look in her direction.

The old woman lifted her hands, one still clutching her staff, into the air and faced the crowd - the bloodthirsty crowd that had begun to quietly chant their desire to see death. "The time walker speaks and Brym will listen. The Outlanders are not to be fed this day." Turning back to me, she lowered her voice and said, "Fail me and they all die, the girlie included. No curse of yours will stay my hand."

I decided not to tell her that I had no idea how to curse anyone. That until Rensi had spoken of Fentra and her curse I hadn't even known it was part of an oracle's gift. Given the fact that an oracle hadn't existed in three hundred years, I wasn't sure my gift was even the same thing as the gift Fentra had.

She grabbed my arm with the hand not clinging to her staff. "Come, my little time walker, it is time we got acquainted, you and I."

CHAPTER 18

I STARED UP AT THE ROPE ladder as it was tossed to and fro by the great gusts of wind. Beside me, Brym stood, waiting. I had my doubts about my being able to climb the thing and hold onto it against the pull of the wind. There was no way she could do it. Beneath all the furs, her body was as frail as a newborn's.

"Climb, time walker."

My right hand throbbed as I closed it around the rope rung, the skin inside the bandage stretching and pulling uncomfortably with the movement. I wasn't sure it would bear my weight as I climbed that first step. I still wasn't sure by the time I'd reached the fourth or fifth rung, but I was now committed. Even with my weight on it, the ladder swung into the wind. I made it about halfway up before succumbing to the temptation of looking back.

It was a dreadful mistake.

I'd never been higher than a horse's back and now I was precariously suspended above the top of the world, blowing about as if I was no more than a leaf on a tree.

Below me, I could see the entire valley that made up the gap in the mountains. I could see in the distance the trail we'd come up and the patches of mud brown and gray rock that had been exposed by the tramping of many hundreds of feet. From up there, I could see a thin waterfall, surprisingly unfrozen, descending into a stream. The people who were still gathered in that valley were like little black insects scurrying around.

A wave of lightheadedness washed over me, and I gripped the ropes harder, pressing my forehead to the back of one hand and shutting my eyes until I felt the dizziness pass.

"It's a beautiful sight, eh?"

Lifting my eyes, I saw Brym hanging beside me, not on a ladder as I was but seated in a sling of rope and fur and leather hides. A rope was attached to the top of the sling, going all the way up the cliff and over some sort of beam they'd fixed at the top. Far below us, two or three men pulled on the other end of the rope, hoisting the sling higher and higher. I had to admire their genius in finding a way to move even the weak and elderly around such a forbidding and dangerous place as Dragon's Nest. Out in the plains, we often just abandoned ours when they could no longer keep up - a fate I would no doubt have suffered along with the others but for my father's intervention.

I didn't think I could get any words out to answer Brym, so I just resumed my climb. The sooner I reached the top the sooner this part of the nightmare would be over. I didn't let myself think about the fact that if I were climbing up now then at some time in the future I would have to climb down.

The ladder came to an abrupt end on a ledge that led into a cave. The mouth of it was small enough that I had to crouch down as I pushed aside the animal hide that hung over it to enter but once inside it opened up into a spacious room. The same musty scent that I'd noticed in Borssa's cave filled this one as well. Added to it was the lingering fetid odor that I assumed came from Brym's rotting teeth.

Shelves were carved all along one side of the cave and an assortment of clay and glass jars filled the shelves, lined up several deep. The light was dim, a shaft of it coming through a small square opening that went through the ceiling and all the way to the top of the cliff. Just beneath that, a ring of stones contained a fire that sent its smoke up through the hole. A candle of yellow wax added the final bit of lighting to the room, set on a wooden trestle table in the very back of the room. Passageways led out of the room, deeper into the mountain, but they were too dark for me to see what lay beyond.

The stone walls were broken up in parts with more animal skins and furs - probably in an effort to trap in the heat of the fire and to make the entire thing seem more comfortable than it really was. Whoever thought the inside of a rock was a satisfactory abode must have been desperate for a place to call home.

Brym walked past me and lit another candle, illuminating another corner of the shadowy room. I think it would have taken a hundred candles at least to make the place seem warm and inviting. Brym lit no more than that one, though.

"Come, come, time walker, welcome to your new home." Brym's scratchy voice echoed in the chamber, bouncing off the stone walls.

A hand on my shoulder nudged me forward and I twisted my head around to see who it was behind me. I hadn't known anyone had followed me up the ladder. It was Blue Eyes, looking as cold and hateful as ever. He paid little attention to me but gave Brym a look like venom when her back was turned to him.

His hand guided me forward to a space on the back wall that was unbroken by passageways. There was a chain anchored into the wall, its metal old and dull in the uncertain light.

Blue Eyes picked up the end of it and bent to fasten it around my ankle. The iron band was uncomfortably snug. Judging from the amount of loose chain that lay coiled on the dirt, I guessed that I could make it to the ledge outside the cave before reaching the end.

"Why?" I asked Brym. "I'm already tethered."

Her smile made my skin crawl as she hobbled toward me. "But not to me, you're not. One can't run, but two can. And you, my little time walker, aren't going anywhere."

Since she stood no higher than I, it was aggravating to be so frequently referred to as little. I wasn't in a position to complain, though, especially not with Blue Eyes still in the room. I'd seen just how quickly and easily he could slit a man's throat.

"What is it you want from me?" I hoped it was not some other ritual.

"From what you are now," Brym paused to spit again, "nothing. But from what I can make you, great things. Many great things. The gift of the Fates is mine to use now and use it I shall. Many times you shall walk for me, little time walker, and you will show me the best paths. Oh, yes, you shall show me all the best paths."

"What you can make me?"

But Brym was done speaking to me. She disappeared down one tunnel, carrying her candle with her and talking to herself, and Blue Eyes retreated out of the cave entirely. With nothing to do and nowhere to go, I settled back against the wall and tried to make some sense of my current situation. Until, that is, exhaustion took over and I fell asleep.

~ ~ ~

It was the rustle of someone moving about the room that roused me again many hours later. The gray winter light of day had faded and now only the fire and the candle lit up the room.

Brym had returned but she was not the one moving around. She was seated on a pile of thick furs by the fire, her eyes shut, and her hands clasped around whatever ornament hung from the leather thong around her neck. She swayed back and forth and murmured softly to herself in a chant.

The movement in the room came from Rensi. I noticed her before she realized I was awake and for a long moment I said nothing to change that, merely watching as she moved to set a small pot she'd just filled with some sort of food over the fire. Her hair was tied back in a braid for once, giving her a sharper look than usual and there was a redness to her eyes that belied her stony expression.

With the pot on the fire, she sat facing me on a low stone bench that ran along one side of the fire pit and that's when she saw I was awake. An odd look passed over her face like a shadow as she met my eyes. I frowned and shrugged to show her I didn't understand its meaning.

"You are permitted to speak to each other," Brym said, her eyes still shut tight. "But know this, time walker, you bought your friends' lives on the promise of your cooperation. Anything other than cooperation, and I will start killing them off."

The warning was as clear as it had been hours before. But that didn't stop my mind from racing through possibilities. Many, many possibilities. Sadly, I couldn't think of a single plan that could work without Rensi severing the tether that bound me to her. If she did that, I would run regardless of what that meant for Drakkus' men.

I was curious, though, to know just what Brym planned to do with Drakkus' men. And I was curious, too, just how much she would give me for my cooperation. I'd never bargained with my gift as I had with her that day.

"Where are the others?" I asked her as soon as the thought came to me.

Brym paused in her swaying and cracked one eye open to look at me. "They are safe and safely locked away."

"How do I know you didn't just kill them while I slept?"

"You don't."

She went back to her swaying and crooning, and I went back to my thinking. The silence lasted only a few moments before a new thought came to mind.

"You must let me see them every day or I give you nothing." I watched her carefully as my words reached her. I watched for any anger or impatience at my testing.

"Adding to the bargain, time walker?" Brym smiled, keeping her mouth closed this time so that she did not reveal the half empty rows of rotting teeth. "Very well. But then I get to add to it as well."

"What else could you possibly want from me?"

Brym's smile widened and turned fierce. "I have not yet decided but I will be sure to let you know when the time comes, time walker."

"I have a name, you know."

"Aye, I imagine you do. But you've not yet shared that with me, have you?"

"It's Korris," I said, trying to hide my growing irritation. I should have just let the matter of the other prisoners' rest. I'd already done more for them than they deserved, and I had no wish to bind myself further to Brym. Still, it was reassuring to know that my gift was valuable enough to make such demands.

"Eat well, time walker," Brym said with her frightful grin. "Tonight, you eat and rest and tomorrow you work." She opened her eyes all the way, dropping the ornament she'd been cradling in her hands back down inside the front of her shirt. "You, girlie, feed him well. He'll need his strength come tomorrow."

With that she rose and disappeared back down the same passageway she'd used before, her tottering steps fading away as she made her way deeper into the mountain.

Rensi didn't move from her seat by the fire, one arm outstretched to give the contents of the pot a small stir. A tangy aroma wafted up from that pot, mingling with the less pleasant odors that inhabited the cave. Whatever was cooking, it was something I'd never eaten before, but I was hungry enough to be excited about trying it.

"That was...," Rensi started and then stopped, chewing on her lip, and bringing the tail of her braid over her shoulder to toy with. The tip of her brown hair twirled round and round on her finger. "That wasn't something I expected you to do."

Tipping my head back against the wall, I let out a sigh but didn't say anything. A pain was starting in my head - the first in a week.

"I'm glad you saved them. Father would..." her voice faded off at the sour look I shot in her direction. Drakkus had nothing to do with my decision to bargain for his men's lives. I wanted to say something to that effect but stopped myself when I remembered he was dead and the redness in Rensi's eyes. "You didn't owe them that."

"No, I didn't."

Whatever was in the pot began to bubble and boil, steam rising and following the smoke of the fire. With my eyes half shut I watched it escape the cave, drifting up into the night sky where the wind would catch it and pull it away. I shared a certain kinship with that wisp of steam and smoke. A kinship born entirely out of how helpless we both were to take any control over the direction we were taken. At least the smoke got to breathe fresh air. The air inside the cave was anything but fresh.

"What do you suppose she wants with you tomorrow?"

Shrugging, I finally left my spot on the wall and made my way over to the stone bench Rensi occupied, mostly in the hopes of getting food sooner. It had been many hours since we'd been fed anything at all and despite the growing pain in my head, and the tired ache in my limbs, my mouth watered for food. Rensi slid over enough to make room for me, staring down at the chain I'd dragged, clanking, across the room with me.

"She knows you can't run, doesn't she?"

"Unless you run with me. That's what she's afraid of. Although it would have been nice of her to chain you up instead. I think I've been bound enough lately."

Rensi ignored my last words. "I can't run. Not while they have..."

"Your father's men," I finished for her. "I know."

And that was the cold, naked truth of our situation. Rensi wouldn't run out on her father's men, and I couldn't run off without her. We were well and truly trapped by these savages of Dragon's Nest until they either got what they wanted from me or tired of trying. And if either of those things happened, I was pretty sure our next step would just be death.

We ate our meal in silence, both too lost in our own thoughts to pretend to be interested in the other's. Besides, my headache was worsening rapidly.

"You're going to have one, aren't you?" Rensi said, watching me as I set my bowl, still half uneaten, aside and held my head between my hands.

I didn't even get to nod before I was no longer sitting in a cave on a cold mountaintop.

Chapter 19

BRYM HELD MY INJURED HAND in hers, her head bent to examine it as she turned it over.

"What happened to it?"

"It's from a ritual."

She tapped a long nail onto the cut, beginning to pry open the barely sealing scab and I jerked my hand back away from her.

"What ritual?"

I looked down at the cut. It was starting to bleed again where she'd jabbed it and I hated the sight of it, so I shut my eyes and forced my mind back to that night. There were still whole hours of it missing from my memories. "The man who had me before tried to take my gift and transfer it to his son."

"Why?"

"They said something about...," I frowned, trying to piece together the mutterings of an old man that hadn't made any sense then and still didn't. What was it Borssa had said when my thoughts were so muddied by incense and drink that I couldn't see straight? "They said something about only firstborns of kings being able to have the gift of foresight..."

"That's a silly name," Brym said.

I fell silent then, unsure if she wanted me to continue or not. Her sharp gray eyes flashed, and she took my hand again, bending a little closer to it as if that might reveal some secret she'd hitherto missed. Why my hand and its wound fascinated her so, I had yet to discern. She'd come back to it again and again in the past few hours.

"Go on."

"There's not much else to tell about it. He tried to take it and it failed. I still have it."

"Hmmm." She began picking at the scab again and I pulled my hand away a second time.

"Stop doing that." Once I'd tucked my hand safely under my arm, I asked, "Why did you say that foresight was a silly name?"

"Because it is."

I bit down on my lip hard to keep from saying anything and lowered my head to hide my exasperation. A more infuriating person to be trapped with, I couldn't think of. She'd roused me well before the sun came up and made Rensi prepare a meal for me. Then she'd taken me back into another room branching off of the main one. I could only reach the middle of the room with my chain on and there she bade me sit while she sat in front of me, so close that our knees were touching. When I'd tried to back away, I discovered that she was in possession of a thin switch. A flick of her wrist and my knuckles were stinging.

We'd been sitting like that, knee to knee, since then and I was no closer to discovering what she wanted of me than I had been the night before.

All I did know was that the residual ache in my head was becoming a torment in the close air and stiff, unmoving position. I still wasn't sure what to make of the vision I'd had the night before.

I'd thought at first that it was the same world ending one that I was used to and perhaps it was. But if it was, it was a part I'd never seen before. There'd been no walled city to see, no screaming voices of the masses as they tried to flee the inferno. The only thing that was the same was the inferno.

And the voice.

Except, that inferno was trapped inside a mountain, in a cavern so vast that it could easily have fit half the tribes of the plains inside it. And the voice when it spoke, was little more than a whisper. It uttered the same two words it had before, *"Free me,"* and nothing more. The tone of the voice was different, though, full of sorrow and pain and anguish.

I'd come out of the vision with Brym only inches from my face, studying me hard, her sharp gray eyes soaking in every detail of what she could see. She'd ordered me to bed when her inspection was through and, since there was no bed, I curled up near the fire, content to be allowed to sleep for the next few hours so that I might recover some of the strength that the vision had pulled from me.

Brym's switch snapped across my left hand again and I was jolted out of my thoughts.

"You let your mind wander too much. You're no good to me that way."

"Perhaps if you told me what it is you expect of me, I could try to do it."

She shook her head, sending the few strands of white hair that she had back and forth. "You're not ready for what I want. But I will make you ready and you shall let me, or friends will begin to die."

"You don't have to remind me."

"Don't I, time walker?"

I'd given up trying to get her to call me by my name. It made sense, I suppose, for her to refer to me only as time walker. That's all I was to her. Her tool. Her game piece. Her weapon against the rest of the world.

"Why do you call me time walker?"

"Ah," her face lit up in a pleased smile, "now there is a question worth asking. Let's play a game, shall we? A question for a question, an answer for an answer. No refusals. Not from you, not from me."

I shrugged and nodded. If we were going to sit here all day staring at each other, I might as well try to learn something. I'd wasted most of my opportunities with Drakkus to learn more about my gift and I was beginning to regret that. I wouldn't make the same mistake here. There were questions I wanted the answers to and if I had to ask an ancient woman who was half mad and holding me captive, then I supposed I might as well get started.

"Why do I call you time walker, eh? Well, that's what you do, isn't it?"

"Not exactly. I just see things in the future sometimes."

"We all see things..."

"Not in the future."

"The past is present; the present, future; the future, past. Round and round time goes. We all see time. It just so happens the rest of us have to look back at it and we call it memory. But you, you can walk it all and that is a gift."

I leaned forward, resting my elbow on my knee and cupping my chin in my hand, trying to make sense of her words. And then I concluded that there was no sense to be made from them and then I just tried to appear as if they made sense to me so that we could move on to something that really did.

Brym took the switch in her hand and scooted back enough to open a little space of dirt floor between us. With the thick end of the switch, she drew a circle in the dust.

"Time," she said, tapping the circle.

I raised an eyebrow at her and she slapped her hand to her forehead.

"You are an infant to the workings of the world, are you not?" She didn't give me a chance to answer which was probably for the best. "Time's a circle, see? If you live long enough, you get to see it repeat itself. Rises and falls. Ups and downs. It all comes and goes, over and over again. We each get to enter and exit at our own points, but time never stops going around for that."

"I see." Even though I didn't. I stared down at the circle as if it were making sense to me in the hopes that we could move on. Even if I did understand what she was saying, I wasn't sure what the purpose of this was. "What's your question?"

Brym didn't ask her question right away. She continued to tap the ground with her long nails. Her eyes were shut and after several minutes had gone by during which even her finger had stopped its tapping, I began to fear she'd dozed off. I held myself still just in case she hadn't. Her switch was a painful thing on my fingers. Voices came from the main room and still she did not open her eyes again. I strained to catch whose voices they were and tried to quell the knot of anxiety that came when I heard Blue Eyes as well as Rensi.

"Who is your father?"

Her voice was soft, softer than I'd ever heard it and when she spoke like that it lost some edge of its agedness. She'd leaned in close to me to speak, her rancid breath a torment to my nostrils, and I turned my head to the side.

"He's just a chieftain of one of the plains' tribes." It was strange to finally admit that secret. It made me think of Drakkus and I wondered if he ever guessed, if he'd ever given the matter enough thought to put together the pieces.

She laughed at my answer; it was as soft as her words a moment ago. "No, he is not. What periapt does he carry?"

"It's a...," I stopped, a whisper of doubt fracturing my thoughts. I couldn't say why I didn't want her to know what periapt was his, but that information was suddenly precious and not to be shared with someone like Brym. Besides, what did she mean by saying he wasn't a chieftain? "I don't know for sure. He never let me see it. Why don't you believe that he's a chieftain?"

"Do you know what periapt I carry?"

That she carried one came as no surprise. Why else would the entirety of Dragon's Nest listen to her commands? She was their oldest, frailest member. Men like Blue Eyes would have thrown her out of power ages ago if she hadn't had a different power to wield.

"I don't."

Excitement danced in her eyes, reminding me of the way Ahashi would look when she wanted to show off one of her special collections of crushed flowers or pebbles that she'd picked up along the way. She motioned me to lean closer.

"I don't let many see mine either," she whispered and smiled as if we shared some conspiratorial secret. "Would you like to see it?"

I nodded, her behavior awakening a burning curiosity in me. I'd only seen two periapts in my life – my father's and Drakkus'.

"Guess what it is?"

I scrunched my face up and thought for a moment. "I have no idea. Dragon's tooth?"

Brym laughed and reached down inside the front of her shirt, pulling out the leather thong that hung around her neck. There were two items hanging from it, a small key, and an ornament.

Without taking the necklace off, she leaned forward and held out the ornament pinched between her thumb and forefinger, letting the key slide back down to her neck. Many shades of green and flecks of gold were trapped inside the glass orb, catching the flickering candlelight, and tossing it back out in splintered rays. A black center contrasted the colors by absorbing the light rather than reflecting it.

"What is it?" I reached out a hand and Brym permitted my curious touch. It was smooth and cold, despite having been resting against her skin.

"Eye of a dragon. It is one of the great periapts. Not like those harvested from the scales or claws. It is power, time walker, great power. It gives me the ability to look anywhere I choose."

"Then why do you need me?"

Those few hours of conversation had made me forget just what sort of person Brym was. Her vicious smile reminded me of the truth. My heart thudded in my chest at the sight of it and I remembered how quickly she'd ordered the others fed to the Outlanders.

"I need you because this," she shook the eye, "isn't enough. It's never been enough. It only lets me see what I choose, but how am I to know what to choose? It only lets me see things that are happening right now. It does not let me see the future. And I need to see the future." A wild light filled her gray eyes. "There's a war coming, time walker. I think you've seen it. And I'll not be left behind in it. I plan on bringing the war. Dragon's Nest will bring the legions of the Outlands to the plains and to Abirell, to Ludys and to the Iron Towers. And you, my little time walker, are going to be the reason I win where all others have failed. You will tell me where to strike next, you will tell me where to avoid, you will show me the path I must take to reach victory. There's a war coming and this time the right people are going to win it."

The mad joy in her face as she spoke made me shrink away from her.

It was madness.

I could see the lunacy of her words in her eyes. The legends surrounding dragons all agreed that their greed was their driving force, the most compelling instinct they possessed. It was that innate need to keep, to possess, to control that powered the tethers.

And some said that the same need could fill the heart of a person bearing one of the great periapts if they held it long enough. It was power humanity was never meant to own, some said, and the price for that power was sometimes succumbing to the same mad greed of the dragons. Myths and legends, all of it. But looking at Brym, I could believe the stories.

"I can't do that. I can't control the visions - when I see them or what I see."

"Not yet you can't," she snapped, coming out of her gleeful reverie. "That's why I will teach you and you will learn. And the first thing you must learn is focus."

CHAPTER 20

"FOCUS."

"Concentrate."

"Pay attention."

"Control your mind."

If I had kept count of the number of times I heard those words in the following days, I'm quite sure it would have neared a million. I'd never known how distracted I was by everything until Brym insisted I practice blocking it all out.

I was sitting out on the ledge just in front of her cave entrance, trying to block out the sound of the wind whining as it sliced through the valley and focus on the scratchy sound of her voice coming from the room behind me. It was an exercise we'd tried before and that I'd failed before. The bitter cold didn't help. Nor did the blindfold she'd tied over my eyes to force me concentrate just on her voice. It scratched against my frozen skin, leaving it feeling raw.

My mind sought relief from the cold, from the harsh winds and the pelting frozen rain, from the chain around my ankle and the tethering band on my wrist, from the constant weight of worry about my family that hung about me. It wandered south, to winters passed spent in the warm sun that always shined on the Iron Towers and I offered no resistance to the wandering although I knew I should.

I was supposed to be learning what Brym wanted to teach me. Lives depended upon it. Besides that, I wanted to learn. If there was a way to control my gift, I wanted to know it. But learning it was hard.

"You're useless to me," Brym said, her voice sharp in my ear.

I jumped a little. She'd come up behind me noiselessly and had caught me daydreaming. With the blindfold on, I had to guess at exactly where she was standing and placed her just inside the opening of the cave.

"When will you try?"

"I've been trying."

"Hmph...not good enough, time walker. Is it so hard to listen to my voice and nothing else?"

I shrugged and felt her switch across my hands that were resting palm down on the rock behind me. Straightening up, I pulled them back into my lap with a hiss of pain. It hurt worse since my knuckles were well nigh frozen.

"I want answers when I ask questions. Not whatever that was."

"Yes, then. It is hard to listen to just your voice."

Whether as a reward for my answer or just because she felt like it, Brym loosened the knot of the blindfold and let it slip free. I blinked at the bright sunlight. It was the first cloudless day I'd seen in Dragon's Nest but even sunlight couldn't make the place look any cheerier or more appealing. It was too harsh, too jagged, too desolate.

I tipped my face up to feel the light and slight warmth of the sun on my skin, trying to feed a need that my memories of the south in winter had awakened. It was a pale comparison, but I soaked it in anyway.

"Inside," Brym ordered, and I grudgingly got to my feet. "Perhaps we need to try something different."

I followed her into the miserable cavern she insisted on calling my new home, reminding me often that I wasn't going anywhere unless she decided it, dragging my chain with me. It clanged with every movement I made, often jarring me out of my sleep during the night. I'd yet to accustom myself to its presence. I didn't want to adjust to it. If I did, I feared I'd lose what little of myself I had left.

"What else is there to try?"

Brym didn't answer, just beckoned for me to follow her down another passageway. It was one I hadn't even known existed because its opening was concealed by an animal skin tacked into the stone wall. She lifted it just enough to slip inside and I did the same.

Hot, moist air hit my face, stealing away my breath for a moment. Sweat sprung up on my forehead almost at once, running in beads down my face in the heat. Steam shrouded the air making it difficult to see much of anything. I wondered how she heated the room and how she trapped the heat so thoroughly inside it. Although a fire was always burning in the front room, a chill still lingered, never fully driven off.

I made it a little way into the room before I stopped, not because I'd reached the end of my chain but because there was a pool of water that I was dangerously close to stepping into. A pool of water that looked bottomless.

Steam rose in curling strands from the water. Brym stood on the other side of, her smile ghastly in the warped air like some ghoulish vision come to haunt me.

"We are going to try this."

"A bath?" I asked, raising an incredulous eyebrow. I wouldn't have minded one, especially since the water was clearly warm. It might have been warm enough to finally rid my bones of the chill that had settled in them. But I had my doubts about its ability to aid in any part of my gift.

She let loose a soft laugh. "Oh, no. That's not what I had in mind. Sit."

It was that soft laughter that was the most frightening. It never matched the crazed, wild light of her eyes.

I tensed but sat down, crossing my legs beneath me and folding my hands together in my lap to resist the temptation to touch the hot water. My fingertips were still frozen from a morning spent outside trying to focus on Brym's voice. The steam brushed up against my skin making it tingle with the promise of warmth and leaving droplets behind to mingle with my sweat.

Brym sat on her own side of the pool, just a few feet away from me. Rather than tucking her legs up to avoid the water, she unlaced her old, worn boots that looked to be about as ancient as she was, and removed them. She let her bare feet dangle in the water and reached for her periapt.

"What do you want me to do?" I asked after she'd shut her eyes and commenced swaying back and forth, chanting under her breath.

"I want you to sit. And I want you to think about time. I want you to search for the threads that make up time and when you have found one, I want you to follow it."

"Threads of time?" I sighed and gave into the temptation to put my hands in the water. The heat burned savagely on my icy skin, and I pulled them out at once with a scowl. "And what are these threads of time that I'm looking for? What do they look like?"

Brym broke off her chant a second time and shot me a withering look of annoyance.

"You know nothing, time walker. Why the Fates chose you is beyond me. It's little wonder the last man who had you thought to give your gift to another. As a time walker, you're useless."

Her words were like a lash across me, stinging in their assessment and judgement. Pressing my lips together and blinking fast, I took a deep breath, determined to say not another word. I hadn't asked for my gift in the first place and how was I supposed to know anything about it? Three hundred years between oracles didn't leave much information behind.

I wished I'd asked Drakkus more. He seemed to know quite a bit about oracles. And however much I'd hated him, he'd been slightly easier to ask questions of than Brym. At least he didn't choose to speak in riddles and puzzles half the time. Actually, when I allowed myself the luxury of wishing, I wished that I'd warned him of the attack. If I had, perhaps it would have been prevented and I would truly have been on my way home, free of the tether. Not that I would ever confess that regret to Rensi.

Steam clouded around me, its vapors making me drowsy. I let my eyes fall half shut as Brym resumed her chanting and rocking back and forth on the other side, her own eyes closed. With the periapt clasped in her hands, I could only assume she was taking the time to look through it. I wondered what it was she stared at so often. Her settlement in Dragon's Nest, perhaps? Or the border between Dragon's Nest and the Outlands? Were there troublesome members of her tribe that she felt the need to check in on every day? Since she could only see what she knew to look for and what was happening in the moment, I was beginning to think the eye of the dragon wasn't quite so powerful a periapt as she wanted it to be.

Sweat tickled the back of my neck, dampening my hair and reminding me of how long it had grown in the last weeks. My mother never let it get so long. I shut my eyes and tried to see her face - not as I'd seen it in my vision, twisted with terror and pain. No, that wasn't how I wished to remember her.

Instead, I thought back to the last time I'd actually seen her face to face. I'd been resting in the elder's yurt, only hours away from being snatched from my tribe and taken with Drakkus and his. Mother and Ahashi had come together to visit me, a slightly wilted, slightly crushed assortment of flowers in Ahashi's little hands.

Mother had sat with me then, quiet because my head hurt. Just there. She was good at that. She was good at just being there and not needing to fill the silence up with useless unwanted words. She'd brought a leather jerkin she was stitching for my brother, Jarris, with her and sat, her round, smiling face bent over her work while I watched and rested. From time to time, she would hold her work up and inspect it, her quick, brown eyes scanning every inch to catch any mistakes she'd made.

"You are thinking of someone?" Brym's scratchy voice reached out to me from across the steaming pool of water.

"Yes."

"Good. You are thinking of a memory of them?"

"Yes."

"Good. Very good." Brym clapped her hands together as if I'd achieved the greatest success I could just by calling up a memory. "You've found a thread. Now follow it. See where it goes. See whose threads it is woven in and out of."

"That doesn't make any sense."

"Because you are trying to make it make sense. Walking time doesn't. If it did, it wouldn't be a gift from the Fates, would it?"

That made even less sense.

"What exactly do you want me to do?"

Brym let out a growl of frustration and dropped her periapt back down the front of her shirt, giving me her full attention.

"Take the memory and follow it."

"There's nothing to follow. That's it, the last one I have of her." My voice broke a little over the words and I hoped Brym missed it. "I haven't seen her since so I don't know what comes after. I can't follow what I don't know."

"If you were like the rest of us, you couldn't. But you aren't like the rest of us. You can walk time backward and forward and so you are the only one who can see what happened next. Bring the memory back and try."

Because I knew it was pointless and a waste of time, I tried to distract her. "So, if I have to start with a memory, I can only follow the threads, as you call them, of people I know?"

Brym laughed again but it wasn't her soft one. It was loud and bounced off the walls of the cave, filling the air as thoroughly as the lazy tendrils of steam did.

"It's just the start, my little time walker, just the start of great things. When you can do that, many doors will be opened to you. Time walkers have always had the greatest gift. It's why people have coveted them so, why they've tried to control that gift and make it their own. Now, try."

With a sigh, I settled back into the effort of remembering. But it wasn't my mother that I searched my mind for this time. Curiosity and apprehension warred inside of me, and I let apprehension win that time. If there was the slightest chance I could follow that memory into the future, I didn't want to know what happened. Not yet. Not while I was sitting across from Brym who had an uncanny knack for reading all my thoughts, especially the ones I wished to keep private.

So, I sought for another person whose future I didn't really care about but whom I had enough memories that I could latch onto one.

I found Rensi.

I'd seen her only the night before when she'd been brought in to fix Brym and I's meal. She'd been different. A bruise darkened her cheek just beneath her eye and more bruises created an ominous pattern on her neck. When I'd asked out of curiosity where they'd come from, she'd snapped and told me it was none of my business and that I didn't really care anyway.

"You're right, I don't care. Why should I?" I'd answered her.

She'd just looked away from me then, hiding her face from me and we hadn't said another word to each other until Blue Eyes came to take her back to wherever she was kept.

That was an easy memory to pull up. I turned it over in my head, giving at least some effort to the searching of a thread, even if I had no idea what a thread was supposed to look like or how to tell if I'd found one. The silence that hung between Brym and I told me that she was watching me with that greedy intensity that I'd begun to grow accustomed to.

An ache formed in the center of my head as I pictured every move Rensi made, the way she kept flicking her braid over her shoulder, the way she winced when she leaned forward to stir the simmering pot of food. I imagined the look on her face as she'd answered my question, her eyes not matching the anger in her voice. Her eyes telling an entirely different story, actually. I wondered how I'd missed seeing it then. Her eyes had told of fear and pain.

I saw through the memory when Blue Eyes entered, and I noticed another thing I'd missed the night before. I'd missed the way Rensi had stiffened at his arrival, shrinking away from him.

The ache in my head was getting stronger and I knew my face was twisting up in a grimace from the pain of it.

But I wasn't ready to let go of the memory just yet. Now that I was trying, I wanted to see if anything Brym said was true. And I wanted to know what happened next. That desire overruled any pain. It overruled everything. I needed to see what happened next no matter how hard it was.

Blue Eyes took Rensi by the arm. I'd seen him do that. It was still just a memory, just a part that already existed in my head. I watched as he pulled her back toward the entrance and pulled the animal skin door aside. That was where memory ended. That was when my mind lost sight of her.

Or at least, that's when it should have lost sight of her.

It didn't.

With a flash of pain so harsh it almost turned everything black, my sight followed her out of the cave, onto the windswept ledge and down the ladder. To another ledge. Another cave. Blue Eyes right there with her the entire time. Shoving her inside. Following her inside. My sight saw her stumble against a table in the room, clutching it to hold herself up. She was turning to face Blue Eyes. She was saying something, but sight was all I had and I could only guess at the movement of her lips. She was begging him, I think. Shaking her head, one hand stealing up to her throat, closing in a fist around the collar of her coat. Blue Eyes was stepping toward her, his back to my sight.

I saw his hand rising and then falling, striking Rensi across the face with a force that threw her to the floor. Then he was bending over her, his hand jerking hers away from where it held onto her coat, his hand working the fastenings open.

I gave a violent jerk as understanding came to me and the sight was lost. I no longer wanted to see where it ended. Sight ended and in its place was a crushing pain inside my head that sent me crashing to the rock floor, unable to hold myself up now that I was aware of myself. Moisture trickled from my nose and ears. I brought a hand up to my nose and it came away bloody.

"Well done, time walker," Brym said from across the pool. "You've walked time, have you not?"

I couldn't even answer her - both because of the raging pain in my head and what I'd seen.

Brym came around the pool, her staff tapping the ground with each step informing me of her advance. She knelt beside where I lay, and the papery texture of her hand's skin brushed against the trickle of wetness coming from my ear.

"Hmmm."

Apparently, the blood was a surprise for her too. I'd never had such a thing happen with the visions that came to me. I'd never thought that there would be such a physical difference between visions that came on their own and ones I'd chased down.

CHAPTER 21

BLUE EYES MOVED ME BACK to the main room. I was incapable of even picking myself up off the floor, my limbs feeling like puddles of water. Once I was lying in there, near the fire, I noticed that Rensi was there as well. Brym flicked her hand from Rensi to me.

"Take care of him, girlie. I need him well or he's no good to me."

Brym and Blue Eyes left the two of us and I shut my eyes so that I wouldn't have to look at Rensi's face. I couldn't bear to do that. Not after what I'd seen. Not after what I'd avoided seeing.

A soft, damp cloth touched my face, making me flinch and open my eyes. Rensi knelt beside me, washing away the blood that streaked down from my ears and nose.

Another bruise, this one on the other side of her face and spreading over her jaw, was darkening. Dullness glazed her eyes. There was a stiffness in all her movements, and she was careful not to meet my gaze.

"So, it worked?" she asked after the silence became too long, too bloated with things unsaid.

"I guess so," I murmured, incapable of anything else. "But it hurts." I couldn't keep the complaint from coming out. It hurt worse than anything, as if some part inside my head had burst and been torn out.

"It's never done this before, has it?"

"Never. But I've never done it like this before."

She retreated back behind her silence again and I laid still, letting her. The pain was enough to make that easy for me.

If searching out the future on my own would always end in such agony, with blood pouring from my ears and nose, I wasn't sure if Brym could use me as much as she wanted to. I wasn't sure I could bring myself to even attempt such a thing again, knowing what it cost me.

The muscles in my stomach clenched as a nauseating wave of pain rolled through my head and I rolled onto my side, retching hard. And unfortunately, right in Rensi's lap. She leaped back but not fast enough.

"Ugh...you couldn't have done that the other way?"

"Sorry," I mumbled when my stomach finally stopped heaving.

"It's bad enough I have to take care of you like this. You don't think they'll give me clean clothes just because you vomited all over me, do you?"

It was all over my own jerkin as well and I very much doubted I'd be given new clothes. Just then, that seemed like the least of my worries. I groaned and tried to scoot away, holding my head in my hands. Rensi got up and returned a few moments later with more water and another cloth.

She started to clean up the mess I'd made, first off herself, then the floor and finally starting on me.

"I'm sorry, Rensi," I said again, the roughness of her hands on my face and chest evidence of how upset she was. "I didn't mean to. It's never made me sick before."

Rensi's hand froze for a moment. "I know, Kor."

I gave up trying to appease her and nursed my own hurt into anger as well because she had no right to be upset with me over something I couldn't control.

There we stayed, the two of us, both too lost in ourselves to care a bit about the other. But even in my state of not caring what happened to Rensi, I couldn't fully shut out what I'd seen. And while I didn't care about Rensi, I did care that I wanted Blue Eyes to die. That thought fit quite nicely inside my anger.

When she was through cleaning up, Rensi lifted my head and held a cup to my lips, and I drank the hot broth that it contained. I wanted more than what was in the cup, but I didn't want to ask Rensi for it.

I rolled over and tried to sleep instead. The cold kept me awake. After sitting for so long in the steam filled room, the chill of the front room was miserable. I must have been shivering because a moment later, Rensi covered me with a thick blanket.

~ ~ ~

A haze surrounded the next few days.

Rensi was almost always present, her sole job at the time being to get me well again. Both her knowledge and care seemed to center around keeping me warm and fed. It was a good thing I wasn't truly ill, or she would have been hard pressed to truly treat me. Still, it meant she stayed night and day in the cave with me and I never heard her complain about that. Nor did I. Brym's company was no company at all.

Brym woke me often, poking me with her staff or sometimes with a sharp finger. She always asked the same question. "Are you ready?"

She didn't have to say what she wanted me ready for. There was a burning light in her eyes every time she spoke of my success. And bitter disappointment soured her looks and words when it became clear to her every day that I was not, in fact, ready to try anything like that again.

For my own part, I put very little effort into my own recovery. I dreaded the time when I would be too well to feign inability any longer. Every time I thought about returning to my efforts, nausea rolled through me, and I had to swallow down the urge to vomit. I never wanted to do that again. I was pretty sure I was never meant to do that. If it was true that the Fates had gifted me with foresight for their own purposes, it was easy to believe that the harsh consequences I suffered for time walking was their way of warning me against the practice.

After several days of doing nothing but resting, drinking tea and broth, eating thin gruel, and convincing Brym that I was still unwell, the fetid air of the cave began to gnaw at me. I wanted out of it. Just a few breaths of fresh air was all I wanted.

Sitting up and shrugging off the blankets Rensi made sure were always on me, I made my way to the mouth of the cave. I kept close to the stone wall, stumbling against it and clinging to it with each step. Black dots swam before my eyes but I rubbed at them until they went away.

Brym had never minded me sitting out on the ledge when I felt like it, just so long as I didn't do it when she wanted something from me. With my chain, I was hardly in a position to run.

Pushing the animal skin aside just enough to let myself out, I inhaled the deepest breath I could. The night air was frigid, winter having deepened its already strong grip on the mountains while I had lain useless inside. It was so cold it burned the inside of my nose and hurt my lungs. But it was clean. It was fresh and untainted by the perpetual rot that grew in Brym's cave.

"You're up?"

I jerked my gaze away from the valley and over to the side where Rensi sat, her feet dangling with precarious incaution over the edge.

We'd barely said a word to each other since the night I'd retched all over her; her, because she was still angry with me and me, because I didn't know what to say. What was there to say? I couldn't make things any better for her and the fact that I'd seen anything at all suddenly seemed like a violation of sorts. What if she hadn't wanted me looking into her future?

Since the fact that I was standing outside seemed answer enough to her rather pointless question, I didn't feel the need to put it into words. Instead, I settled myself on the cold, hard rock, crossing my legs underneath me because I couldn't fathom just letting them hang over the edge.

"I wish you weren't," she said, as I tried to make myself comfortable.

"Well, if you don't want me out here so badly, you could just ask me to go back inside. Or use the tether since you insisted on keeping it on me."

Rensi bit down on her lower lip and one hand fingered a stray strand of hair. Her braid was gone, her loose hair flapping about in the ceaseless wind. It was hard to catch glimpses of her face in between the constantly shifting and moving curtain that her hair formed, but I was sure, when I did get a look, that there were tears on her cheeks. Her bruised cheeks.

"It's not like that, Kor. You always assume everyone means the worst about you."

"I wonder why."

Rensi sighed and turned her face away from me. "I know you hate my father for what he did to you..."

"Don't." I didn't want to talk about Drakkus and what he'd done. The scar on my hand would be a permanent proof and reminder of exactly what he'd done. I didn't want to hear Rensi's excuses for it now.

"I miss him," she said quietly. I wasn't sure I was even supposed to hear her say that. "I miss them all so much. I just want to see them again."

"I miss my family, too. And it's all because of yours." It was a poor way to treat her when I knew what she faced but I couldn't stop myself in time. My own desires and wishes had been brushed aside time and again and I couldn't find it within myself to pity another at the moment.

She was quiet for so long that guilt began to creep inside me no matter how hard I fought it. I glanced sideways at her and saw her legs drawn up, her face pressed to her knees and her shoulders shaking with silent sobs. I turned away and stared out at the valley, leaving her to herself.

Heavy clouds blocked out the moon and stars but even so the sky over the valley seemed light when compared to the darkness of the Outlands. Wind cut through the valley in its never-ending race, howling as it sped through the divide. I frowned as I listened with more care. It wasn't the wind itself that was howling, it was merely carrying the haunting sound.

My eyes drifted back to the blackness of the Outlands. That was the source of the noise. The howls were coming from somewhere beyond that impenetrable darkness. The realization sent a shiver all the way down my back.

"What's out there?" I asked, not really expecting an answer.

Rensi sniffed and drew her sleeve over her eyes and nose, wiping away the remnants of her tears and followed my gaze to the Outlands. "Nightmares."

"They're loud."

"They howl like that every night. If they come too close, the warriors will light their fires and chase them away again." Rensi spoke as if she hadn't just been crying hard, as if she was glad to have something else to think about other than her own troubles. "Harysh says whatever lives out there is terrified of fire."

"Nightmares," I repeated her word from before.

"I can't imagine anything being worse than here."

"Who's Harysh?" Once we'd both abandoned our homesickness and loneliness for a shared fright, it was easier to talk without snapping.

"He's the one who...," Rensi couldn't go on, her voice catching, and I had a good guess as to who Harysh was.

"I didn't know he had a name. I just call him Blue Eyes."

"Kor," she paused again, chewing on her lip, "do you think you can at least pretend to be sick still for another day or two?"

I opened my mouth to tell her that I planned on doing just that.

"Don't give me some answer about how I don't deserve your help. Just say yes or no."

"I'll try. But Brym's getting impatient."

"And if you don't cooperate, the rest of us die," Rensi finished for me. "I know. Forget I asked. It just would have been really nice to have another day or two away from... him."

For a long time, the only sound was the wind and the howling it brought with it. I wasn't ready to return to the stale, rotten air inside the cave and apparently Rensi wasn't in a hurry to, either. Out there, alone, suspended above the world, it was just the two of us against the world. And that was a rather terrifying thought.

Chapter 22

THE HEAT INDUCED DROWSINESS threatened to pull me under and it was only Brym's switch across my unsuspecting hands that kept me from dozing. She'd added something, either to the water or burning it in a pot somewhere, that rode on the steam. It had a heavy, sweet scent that thickened the fog inside my head with every breath. It reminded me too sharply of Borssa and his ritual on the mountaintop and the anxiety that memory brought with it tightened around my chest. Whatever hung heavy on the air in that room, its purpose was to rob me of my clear-headedness and as I felt my control slip away, I was terrified.

"I don't want to do this again," I said, before I was too far gone. There was that sickness in my gut again just at the thought of the pain. "It hurt too much last time."

"I believe the first time is the worst," Brym said, her eyes a little glazed, their wildness muted by the effects of the scent in the room. She waved a flippant hand in the air. "The more you do it, the better it will get."

"You believe?"

"If you've changed your mind about your friends' survival, you need only say," Brym said, her scratchy voice turning sharp. She was no longer near enough to use her switch, having instead moved to her customary spot on the other side of the pool. "I will happily feed them to the Outlanders."

With a resigned sigh, I leaned forward, brushing my fingers across the surface of the hot water. I'd done it several times already, forcing my skin to slowly adjust to the heat. "A question for a question?"

"You're in the mood for a game today?"

I shrugged. I was in the mood for anything except for inviting that pain into my head again. "I suppose so."

"Very well, time walker. But I get to ask my question first." Brym shut her eyes the way she always did when she wanted to think. "Whose time did you walk?"

"That's not a hard question."

"Did I say it would be?"

"No. I just thought since you wanted to go first..."

"And yet, you have not answered it," Brym said, her ghastly smile made worse by the fog of steam between us.

"Rensi's. It was Rensi's time."

"Ah. The girlie who didn't want to feed the Outlanders. And what did you see?"

"Isn't it my turn to ask a question?"

Brym paused, her lips pinching together in a frown at the reminder. "So it is."

I took a deep breath as I tossed around different questions in my mind. There was much about my gift that I didn't know and had no other way of finding out. But whatever question I asked, I wanted the answer to be a long one. Long enough, perhaps, that Brym would forget about Rensi and forget about trying to have me walk time again.

"Why is it that I only see some visions once and some more than that?"

It took Brym a long time to answer. She held up three fingers, bent and knobby with age, the overgrown fingernails bearing a marked resemblance to a set of yellowed claws. "The visions are a gift sent by the Fates. The first," she lowered her first finger, "is sent by the eldest, Chance. It is her warning of what will come to pass unless choices are changed. The second," she lowered another finger, "is a gift from the second born, Time. It is her warning that time is running out to change a fate. The last," she wriggled her remaining finger, "is sent by the youngest, Destiny, and hers are the final. Not a warning, but a prophecy. A fate seen three times is a fate that cannot be escaped or altered. It is settled by all three Fates."

"What if an oracle sees it more than three times?"

Either she didn't notice that it was my second question in a row, or she didn't care. She laughed as though I'd asked a question that had the most obvious answer. "Time walker, no oracle sees a vision more than three times. Why would the Fates waste their gift on more visions where three suffice?"

"Oh." I thought about the end of the world and tried to count up the number of times that particular vision had overtaken me. Even if I didn't count the times when I was sick with delirium and fever while traveling with Drakkus and Rayka or in the aftermath of Borssa's failed ritual, it was well over three. Brym seemed so sure of her own answer, of her own knowledge regarding oracles. But Brym was wrong. Even though I didn't see what good it would do me, I wasn't going to let go of that advantage. I was never going to tell her. "What's your question?"

Brym studied me hard, her gray eyes narrowed from across the pool of water. She tapped her chin with her long nails. "What is the greatest number of times you've seen the same vision?"

"Three," I answered without so much as a blink. At least she wasn't pursuing her question about Rensi and what I'd seen. Nor was she insisting I search for another thread of time to follow. "Why did everyone agree that Fentra should die?"

"You have so many bits and pieces, but not nearly enough to see the full picture, time walker."

"Which is why I'm asking."

"Fentra lived three hundred years ago. How should I know why people wanted her dead?"

I didn't say anything else. Just waited for Brym to answer because I knew she knew the answer. She'd known what Rensi was talking about when Rensi mentioned the curse of Fentra. She'd known enough about it to acquiesce to Rensi's demands, and even mine. Something about Fentra still bothered her. Something about her gift or power frightened Brym.

"And who's to say that everyone wished her dead?" Brym went on, working herself up into answering my question. "Who's to say that the stories written are the whole truth and not just a portion of it? You've much to learn, time walker, especially when it comes to what and who you believe."

"None of that answered my question. What was wrong with Fentra that made everyone think it would be better if she died?"

"Enough," Brym said, the sharp edge on her voice startling me a little. Her gray eyes glared at me from across the pool. Her knuckles tightened around the staff that lay across her lap. The wrinkles around her mouth tightened with her scowl. She was angry about my question, which only made me more curious to know the answer. "No questions about Fentra. Choose another."

"But you said no refusals from either of us. That was your rule."

"And it's my game, so I am changing the rule."

"Then I get to refuse once, too," I said.

Brym made a hissing sound and spat into the pool of water between us. "Fool boy. You are mine and do not get to make demands of me. I've given you the lives of my prisoners in exchange for your compliance. But that is the limit of my negotiating. You will do as I say, and not the other way around. Ask me about Fentra again and I will make you watch as I feed one of your friends to the Outlanders. Then you will know not to cross me."

She spat in the water again and got to her feet. It was a slow process and every time I'd watched her do it, I thought for sure that she would tip over headfirst into the pool, but I hadn't had any such luck. If I'd been near enough to her, I might have been tempted to help her into the pool myself.

She came around to my side, her staff in one hand tapping the ground and her switch in the other making a scratching noise as it dragged across the rocks. Pausing in front of me, she gave me a calculating stare, looking me up and down the same way she had when we'd first been brought to Dragon's Nest.

"Time for you to keep your part of the bargain, time walker. You followed the girlie's thread. Follow mine."

"Follow it to what?"

"My future, fool. What else? Follow it until you see how I win. Find the future that holds my success."

She was gone in a stooped bustle of furs, and I was left to myself. Left with nothing but her instructions and a curiosity that burned through me as viciously as any fire could have. I needed to know about Fentra. Brym's anger at my questioning assured me of that. There was something more to the story than what Drakkus told me, something more that Brym wouldn't tell me. I wondered if Drakkus even knew or if he only knew a portion of the truth as Brym had suggested. It was too late to find out. He was dead and any chance I might have had to question him was lost.

The sweet aroma that had been steadily clouding my mind grew stronger without Brym's presence. I wondered if she'd added to whatever was making it or if it was just the absence of the stench she carried with her everywhere that allowed the sweet odor to finally shine through fully. Either way, it made my thoughts slow and vaporish, falling apart before I could catch hold of them. I wasn't sure if she thought that would help me walk time or not.

Drawing in a shallow breath, I shook my head in an effort to rid it of the lightness. I shut my eyes and tried to draw up the memory of Brym as she exited the room only moments before. The memory was close to the surface and not at all difficult to recreate. Holding onto it and following it was a different matter, though.

Just like with Rensi, my sight followed her through the memory. Unlike with Rensi, I knew the pain that came from following a thread of time, and as the memory came to its end, my body balked against my mind. I lost my hold on the sight and the failure was a relief. I didn't want to walk time. It was bad enough to have visions thrust upon me whenever the Fates felt like giving humanity a warning about their actions.

I tried again.

I failed again.

On and on it went. Over and over again. I tried, I failed. I tried again. With each attempt, the pain grew and with each failure it subsided back to a reasonable level.

Brym lived in my memory, but I couldn't follow her into the future. Not when every instinct inside my body was screaming to stop, to spare myself the damage. It was a hurdle I couldn't leap, that I couldn't force myself to leap. Hours passed in that steam-filled room with my head desperately trying to satisfy two needs that couldn't both be met at the same time.

When Brym returned, I had no way of knowing how much time had passed. My stomach gnawed at itself with hunger and my eyelids drooped shut of their own volition, so I guessed that night had come at last. I only knew Brym had entered the room by the tapping of her staff as she came closer. I shrank away from her.

"Well?"

"I can't do it," I said softly, desperately hoping her anger from earlier had disappeared.

“Won’t do it, you mean. You’ve done it once and that means it's possible for you to do it again. So why won’t you?”

“It hurts so much.”

Brym seemed to truly consider my words, but there was a maniacal light in her eyes, and I guessed that her anger had only spent the past hours brewing into something far worse.

“Then it seems the solution is to make the pain of not doing it worse than the pain of doing it.”

“No,” I cried out. “No. I’ll manage it. I swear I will. I just need more time. Just a little more time.”

“Hmm... we’ll see. Still, some form of motivation seems necessary. I’ll think on it.”

Chapter 23

THERE WAS ONE TIME EVERY day when I was free of the chain. That was when Harysh took me to see the others in accordance with my agreement with Brym. I'd persisted in my insistence on the matter solely because it was the only time I was free of the chain and its noise and weight. It was the only time I saw something other than Brym's cave and the ledge beyond it.

The first time it had happened, I'd worried about having to descend the flimsy ladder, but Harysh hadn't taken me outside at all. He'd unlocked the chain and led me down a passageway. There were stairs at the end of it, chiseled out of the rock. Whoever had fashioned those caves into homes must have been incredibly strong. So much of the rock was hewn and cut and carved to fit their needs. It was an incredible feat of determination if I'd had the mind to appreciate it. I'd learned, on that first trip, that the caves themselves were a vast colony, connected by the passageways and staircases and that you could reach one end of the canyon from the other without ever setting foot outside.

I'd memorized the path down to where they housed the others. It was hard not to since I went there every day and Harysh never bothered to be subtle. He never tried to trick me by leading me along different routes. It was always the same. Just Harysh and I.

That day, though, the day after I'd failed Brym, it was different. Brym accompanied Harysh and I. She tottered down the stairs ahead of me, so unsteady that the tiniest of shoves would have sent her tumbling. I thought back to the night Drakkus and his men took me, to the moment when I'd shoved Rensi into the water with a well-timed stumble. The temptation to do the same to Brym was far stronger and it was only Harysh's presence behind me that restrained me.

Brym turned to me as we descended, a shrewd look in her eye that told me she was scheming. That came as no surprise. Brym never stopped scheming. Still, I wondered why she was accompanying us. She'd said nothing about my failure earlier that morning, only told me that we would try again today and that if I failed again, there would be dire consequences to my person. My imagination had run wild with the possibilities her words opened. That she would stoop to torture me, I did not doubt. I only wondered how she would do it.

"A question for a question?" Brym said as she turned back around.

"Fine," I answered, more to break up the silence and distract me from the knot of tension that was growing in my gut than anything else.

"Have you ever seen an Outlander either in your visions or in person?"

"No." I frowned. It wasn't the sort of question I'd expected, and I wasn't sure what to make of it. Brym always had a purpose to her questioning. "I'm pretty sure if I saw one in person, I'd be dead, wouldn't I?"

She turned, flashing her rotting smile at me. "Not always."

I thought about the questions we'd exchanged the day before and the anger in Brym's reaction to my mention of Fentra. Something hadn't made sense about it all. Something about Brym didn't make sense. She knew too much. She had knowledge of oracles that had never passed down through the written texts of Abirell or the Iron Towers. Her knowledge was old.

Three hundred years old.

It was the sort of information that people said was lost to time. So, how did she have it? And, with that thought, I knew what my question would be.

"How old are you?"

Brym's soft chuckle floated back to me. She didn't turn around but fluttered a withered hand in the air over her shoulder. "Not so much of a fool as I thought, eh? When you put your mind to it, time walker, you can be a bit clever, can't you?"

"How long have you lived?"

"Far past my time, time walker. Far past it. More than three hundred years I have walked this world and perhaps for another three hundred years I shall if the world's end should be that long in coming. As I am cursed to do."

I choked down my exclamation of surprise and turned it into a single word, "How?"

Her face was hidden from my view, but I saw her hunched back stiffen and her staff tapped the ground just a bit harder. She continued her descent in pointed silence, and I gave up waiting for her answer. I gave up waiting for her to ask me her own question in turn.

It was a long way down. So far, in fact, that the tethering band on my wrist began to send out the first subtle pulses of pain by the time we reached the room they used as a prison. The heat of it hung precariously between discomfort and pain. It was just on the edge of my invisible boundary.

The stairs opened to an enormous cavern that echoed every sound made inside it. Water was always dripping from some dark recess inside it. The torches that lit it up only barely touched the darkness, leaving plenty of shadows behind. In the very center was our destination - an iron cage that was made to hold something much larger than a man and therefore housed their dozen prisoners quite easily.

Our daily appearance had ceased to garner any reaction from the men held inside. And I'd ceased to take much interest in them myself. It was my only chance to do something other than sit with Brym and that was all.

Although Brym had kept her end of the bargain and had fed none of them to the Outlanders, she'd done little else for them. And I hadn't wanted to add anything more to my bargain. Their wounds had been left untreated, their meals poor. Trapped in the perpetual darkness of the cavern, they would all eventually succumb to death unless they found a way to escape. I had no way of preventing that, nor was I inclined to do more for them than I'd already done. If Rensi had just taken off the tether, I would have left them all to rot.

"Hurry, hurry, my little time walker. We've not much time to waste today, have we?" Brym said, crossing the open floor of the cavern toward the cage. She stopped in front of it and leaned her staff against it waiting, her gnarled hands rubbing against each other. "So much to do today. So much time to walk. Let's get started."

Harysh's hand fell heavy on my shoulder and he guided me forward when my steps slowed. My breath had quickened, and I was trying to rein in the wild racing of my heart as I came to a stop beside Brym. She was smiling her grotesque smile, but she wasn't looking at me.

"Brym, I'm going to do it. I will. I told you that yesterday," I said, my voice rising a little as she continued to study the men inside the cage, a hungry light in her gray eyes. I thought the look shared a likeness with the great cats that prowled the plains.

"Oh, I know you will, my little time walker. I know you will. But now's your chance to prove it to me."

"What do you want me to do?" My voice rose and ended in a squeak of uncertainty. The racing in my heart had grown stronger, faster, its cadence a wild thing.

Pinching her lips together, Brym tilted her aged head to one side. She pointed at one of the men lying down, too wounded to get to his feet. Although blood and dirt and grime made it difficult to say for sure, he appeared to be the youngest out of the group, only a few years older than I. "Since my time is so distasteful for you to walk, walk his. Tell me what his future holds. Unless you need a bit of motivation first."

She looked past me to Harysh, and I twisted around to look at him as well. The smile he gave me made me turn cold for it was the same ravenous smile I'd seen on his face when he hurt Rensi. In his hand was a coiled-up whip.

A ragged breath pushed out of me as I realized what form Brym's motivation would take.

"So? What will it be? Walk his time."

It wouldn't be that bad, I told myself. It wouldn't be as bad as what Harysh would do to me. I only had to repeat what I'd done with Rensi. Brym was watching me, waiting for my response and I managed a weak nod.

Closing my eyes, I pulled up the memory of seeing that man lying on the ground that was no more than seconds old. That part was easy. My sight latched onto the image of him lying there, a permanent grimace on his dirt coated face, blood dried to the top of his forehead and matted in his hair and more blood staining his clothes around a giant tear.

I reached out with my sight to follow that thread, gritting my teeth as I reached the same barrier I'd thrown myself against the day before. My body sought an escape from the pain it knew was coming. But unlike the day before, I was sure that failure would end in my having to watch someone die a gruesome death and with that thought firmly in place, I forced my way past that barrier. I forced myself into the pain. I followed the thread of that man's life. A man who's name I had never even learned. I hadn't bothered to speak to any of them when I was their captive with Drakkus, and I hadn't bothered to speak to them when we were all prisoners together. I didn't need a name, though, just a memory to start with.

The memory was short, ending quickly. I followed past that with my sight. I watched as the door of the cage opened and Harysh stepped inside. Like with Rensi's thread, I could hear nothing, only see. I saw Harysh's hands slipping under the man's arms and dragging him backwards out of the cage. Dragging him towards one of the deep shadows in the cavern. I saw the man's mouth moving but could hear no sound coming from him. I saw as another mountain man brought a torch into the shadow, illuminating it for us all to see.

Another cage lay inside that darkness. Something paced inside it. Something that absorbed the darkness around it, something shrouded in shadows so deep and thick that they didn't flee the light of the torch. I saw Harysh opening the door of that cage and shoving his captive inside. And then I saw it.

An Outlander.

No one needed to tell me what it was. It was a monstrous being, prowling back and forth on its massive paws, its ridged back standing higher than a horse's. Sharp claws curled against the rock floor, leaving gashes in its path. Its face resembled that of a wolf, but its snout was thicker and wrinkled with an excess of skin, its maw hanging open in a snarl, and there were no ears visible on its head. Milky eyes rolled slowly in its head as it stepped forward, looking over its new prey.

I saw the moment it crouched and sprang, tearing into the man left inside its cage as if he were nothing but a ragdoll, batting him around in much the same way a cat plays with its field mouse.

"NO!" I yelled, breaking free of the sight. I was no longer on my feet. At some time during my time walking,

I'd sat back on the ground hard. I stared up at Brym and shook my head, the tightness in my chest swelling. "Please don't do that, Brym. I'm doing it. I'm doing what you want me to. Don't make me watch that."

"What did you see, time walker?" she said, that same hungry, crazed smile lighting her face up. "Why don't you tell us?"

"No. Brym, please, don't do it."

She shot a look at Harysh who moved toward the door of the cage, and I tried to jump to my feet. Blood was trickling from my nose and ears again, the same as it had the first time, and pain throbbed inside my head but that didn't stop me. I staggered toward Harysh, the last of my strength enough to propel me into the space between him and the cage. It was useless to stand in his way, but I was too far gone in horror to care. She was going to make me watch and the thought sickened me beyond reason. No amount of anger towards Drakkus' men could make me want to witness such a sight.

"Stop, please. You can't punish them for me. That's not fair."

"Tell me, my little time walker, what part of your life has ever been fair?"

None. None of it had ever been fair. I hadn't asked for my gift. I hadn't asked to be used again and again for my gift. I hadn't asked for anything. But that didn't matter. All that mattered was that I could not bear to watch another killed so horribly just for my own failure no matter how I might dislike them. No one deserved that death.

Harysh knocked me aside with ease, not even breaking his stride. I was too dizzy to keep my feet under me then and as I fell with a crash to my side, I watched in helpless dismay as my sight unfolded itself in the present. Harysh opened the cage door just as I'd seen him do, grabbed the man just as I'd seen him do, dragged him backwards out of the cage just as I'd seen him do.

And all I could do was lay on the ground, cursing the uselessness of my gift. There was not a single person I'd managed to save with it. Not one.

What the thread of time could not show me was the sound that accompanied the act. Hearing a grown man scream in pain and terror is a sensation unlike any other in the world.

I pressed my hands over my ears as I lay curled up on the floor but that did little good. The fierce snarls mingled with the sound of wet, tearing flesh, bouncing off the walls of the cavern so that there was no escape from it. Whatever monster that lived in that cage, it made no effort to kill quickly. I'd known it wouldn't. Instead, it toyed with its prey until I was silently begging for the man to just die. Until I longed for the silence of death.

Was it minutes until it was over? Hours? I didn't know. I didn't know anything except the knot of hatred that Drakkus had begun in me had grown and hardened in that time. My breath tore in and out of me faster than

I could sustain and that tightness in my chest was suffocating. But even so, the only coherent thought I could put together was that Brym would pay for what she'd done to me. I would learn to curse time just as Fentra had and I would lay my curse on her.

Brym wasn't through with me yet, though.

Harysh returned from his task, dusting his hands off on his pants as if that simple act absolved him of all guilt. As if he'd done nothing more than clean up a mess and not just ended someone's life in a most horrible fashion. I glared up at him from where I lay still on the floor. My heaving breath was the only sound in the room for several minutes and Harysh and Brym both watched me pull myself together with mild interest.

"A question for a question?" Brym said, her voice as casual as if we were sitting across from each other at the pool. Even her eyes were the same. She truly didn't care about the life she'd just taken, as long as it got her what she wanted.

Still bleeding from my nose and ears, breath still harsh and ragged, I knew that I had no choice but to play her game. I swallowed down the lump in my throat and nodded, pushing myself up into a sitting position.

"Have you ever seen an Outlander either in your visions or in person?" she repeated her exact words from before. Such callous words that twisted inside me like the blade of a knife.

"Yes." The word was a hoarse whisper, loud in the ringing silence. "Both."

"That is but a taste of what the Outlands contain, time walker. They contain plague, famine, sorrow, ruin, death. And they are mine, my little time walker, the same as you are mine. They are mine to command. All these many years I've had to study them, to learn of them, to understand them. And now they are mine. I will bring the wrath of the Outlands through the gateways and our world shall bow to me as they were meant to do three hundred years ago. You will tell me which gateway I must take first." She waved a hand toward Harysh, signaling him to do something I was sure, but I was too focused on what I saw on the palm of her hand to spare Harysh any thought at all. What I'd never noticed before.

A thin scar.

Made by a knife, same as mine.

Harysh moved toward me, but I slipped out of his hand at the last moment. "I still get my question," I said, meeting Brym's cold eyes. "Whose gift did you try to take?"

Chapter 24

THE HISS OF ANGER THAT escaped from Brym's lips as she snapped her hand shut told me that I'd asked the right question. Even as I knew she would never answer it. I didn't need her to.

Harysh's hand clamped down on my arm and cold iron locked about my wrist, but I didn't bother to look down at the chain I knew was there. "It was Fentra's, wasn't it? You tried to take her power from her, and she cursed you, didn't she? You can't die until you see the end of the world. That's why you want to bring the Outlands in. You want to end the world in your own way." I was babbling again, words running out of my mouth without thought or control. Because all the pieces had just slipped into place. "But it doesn't end like that. I've seen it and you're not in it. No one bows to you. No one even knows who you are. It's fire that ends the world, not your monsters..."

"Enough," Brym shrieked. A second iron band fastened over my other wrist but still my eyes were locked on her. "You know nothing. You are nothing but my game piece. You do as I say, or you will watch more of them die and I will let Harysh have his way with you. He'll make you beg for death but I'm not going to let you die."

I opened my mouth, but Brym wasn't finished. Her lips twisted in a cruel sneer. "Go ahead, time walker. Throw your curses at me. They mean nothing to me. I've been cursed for more than three hundred years. Your words are empty threats to one who has lived as many lifetimes as I have. What will you curse? My family? I've watched them all die already. My friends likewise. My body? It already decays but never dies. For more than three hundred years I've lived with that and will continue to live until the end of the world is seen. But you, my little time walker, can and will die. I will break you here as I broke Fentra, but I'll never let you go. When you've gone mad with the future, I'll breed a new oracle on you. And then I'll kill you, but I'll never let you go."

A thousand thoughts dashed across my mind at her words, coupled with the new presence of the chains Harysh had placed on me but one stuck out above the rest, holding onto her final words. "You'll what?"

Brym laughed again, a wild, raucous sound. "Oh, yes. The gift of foresight passes through the bloodlines of the gifted. The Fates made it so. There is no great mystery to our Silence like others pretend there is. The gift died with Fentra because Fentra had no children. I'll not allow the same to happen with you."

I staggered back, heat flooding my face and I was glad for the uncertain light and the shadows. I was glad for the streaks of blood left behind from my nose and ears because they distracted from the deep flush that I'm sure crept over my cheeks.

The chains on my wrists went back to the nearest wall where their ends were embedded in the rock. It was a much shorter length than I'd been allowed up in Brym's front room. I backed all the way up to that wall, my knees shaking hard the entire time, and sank down with my back to the rock.

Her fit of laughter over, Brym's anger evaporated and when she spoke next it was with the same casual tone she'd used before. "Now, you'll stay here instead of upstairs, and you will walk time until you can tell me which gateway I must go through first and how. Fail me, and we do this all over again and worse. As many times as we need to."

She left me then, alone aside from the other prisoners who were all trying hard to pretend they weren't watching me. Likely, they hated me for my failure. I'd thought I was past caring about the unwanted attention, but as I felt their surreptitious eyes on me, I wanted to yell at them to just leave me alone. I wanted to crawl into some hole in the ground where no one would ever find me again. Where no one would ever use me again.

I shut my eyes but all that did was open my memory up and I saw again the hapless man being shredded by the Outland monster. I heard again his screams and cries for mercy.

I'd failed.

I'd been so afraid of the pain that I'd failed.

Guilt dug its ferocious claws deep inside me, eating away at me. I'd failed those men who were staring at me now, men who had done me wrong but who didn't deserve that end. I could almost sense their accusation in their gaze, and I wanted to fall on my knees and beg their forgiveness for allowing such a horror to take place. But I think I was damaged more than they were. I'd seen it not once, but twice. And the pain of time walking was still mine and mine alone.

I wished Otho had taken my gift. I wished the ritual had worked. If it had, none of this would have happened, or if it did, I wouldn't have known any part of it ahead of time so I wouldn't have had the same sickening dread. If only Otho had taken my gift, then I might have been free.

Swiping the back of my hand across my face, I wiped away the drying blood as best I could and tried to put the pieces of myself back together. It was a bit like trying to fit together the sharp broken pieces of a shattered clay pot. Nothing fit right and the cracks ran deep, forever marring the whole image. Whatever else happened, I knew the scar that Brym left behind in me was never going away.

Brym was right about one thing, the second time hadn't been quite as painful as the first. True, I'd still bled from it, but the pain wasn't quite as bad. Although, that might have had more to do with the desperation that had fueled me right after I came out of the vision. Knowing what would happen if I failed her again, I knew I would find a way to push past that barrier every time. The alternative was just too horrible to contemplate.

Cold rock dug into my back and moisture seeped slowly through my clothes as the hours slid away in ceaseless monotony. I had sunk into a daze of sorts, shutting out as much as I could of the day's events. I wasn't sure when Brym would return to question my progress. And even if she'd given me an amount of time, there was no way for me to tell how much of it had passed. The steady staccato of dripping water wormed its way into my aching head, dulling everything further. I shut my eyes and brought my hands up to the sides of my head, trying to massage away some of the pain. The sooner I could walk time again for Brym, the better it would be for everyone. Everyone except me, that is.

~ ~ ~

I picked Rayka's time to walk.

Brym's would have to come later, when I could stomach what I knew I'd find there. Her mind and heart were set on bringing destruction to the only world I knew. Walking her time would be unpleasant for many reasons, including that. I'd seen my fill of death for the day. At least, I thought it was still the same day when I had woken up from a heavy sleep.

Rayka had been kind, as kind as anyone could be to their unwilling captive. Certainly, she had been kinder than anyone in Dragon's Nest. She was the best option after my own family and I was still hesitant to look into their futures, still afraid of what I might see. I didn't think I could bear witnessing their deaths again.

Following my final memory of Rayka, standing outside of Borssa's cave, fussing over my hand and my coat, I began.

She'd watched us, arms hugging herself against the cold, until we'd disappeared from sight. Then she'd retreated to another part of the same cave I'd lain in for so many days, to where Otho lay.

A gray pallor clung to his sunken cheeks and his eyes were dull as she bent over him, her hand running lightly across his face. She was speaking to him, her words lost to me, but there was an urgency in her manner, a current that ran beneath her calm. I could see it in the tightness of her smile, in the way it never touched her eyes. Something was wrong. I thought perhaps that it was Otho that troubled her.

Borssa came into the room, leaning over Rayka to get a look at Otho. The words they exchanged were brief, sharp. Rayka's lips pressed together in a thin, tight line and she slapped Borssa's hand away when he reached out toward Otho.

The sight wavered, my hold on it weakening, my body's strength sucked dry already. But I wasn't ready to let it go. I wanted to see what happened next. Curiosity drove me on, a hunger awakened that I needed to satisfy. Something was wrong and I needed to know what.

It disappeared and left me lying on the floor in the present. The cold, hard, damp floor with Drakkus' remaining men only a few feet away from me, watching me. Afraid of what I'd see in their faces, I turned my eyes away from them. I drew my hand across the now familiar streaks of blood and tried to sit up. Weakness held me down and I gave into it.

Footsteps descended the steps, and I forced my burning eyes to focus on the opening of the stairs. I hoped it wasn't Brym yet. I hoped it wasn't Harysh.

It was Rensi, staggering under the weight of the heavy pot she carried. She set it down outside the makeshift prison without so much as a glance in my direction. Harysh followed her down a moment later and unlocked the cage. I watched as Rensi served each man a bowl of whatever was in the pot. Then Harysh closed and locked the door and jerked his chin in my direction.

"Brym says to take care of him while you're down here."

Harysh must have been quite confident in our collective inability to escape because, once the cage was locked again, he left Rensi alone with me. Probably Brym was sitting up in her cave, rocking back and forth and watching us through her eye of a dragon periapt.

Rensi approached with another bowl in her hands, her eyes downcast to avoid mine. I propped myself up against the rock and took the bowl from her shaking hands. My own fingers struggled to function properly, trembling with the after effects of not just the time walking, but of all the other events of the day.

"How could you let her kill Alkan?" Rensi asked in a voice so soft that only I could hear it. "All you had to do was find her future."

The bowl slipped through my fingers and clattered to the floor, splattering its contents on both Rensi and I but neither of us paid much attention to that. I didn't give her time to pay attention to it. Her words had awakened all the horror of that death and ignited the fury I'd been unable to fully unleash on Brym. It boiled up inside of me at her accusation. She had no right to that accusation. She, who kept my tether on for the sole purpose of ensuring her survival, had no right to be angry with me. I owed her father's men nothing.

I struck Rensi.

The iron manacle on my wrist caught on her jaw, tearing open a thin cut along it. She fell back with a cry. Her hand flew to her face as she stared at me, hurt and betrayal flooding her eyes. I was too lost to the churning rage inside me to care.

"It hurts, Rensi," I spat each word at her, trying to push some of that pain away from myself for once. "That's why. It hurts every single time I see the future. It never stops hurting. The pain never goes away. I'm tired of it. Nobody cares as long as they get what they want from me. And you're not better than anyone else. You keep this," I gave my right arm an emphatic shake, "on me just to make sure you stay alive."

There was so much more I wanted to say, so much more that I thought I could say, that it surprised me a little when the words choked up inside of me and refused to come out.

It terrified me when a hysterical mix of crying and laughter rose up inside me to take the place of words. I picked up the bowl with its remaining contents and flung it as hard as I could across the cavern floor before burying my face in my arms. It hit the rock hard and rolled, the sound of its clattering all that could be heard in the stillness after my outburst.

I felt Rensi's hand brush against my shoulder and shrugged it off. "Get away from me."

CHAPTER 25

KORRIS."

I heard the voice from a great distance, coming from somewhere outside the future I was witnessing then.

It was Rayka's again. Despair had driven me to it, hoping to lose myself in someone else's future for a time. That was easier than facing my present.

I'd chased her thread passed those first few hours after my last memory of her and was reluctant to give space to the present. Something important was about to happen, I knew. Rayka was on edge, all of her movements laced with tension. She'd sat by a fire with Borssa until the old man disappeared into his own room of the cave system. Even after he'd left, she sat unmoving for some time, staring into the flames as if they held some message for her and her alone.

"Korris," the voice came again, insistent in its interruption but I clung to the future. I had to see. I had to find out what was happening. Worry tried to wriggle its way inside my mind, warning me against spending so long in the future but I ignored it. Rayka was getting up, her footsteps measured and careful as she approached Otho's bed. I could imagine she made not a sound as she crossed the ground. Her hand was shaking him gently, nudging him out of his sleep. He was sitting up, nodding at whatever she was saying.

They were slipping out of the cave, out into the dark night, taking only what they could carry on their backs. Rayka was glancing over her shoulder every few steps. She was watching for someone to follow them.

They were running from Borssa.

"Korris," the voice said again and this time it dragged me back to the present.

I was laying down on my side, gasping in shallow breaths. Pain locked around my head, but it wasn't unbearable. I rubbed a hand under my nose, but it came away clean. No blood. So that was another thing that got better after I'd walked time the first time.

Shifting to get my elbow under me, I pushed myself half up, blinking slowly at the shadowy scene before me as I came out of the future induced haze that held me.

There was the cage, with its captives; the cavern, with its secret recesses containing captured Outlanders.

Present.

I was back in the present.

Exhaustion swept over me as I pivoted my body up into a sitting position, my back to the wall. A yawn stretched my jaw painfully wide, and I thought if I closed my eyes I could probably sleep and not wake for many hours.

I frowned.

Something had brought me back to the present. I hadn't wanted to abandon the future I was following but something had brought me back. Glancing around, I could see the men in the cage were watching me. One in particular seemed to be waiting for something from me.

"What?" I said, unsure if it was the right response but completely incapable of coming up with something better.

"How close can you get to us?" the man said.

I shrugged. I was too tired to experiment with the length of my chains. I had spent too much time in the future to worry about how far I could go on my chain.

The man gave an impatient gesture, motioning me to come nearer. I sighed. But I also left the wall and crawled, unable to get to my feet, to the end of my chains. They allowed me to reach the cage. There I sat, my legs folded up beneath me, staring with dull eyes at my former captors, leaning one shoulder up against the bars of the cage. Staring, specifically, at the man who I'd recognized as the one who'd carried me when they stole me out of my tribe's camp and who had held my arm while Drakkus tended to my wounded hand. He was the one who'd motioned me to them, the one whose voice had brought me back to the present.

"What?" I repeated. I knew my voice was sullen, but I made no effort to change that.

"What would it take for you to escape?" he asked in a whisper so quiet that I had to lean forward and focus just to hear his words.

The question surprised me. The fact that he was asking about me at all, and not about himself, stunned me. I stared down at the iron shackles on my wrists, ready to say that they prevented any hope of escape, but that wasn't quite true. My wrists and hands were thin enough that with patient, careful work, and a bit of raw skin, I could probably wriggle free of them. No, it wasn't the chains that held me in place.

"It would take either all of you escaping with me or all of you dead. And it would take Rensi severing this," I held up my right arm with its band, "or coming with me."

The man nodded, apparently not at all troubled by what I'd said. "Why?"

"Because Rensi has me tethered to her and she won't leave without you all so we either all die here together, or we all run together and one of those options seems a great deal more likely than the other."

"No. I meant why'd you even try to save us in the first place? You ought to have just let us die." He asked for no pity in those words, made no accusation about my failure. He merely stated it, his now gaunt face carefully passive.

I ought to have. It would have spared me a world of nightmarish memories.

But I hadn't.

Because of my mother. Because of what she'd told me when her and Father first realized that I truly had the gift of foresight and not just an overly wild and mad imagination. Because she'd said that the Fates gave gifts to those strong enough to use them right, to those who would use them to save lives. That was the purpose of my gift, she'd said. Because I'd believed her.

I wasn't sure anymore, though. The number of lives my gift had saved was exactly zero. And if I did as Brym wanted, the number of lives my gift would cost would be innumerable, likely including my own. I wasn't sure I believed her words anymore. They seemed like nothing more than empty comfort offered to her confused and pain ridden twelve-year-old son.

But I couldn't say any of that to those men. So, instead, I shrugged and said, "Because I felt like it."

His quick look told me that he only half believed me. I only half believed myself. Not that it mattered anymore why I'd done anything. With Brym's threat of letting Harysh torment me, I had no heart to rebel.

"You can't let her win, Korris," the man said in the same quiet, measured voice as before.

"I can't' stop her."

The man said nothing, but I felt something brush against my hand and looked down to find him pressing a portion of hard bread into my hand. The sight of it reminded me of my hunger and I was not strong enough to refuse it.

"Why?" I asked, looking up at him, seeing how thin and gaunt they all were. They needed food more than I.

He smiled a very small smile and said, "Because I felt like it."

~ ~ ~

Brym's thread of time was wrong. It was all wrong.

I had only just managed to force myself past my memory of her, through the wall my body threw up in my way as defense against the pain and into her future, when I sensed the wrongness of it. If a slight aura of decay hung about her in the present, it was multiplied tenfold in her future. It was death, I knew without understanding how I knew. The death she wasn't allowed to have yet, clinging to her, waiting for the day the end of the world was seen. It cloaked her in its rotten vapors, darkening every image of her as I followed her thread.

And every moment I lingered in her future felt like a race toward an inevitable horror. Even lost in the throes of her future, my stomach churned at the wrongness of it all. There was no path left to Brym that did not contain multitudes of death and ruin.

I hadn't gone far into her future, but I felt it still, that darkness that she was running towards, a darkness that sprung from her soul. I'd only gone far enough to see her seated by her hot pool of water rocking back and forth and chanting. At least, I assumed it was her mindless chanting. I still couldn't hear anything when I walked time. And still, I could see all that darkness.

It was the wrongness that drove me back into the present that first time. That wrongness left a putrid taste in my mouth even after I'd fully released my hold on her future. It left a burning, fetid scent in my nostrils. I wanted to spit it out and never taste it again.

I gulped down the water I was left in an effort to rid myself of the flavor of death, but it did little good. There wasn't a way to escape it. Not when it was her time I had to walk, her thread I had to follow, her future I had to find. Just the thought created a pit in my stomach and brought bile to the back of my throat. It made cold sweat break out on the palms of my hands. Something horrible lay in her future and I had to find it.

~ ~ ~

I was so tired.

All that waited for me in the present was that exhaustion and the constant, sickening fear that I would be punished for my failure. I came back from the future only to curl up, weak and drained, on the floor, letting sleep claim whatever time I wasn't walking. Even food, left within reach of my chains, held no appeal. More often than not, I simply lay where I was, staring at the wooden bowl until my eyes dropped shut.

My head ached with a constancy that wore through me. It whittled away whole chunks of my mind until I couldn't put together any coherent thoughts. The pain simply never went away.

Never.

My only consolation lay in the fact that, since I'd begun walking time on my own, no spontaneous visions had appeared to me. Still, the tightness inside my head that pulsed and pounded behind my eyes never went away. It grew worse until the only relief I had in it was slipping into the future. That distanced me some from the pain although it couldn't take me away from it altogether.

In the few times I was not only awake but present when Rensi came down to deliver our food, she said nothing to me. If she had been allowed to, I thought she might neglect me entirely. The thin cut I'd given her had scabbed over and the bruise had begun to fade.

Still, whether because she was still angry at me or perhaps because I looked as unapproachable as I felt, she barely spared a glance in my direction, spending all her time after Harysh had left talking to her father's men.

Their voices were always pitched too low for me to hear any of their words, but more than once I caught their pointed gaze in my direction.

They were planning something.

I couldn't bring myself to care.

CHAPTER 26

IT WAS THE RHYTHMIC *tap-tap-tap* of Brym's staff that warned me of her arrival before she appeared in the shadowy doorway at the foot of the stairs. Rensi and Harysh followed after her, Rensi carefully staying just outside of Harysh's reach, and went about their usual routine of seeing to the other prisoners. Brym, however, didn't spare a glance in their direction. Her greedy gray eyes sought me out at once as I sat huddled against the wall, as far from her as I could get.

"Well, well, my little time walker, it's been as good as a month now. Surely you have something for me."

I ground my teeth together and dug my nails deep into the palms of my hands in a desperate effort to keep myself awake. My head wanted to tip to one side or the other or back against the wall. It didn't much care which direction, just so long as it no longer had to hold itself upright. My eyes blurred the image of Brym's approach as they dropped shut only for me to force them back open.

An untouched bowl of cold, congealing stew lay on the floor just inside the reach of my chains and Brym paused beside it, knocking the end of her staff against it with a look of disgust flitting across her face.

"Starving yourself? That's not wise," she said.

It took several tries, but I finally managed to give her a small shake of my head. "Too tired," I mumbled as she raised an eyebrow.

"Hmmm... can't have you wasting away on me now. I've too much use for you." She came toward me again and lowered herself to the floor. "Now, tell me what you've found."

My mouth didn't want to work. I tried to piece together the words I needed to say in my head, but they scattered. "I... I..."

"Yes, you. What have you seen in my future? What gateway must I take first?"

My eyes were burning. I shut them and brought my hands to my head, cradling it as the pain settled in deeper than usual. Present and future melded together into a web of images I could no longer decipher.

It wasn't right.

None of it was right.

I was sure of that. The Fates had never meant for their oracles to chase down futures on their own. They meant only for me to see their chosen visions, nothing more. Every time I ventured past that, some part of me was chiseled away, some part I didn't think I'd get back. It left a growing hollowness inside of me.

And it left me so tired.

So very, very tired.

I couldn't think, I was so tired.

A slap stung the side of my face, and I jolted forward with a gasp. I'd fallen asleep. With Brym right in front of me, demanding answers, I'd fallen asleep. My mouth was hanging open as I blinked up at her, trying to remember what it was she'd asked me.

"What have you seen?" she repeated the question, this time biting off each word for emphasis.

My face scrunched up as I tried once more to sort through the tangle of time that rummaged around inside my head. Too many threads. Too many futures. Too many possibilities.

"Plague." I got the word out, remembering its significance but none of the details. "There is plague from the Outlands?"

"Ah, yes. One of my favorite creatures. Shall I show you?"

I shook my head, both to inform her that I had no desire to see the plague and also to clear my own thoughts.

Through the sleepy haze that hung over my eyes, I saw Brym's mouth pinch up tightly, shifting the many wrinkles of her face. Her gray eyes narrowed, and she reached forward. My body was too sluggish, too much like trying to move a sack of dirt, for me to retreat from her grasping hand. She held my chin and pulled my face toward hers. Turning it to one side and then the other, her tightlipped scowl deepened.

"But my patience is worn very thin with you, my little time walker. You've given me nothing yet and you're not taking enough care of yourself to be useful. So perhaps a demonstration is necessary. Or perhaps a little time with Harysh."

"No," I murmured, stretching my hand out in a mute plea for her to stop whatever it was she planned but it was too late. If Harysh took his whip to me, I did not think I would survive.

Harysh was already moving and to both my shame and my relief, it was not in my direction.

He had the cage door open and another man out of it before the others had caught on to the turn Brym and I's conversation had taken. The man was not as weak as Alkan had been. He fought against Harysh, but it was still a hopeless fight. Another of Brym's men led the way with a torch, revealing yet another creature of the Outlands locked away beneath the mountains.

I turned my head away and squeezed my eyes shut. "I'm trying, Brym. I'm trying so hard. Don't make me watch this." Because I couldn't take any more nightmares. They robbed the restfulness out of the little sleep I got.

She grabbed my chin in one hand again and forced my face to turn toward the scene of murder unfolding before us. From somewhere in the distance, Rensi was screaming, and I assumed someone must have been holding her back because otherwise she would have been tearing into Harysh from behind.

I wished I could do something. Wished that I could at least hold my own head up. Wished that I could say something clever that would remind Brym that I was the time walker, and I could somehow curse her if I wanted to, that I had power she was supposed to be afraid of.

The creature inside that cage was as different from the first as possible. The form was that of a man but instead of flesh it was a thick white smoke that covered it. Wisps of that smoke peeled off the body and dissipated into the air inside the cage.

It took only seconds from the time Harysh shoved his captive inside for a tendril of smoke to find the man's skin. It turned it at once into the white, rotting flesh of the plague. A plague that I'd seen once before in a vision.

Abirell. Sea city and gateway of the west.

It came flooding back to me then.

The vision.

The future I'd found only hours before - at least, I thought it was only hours before. They were the same.

Abirell full of the dead and the dying. Plague stalking her streets like a living thing. It was a living thing. A living thing Brym could send.

I knew the answer to her question.

If I had been Drakkus, I would have counted my own torment as nothing against the need to save so many others. I would have weighed the lives of the prisoners in front of me against the lives of those living in Abirell and I would have saved Abirell. I would have let the men in front of me die to save Abirell. The few for the many. After all, that was what he'd decided about my family, about me.

But I wasn't Drakkus.

I couldn't force myself to endure any more pain than I already lived with. It made me a coward, I know, but the threat of Harysh hung over me, a shadow that followed me through all my waking hours.

And I couldn't sit there and listen and watch as one by one Brym murdered an entire group of men, even ones I disliked. I couldn't take living with the memories of that implanted in my mind. As I watched the plague spread slowly across the man's body, I knew what I would do even if it was the wrong decision in the end. Even if it cost more lives in the end.

I pulled my face out of Brym's grasp and turned to her. "Take Abirell first. Use the plague."

"Kor," Rensi cried out from across the room. "No."

I wasn't sure what it was she wanted. She'd been furious when Alkan died. Hadn't she wanted me to play along with Brym's game? Hadn't she wanted me to cooperate and spare the lives of the others? If she hadn't, then why had she been so upset?

I was too tired, too empty to make sense of any of it. I hated her for not making any sense. I hated her for always finding a reason to be angry with me. I hated her for pretending she was so much better than me even though she'd never been forced to choose like I just had. Mostly, though, I hated her because I couldn't make myself do anything else. Every torment of the last few months piled up, seeking a target, and Rensi was the easiest one.

Brym smiled at me, her rotting teeth just the beginning of the rot inside of her. Her soul had rotted and shriveled up a long time before, I knew. That was part of what made her time so dark.

"Well done, my little time walker," she said and patted my cheek. I lacked the strength to pull away from the touch. "Great things we will do together. We'll bring the end to the world. But for now, rest. You have done well and now you must rest and regain your strength for there will be other paths you'll need to find for me."

~ ~ ~

When I woke, it was to my name being softly called.

I stared at the man in the cage who had called to me, the same one as before. Buried deep beneath the exhaustion that had turned my insides to dust, I was strangely and selfishly glad that he was not the one Harysh had taken to be killed. He'd been kind to me for just a moment and that was more than anyone else in that wretched place. I knew he wanted me to move, to come near to him so that he could speak and not be overheard. But try as I might I couldn't find the will to even lift my head off the ground.

I hated myself too much for what I'd done.

Abirell would fall.

And it was my fault.

It was all my fault for not being strong enough to choose the many over the few. I was a coward, picking the easier of two evils. I wouldn't have to watch the death that would sweep through Abirell. I wouldn't have to feel that pain. That was why I'd chosen the lives of the men in front of me instead. It wasn't mercy to anyone except myself. And the people of Abirell would pay for my cowardice. People I'd never met. People I would never meet.

The man gave an impatient wave of his hand, beckoning me to him but I still didn't budge. There wasn't time for me to move before I heard footsteps descending the stairs. Still lying on my side on the floor, shivering a little because of the cool dampness that never went away that deep inside the mountain, I watched as Rensi and Harysh emerged from the mouth of the stairs.

Rensi was even more careful than she had been before to keep her back to me, ignoring my very existence. That was fine with me. Since I couldn't make sense of what it was she wanted, it was better to just not even try.

"See that he eats this time," Harysh said to her as he, his part of the job finished, started for the stairs again. "If he won't, tell Brym."

Rensi held in her exasperated sigh until he was gone. Stepping just inside the reach of my chains, she held out my bowl of food. "You heard what he said, didn't you? Brym doesn't want you dying yet so you have to eat."

Food wasn't a compelling enough reason to force movement into my body. Which was alarming, I realized, considering that I couldn't actually remember when I'd last eaten. I ought to have been ravenous with hunger. Instead, I was nothing. Just empty and tired and weak. And ashamed.

"Well?" Rensi said, her frustration rising when I made no response. "I'm not your slave even if Brym pretends so."

"Ren," the man who'd woken me said softly. She turned to him. "I'm not sure he can move."

He was right, I knew.

Rensi flashed a doubtful glare in my direction before moving closer to the cage. The whispered conversation that ensued didn't have to be loud enough for me to hear to know what they were talking about. They were talking about me. Weariness overtook me again, though, and I fell asleep waiting for them to finish, forgetting all about Brym's orders to eat.

~ ~ ~

Searing agony in my arm woke me up, a silent cry escaping my lips as I tried to piece together what was happening. It lessened as I struggled to sit up and I stared down at the tethering band on my arm. That was where it had come from. It was the same pain I'd felt when Drakkus compelled my obedience, the same pain I'd run against in the woods during a vision. My watering eyes went from the band to Rensi on her knees just in front of me.

"I'm sorry, Kor. I didn't want to do it, but you wouldn't wake up."

She didn't sound quite as sorry as her words suggested.

"Thought the only reason you kept it on was so that you'd live," I mumbled.

"I said I didn't want to use it. But I've been trying to wake you for the last hour and it's like you were dead."

An hour? It hadn't felt like an hour's worth of sleep. It hadn't felt like more than a moment or two had passed since I'd shut my eyes on the sight of Rensi and Drakkus' man talking. And yet, in that hour I'd relieved Abirell's fall in the form of a nightmare. I couldn't escape it or the weight of guilt that had settled over me since I'd given it up to Brym. Every time I shut my eyes, the sight of its plague-ridden streets haunted me. I should have just accepted Brym's punishment from Harysh. I should have just let Drakkus' men die, even if I'd been forced to watch and forced to endure the nightmares that followed.

"Here," she shoved the bowl of food into my hands, "it's cold now but you have to eat it." I just stared at the thickening contents of the bowl. Rensi sighed, but this time it was less frustration and more resignation. "Brym will know if you don't."

I lifted one spoonful of the stuff up and let the glob drop back into the bowl, my face wrinkling with distaste. Lifting another spoonful, I managed to get it into my mouth. Rensi let go of a breath she'd been holding while waiting for me.

"Why'd you give her Abirell?" she asked when I'd made it halfway through my meal. There was accusation in her tone, disbelief that I'd done such a horrible thing.

Lifting eyes that burned still with exhaustion, I stared at her for a long moment. Long enough that she began to shift and squirm. "I can't save everyone," I said at last, a little horrified at how hoarse and raspy my voice was. "What is it you want me to do? Save them," I glanced over her shoulder at the men in the cage, "or save everybody else?"

"Have you even tried?"

"How would I do that?"

"Have you even tried to find a way to save everyone? You can walk time, Brym says. You can see the future, Kor. You could be searching it for another way to get us out. Have you walked any time trying to find another way out of this? Or do you truly not care what happens to everyone?"

The temptation to hit her again was tempered only by my own impotence at the moment. My face didn't hide my desire, though, and Rensi must have seen it because she tensed and shifted away from me.

"Why would I? So that I can be shoved on to the next person who wants to use my gift? Become somebody else's game piece? I'm tired of it. I'm tired of just being pulled one way and then another."

Tears sprang into Rensi's eyes, but I didn't understand them. "Then start pulling back, Kor. Search your own future and find another way out."

"I can't."

"You're the only one who can."

"No, I can't, Rensi. I can't see my own future. I never could."

Chapter 27

FIND ANOTHER WAY OUT.

Rensi's words had meant nothing to me when she'd first uttered them but in the silence that followed her departure they bounced around inside my head, refusing to let me rest. *Find another way out.* Not find *a* way out.

Another way.

Like she already knew of one way. One way that must not have been incredibly promising if she was so desperate for me to find another. I settled back against the rock wall, wishing I could just slip back into the same deep sleep that had held me for so many hours, but her words held me shackled to the world of waking.

I couldn't search my own future. But I could follow Rensi's and then perhaps I would see what way she planned on taking, if there was such a way. I couldn't think of any.

There was no way a dozen of us were slipping out unnoticed by our captors. Especially not when I remembered Brym's periapt and how much time she spent watching through it. It was easy to guess that a considerable amount of that time was spent watching me as I sat in the cavern beneath the cave rooms she called home.

How do you escape someone who can see anywhere they want? Perhaps if there was a way to kill her. I gave up the thought at once. Brym was over three hundred years old because she couldn't die. Fentra's curse wouldn't let her. Nothing Rensi or I did was going to alter that.

The thought of walking Rensi's time made my stomach churn. I remembered the last time I'd walked it, what I'd seen, what I would have seen if I hadn't fled back to the present. Guilt came with the memory. Her life was little better than mine in Dragon's Nest. That wasn't enough for me to forgive the way she'd treated me the last few times she'd seen me.

It must have been night because the other prisoners were mostly asleep in their cage. Or perhaps they just slept because there was little else to do other than sit and contemplate their fast-approaching deaths. Whatever the reason, the only one still sitting up awake was the only one I'd spoken to at all. He was watching me but pretending not to. I caught sight of his gaze out of the corner of my eye but when I turned to face him, he looked away again, finding interest in something about his hands.

For a few minutes, I just watched him. The food he had slipped to me that once was a kindness I could not forget, not when all around me was misery and cruelty.

His time in Brym's care had left its mark on him. Although he was likely several years younger than Drakkus, it would have been impossible to tell. There was not much about him that would have made him easily recognized in a crowd. His hair was dark, almost as black as mine, making it easy to see the green and yellow strips of leather braided into it. Starvation had left his cheeks sunken in and his face thin.

The food Rensi had forced upon me had done more good than I wanted to admit. I wouldn't have been able to lift my body off the ground before. And I definitely couldn't have crawled the short distance from my rock wall to the end of my chains. Those chains clanged together as I moved, the noise caught in the expanse of the cavern and bouncing off its walls and ceiling until I thought everyone in Dragon's Nest could hear I was moving.

He waited for me to speak but just that short exertion had left me out of breath and dizzy. If Brym was right and I'd really been left for a month to walk time, my strength had suffered for it. That alone would make running away a difficult matter, even if Rensi had figured out a way to escape. I leaned my shoulder against the cage and rested the side of my head on its cold bars.

"She has a plan?" I said, when I'd recovered enough to speak.

"It's not her plan. That's why she wants you to find a different one."

"Yours?"

"Ours," he answered, glancing at the others.

"I don't know if I can find a different way." I pulled my legs up, hugging my arms around them and letting my head rest on my knees.

"You shouldn't."

I frowned. "What is your plan?"

"You said that it would take either all of us dying or all of us escaping together for you to run away. You said Rensi would have to either sever your tethering band or come with you. She can't sever the band without it being noticed. And the chances of all of us being able to escape together are... well, they aren't good." He paused, glancing at the others again. None of them had stirred since I made my way over, but when he spoke again, the man's voice was so soft I could barely hear it. "So, when the time comes, you and Ren are going to run and you're going to forget all about us."

"You'll die," I said, shaking my head. The man had to know that the only reason they were alive was because of me. "Brym will kill you all."

"Korris, we're already dead."

I knew that. I knew it was only a matter of time before Brym murdered her way through them. All the bargains in the world couldn't save them while they were here, because Brym would always find failure or lose patience.

"It won't work," I said, instead of arguing with him about their lives. "Brym watches too much."

"She has to die."

I laughed without mirth. "She can't die. That's her curse. And ours."

The man's brow wrinkled up in thoughtful consideration of my words and it was his turn to shake his head. "*'Until the end of the world is seen.'* That's what she said down here after she had Alkan killed. And you said you've seen it."

So, our plan to escape would hinge on the wording of Brym's curse. I was pretty sure it was doomed already. Even if she could die, how were any of us going to kill her? I had no weapon, no access to a weapon. The men in the cage never came out of it unless it was to be fed to one of Brym's Outlanders. That left just Rensi, but she was always under Harysh's care, and I doubted he'd let her get her hands on a weapon.

"It won't work," I said again.

"It might not. But when the time comes, you need to try. And in order to do that, you need to regain your strength."

"Why would I listen to you anyway?" I said, angry all over again at the way he ordered me. "You're not my friend either, you know. You helped Drakkus capture me."

And offered me food when I needed it. And suggested I save my own life over his. As much as I wanted to cling to my dislike for him, it was growing impossible.

"You should listen to me because there are thousands of people who call Abirell their home and if you don't find a way to fix what you've started with Brym, they're all going to die. And after that, you'll help her find her next target - Ludys or the Iron Towers. That will be thousands more dead thanks to your foresight. Then it will be the plains she heads for next. The plains that are full of your people and your family. She's not going to stop until she ends the world herself in her way. And as long as she has you, and as long as you give her what she wants, no one else stands a chance against her. That's why you should listen to me. That's why, when the time comes, you're not going to waste one thought on us, your enemies, and you're going to run as far from here as you can."

I'd shrunk back away from him as he spoke, that man who's name I did not even know but whose words burned a hole inside me. He was right. I hated that he was right, but I could not deny the truth of it. And since I didn't want to face it, I retreated from it, back to the rock wall of the cavern where I didn't have to listen to any more accusations. It was my fault. I shut my eyes and tried to shut out the man's words.

He was right. And when the time came, I told myself I would listen to him. I would find a way to fix what I'd done to Abirell, to the thousands of innocent people who lived there. For the sake of my own mind, I would fix it.

~ ~ ~

I woke to a sharp pain in my side, the result of Brym's staff prodding me. Curling into myself, I groaned.

"Here I am again, my little time walker," she said, with a cheerful savagery. "And here you are again, not yet ready to walk time again."

It was the same thing she said every time she dragged me out of sleep and forced me to converse with her. My murmured protest was too incoherent for her to make sense of, and I felt once more the sharp rebuke of her staff.

"How am I to end the world and bring in the new one when you laze about like this?"

"Perhaps if he had some fresh air, he'd recover faster," Rensi said over my head.

I made a poor effort to sit myself up and found Brym's fingers gripping me by a handful of hair the next moment. She studied me and I held myself limp and yielding. Rensi had suggested just the night before that our chances, slim as they were, would be better if I was returned to Brym's caves. The appeal of fresh air, even if it was bitter cold and could only be taken by sitting on a thin ledge high above the rest of the world, was enough to ensure my cooperation with that part of the plan.

When Brym released her fistful of my hair, I slumped back onto the ground, shutting my eyes.

"Hmmm," Brym hummed to herself. If I'd opened my eyes, I'm sure I would have seen her tapping her talon-like fingernails against her chin. "Perhaps. Harysh, bring him up."

I stirred again only when Harysh unlocked the shackles on my wrists and even then, I was careful to look suitably drowsy. It wasn't hard. Even though I hadn't walked time in days, and I'd eaten everything I'd been given to eat and slept as often as I wished, my body still suffered from the effects of almost a month of time walking. Harysh grabbed beneath my arms and pulled me to my feet. I let my head hang, my chin resting against my chest and made no effort to take a step.

Brym's fingers closed in on my chin, tipping my head back and forcing me to look her in the eyes. Her nails dug like blades into my skin, and I tried to pull back.

"How soon do you think my plague will reach Abirell, my little time walker?"

"I don't know. You didn't ask me to find that."

"True. I did not. But surely you saw something that gave you a hint? A harbor full of boats? Leaves in the trees?"

I thought about what I'd seen. The vision was the clearest image I had of the event, and I couldn't recall it without recalling Drakkus and everything that had happened. It all seemed an eternity ago. That vision had left me as near despair as I'd ever been.

"Well?"

"There were buds on the trees. So, it must have been springtime. Still at least two months away."

Brym smiled, blackened teeth looking and smelling worse than I'd remembered. Maybe I didn't really want to go back up to her caves. "Not so long, little time walker. You've walked so much time in the future, you've missed how much has passed here in the present."

She laughed then at the consternation on my face. She laughed, and patted her gnarled hand against my cheek. And I tried without success to pull away from the touch as if that alone could corrupt me with the same death that clung impatient to her. She laughed harder then.

"When will you accept the fact that you belong to me?"

Never. I would never accept that.

For the first time since reaching Dragon's Nest and making my bargain, the need to escape overcame all other thoughts. Rensi was right even if I would never admit it. It was time to start pulling back.

Even if it meant abandoning those that I'd tried to save before.

CHAPTER 28

WIND WHIPPED ACROSS MY face, tugging my hair to one side. It had grown long enough to brush against the tops of my shoulders, and I hated the feel of it. It drew my thoughts toward my mother, who would never have let it get so long. Such thoughts awakened an ache inside me that I'd been too empty to feel before. Not even that, though, could take away from the satisfaction of breathing fresh, clean air for the first time in over a month.

I shut my eyes to keep the wind from stinging them and let the coldness of the winter air cleanse my lungs. I only wished the sun could also have been shining that day. It was the sun, I think, that I missed most. My skin had lost much of its usual color, turning pale without the sun's warmth and light.

"Just because I've let you come back up here doesn't mean I won't send you back down if you fail to cooperate again," Brym said, standing just over my shoulder. She couldn't allow me to have even one moment of peace, it seemed.

"I know."

"I want you to walk time again for me by the next moonless night."

I nodded. Having so thoroughly lost track of how much time had passed, I had no idea when that would be, but I wasn't about to ask her and invite further conversation.

The tapping of her staff faded as she walked back inside, leaving me to myself. Well, mostly to myself. Only a few feet away, Rensi sat, still obligated by Brym's demands to take care of me. Her face was turned away from me, although a fresh set of bruises was still visible. These spread over her ear and disappeared into the collar of her coat. There was a paleness to the rest of her that made her look frail and wasted.

I'd begun to think that she planned on ignoring me like she had before when she scooted across the ledge to sit beside me. She didn't say anything, and I wondered if I even wanted her to. Since every time we spoke seemed to end with one or both of us angry, perhaps it would have been better if we didn't bother.

Remembering how quick she'd been to laugh and the efforts she'd made to befriend me before Harysh and his men had attacked, it was hard to believe that she was still the same person. She certainly didn't look it – all thin and worn through. I wondered if I'd changed as drastically.

"When is the next moonless night?" I asked, pinching some of the loose, worn leather of my pants between my fingers. I'd lost weight. They had fit much better months before.

"Three nights."

"That's not long."

"No, it's not."

Rensi's legs were dangling over the edge again, swinging in and out with a carelessness that I found a little unnerving. I had to try my best not to look down or my head would start spinning. Allowing any part of my body to hang over the edge would have been inviting trouble.

Our silence wrapped around us so thoroughly that I forgot she was sitting there. I let my mind wander back to my conversation with Drakkus' man. The nameless man who'd carried me away captive months ago and who'd given me his own food and who'd suggested I leave him and the others to die days ago. I wished I'd tried to speak to him one more time before Brym brought me back up, if only so that I could learn his name at last. I wished I knew if he blamed me for Alkan's death. I wished I'd asked him if he regretted any of his part in my capture. It might not have made anything better, but I wanted just one of them to apologize for the wrong they'd done me.

Warm skin brushed against my hand, startling me. I looked down to find Rensi pressing something small and cool and hard into my hand. She leaned in close, her breath hot against my ear.

"In two nights, Brym needs to die."

Her words sent a shiver crawling up my spine. I froze in place, not daring to breathe for fear it would sound too loud, too harsh and bring Brym running to see what was going on.

"Put this in her pool of water but do not touch it or the water."

I closed my hand around the object Rensi had pressed against my palm. It was a small vial, easily hidden inside my fist. I nodded without looking at her.

"How did you get this?"

"We're not the only ones who want a three-hundred-year-old woman dead."

Suspicion clawed at me. "Who?"

"Harysh."

"Harysh?" It was hard work keeping my voice low and quiet. "Harysh is the one who gave you this? He's probably already told Brym all about it." If we were getting help from him, our plans were already as good as ruined.

Rensi sucked in a sharp breath. "He wants her dead because while she lives, he can't have her power. He's the only blood she has left and when she dies, he inherits her periapt and her position. He's not going to tell on us."

"And you believe him? Ren, I know what he's done to you. Why would you ever accept his help?"

Her face went white, blood draining from it faster than I could finish my words and I realized I'd made a dreadful mistake in my confession. "You know?" she said, a deadly softness in her voice. "How?"

"I...," I bit my tongue. It had felt like a violation of sorts when I'd walked her time. I was sure she would agree. "I didn't mean to see anything. It was just... I didn't know who else's time to walk. Brym told me I had to do it and I didn't want to see what happened to my family. I thought yours wouldn't be that bad."

"So, you just watched Harysh..."

"No. No, I didn't. I came back to the present. All I saw was him hitting you."

"You saw him hit me and then you turned around and did the same thing to me," she said. Bitterness wove its way into her tone.

"You shouldn't have said what you did to me then."

"So, it's my fault."

I moved further away from her, needing the distance. "All of this is your fault. If you hadn't shown up in my tribe, spying on me; if you hadn't gone running back to your father to tell him who I was and where I could be found, none of this would have happened. I'd be safe with my family, and you'd be safe with yours. So, yes, it's your fault. You started all of this."

If I'd thought her angry before, it was nothing to the fury lighting her eyes now. She leaned toward me again, this time facing me. If she'd been crying, I'd have pitied her. But there wasn't a tear in her eyes, just coldness. And there wasn't a catch in her voice when she spoke, just icy malice.

"At least I'm not a coward who can't even take a little pain. Our whole world's broken and you're probably the only one who can fix it, but you can't be bothered because you just want to be safe and comfortable."

For a moment, I was too stunned by her words to answer. If there had ever been a time in my life when I was completely safe and comfortable, I did not remember it. "That's," I stammered out at last, "that's not true."

"Isn't it?"

She turned away from me then, crossing her arms over her chest and staring out at the darkness that was the Outlands. Her anger at me and mine at her was almost enough to drive me back into the musty cave with Brym. At least Brym didn't pretend to be on my side sometimes. I always knew where I stood with her, I never needed to question her motives or actions. The only thing that kept me outside still was the need to discover the rest of Rensi's escape plan.

We might have sat there in silence forever if we'd had the choice. Rensi wouldn't even look in my direction and

I fought to gather up enough nerve to ask her for more details. It was remembering that she'd just called me a coward and my own intense desire to prove that wrong that finally came through for me.

"If Harysh knows the plan, he's not going to let us run. He'll want me just like Brym does."

"Leave Harysh to me," was all Rensi said about it.

That wasn't exactly reassuring but I didn't think I would get anything more out of her.

"You ought to be inside resting, time walker," Rensi said. I bristled at the mock sweetness in her tone, but she pretended not to notice. "After all, we wouldn't want you too tired and weak to play your part."

If her purpose was to send me inside, she failed catastrophically. I hunkered down against the cliff wall, determined to outstay her. Determined, that is, until a burning pain began in my wrist and crawled up my arm.

"Don't you dare," I said. She had no right. No right to abuse the tether she'd kept on me. She accused me of wanting to be safe and comfortable all the while keeping herself alive through that tether. She was worse than Drakkus ever had been.

"Get inside," came her command, compelled through the tether. There was nothing I could do to resist it, no fight I could put up that would change the fact that my body was already obeying.

"I hate you so much."

She ignored me.

CHAPTER 29

TIME CRAWLED BY.

Hour by hour by hour. I watched it pass while sitting outside Brym's cave. I marked it by the number of times Rensi came to prepare Brym and I's meals. I measured it in the eagerness on Brym's face as the hours mounted, bringing us closer to the moonless night. And I worried more with the passing of each of those hours. The vial, tucked safely away inside my pocket, grew heavier with every moment.

There was so much about the plan I didn't know. So much Rensi wouldn't have told me even if I'd had the chance to ask, although she made sure I didn't get the chance. I saw her only when she came to cook, and no words passed between us then. So many things could go wrong. Harysh would never let me go any more than

Brym would. And if Rensi was planning on outsmarting him, I thought our chances of success were even slimmer. Harysh would see through her plans, would see through her attempted deception and tricks. He'd wait until Brym was dead and then sweep in and lay claim to me as his time walker.

Hope and despair danced round and round inside of me, twisting me up into all sorts of knots until I could barely keep my eyes shut to sleep at night.

As the hours piled on top of each other and the second day dragged on towards its evening, I was sure Brym could hear the way my heart thudded against my chest. I was sure she could see the pallor of my face and know that something was amiss. I was sure she could taste the fear that I sweated out of me on my palms and forehead. The vial in my pockets had turned to stone and I was sure the lump it formed screamed for someone to notice it.

The temptation to walk Brym's time again, to see if we stood any chance at all, washed over me. I wanted to know, and I didn't want to know. I wasn't ready for the finality of that knowledge. It was something to be feared.

Rensi came and made our supper, avoiding me as carefully as she had been since our conversation on the ledge. Brym noticed and watched with a wicked gleam in her eyes as the two of us held our hatred for each other out in the open. It was probably best that way, leaving Brym to assume we could not stand the sight of the other person. Perhaps then she would believe we could never have a plan to escape together. For my own part, it was hardly an act. I could never forgive Rensi for her insistence on keeping the tether in place. I could never forget her accusations, made from the safety of never having to share my experiences. And I most certainly could never forgive Rensi for using the tether to compel me.

"You are better," Brym announced over our supper of stewed mountain goat and stringy vegetables. "Perhaps we will not wait until tomorrow night. Perhaps you will walk time for me tonight."

Behind me, waiting to clean up our meal when we were through, I felt Rensi stiffen. In front of me, Brym pulled out her periapt and cupped it in her hands. Unlike the other times I'd seen her take it out, she did not shut her eyes. She did not commence her swaying or her chanting. Instead, she peered at me from across the fire, a burning suspicion darkening her gray eyes.

"What is it you want me to find?" I asked, hoping to forestall any accusation or questioning.

"Walk Harysh's time. Tell me how his future connects to mine. Tell me if what I've witnessed in the present through the dragon's eye will come to pass in the future."

I frowned. "What have you seen him do?"

"Plot. Against me."

"Oh. So, you want me to see if he actually acts against you."

Brym's face split open in her grotesque smile. "No. I know he will act. I want to know the best way to make him fail and suffer for it. He forgets I cannot die. He is not the first to have forgotten it." Her smile faded and for the first time since I'd met Brym, sadness flickered across her withered face. "They all turn in the end. Mother and Father, sister and brother, grandchild. They all turn against me."

She dropped her periapt and let it fall against her chest outside her shirt. It clanged softly against the small key that she kept looped onto the same leather thong. She motioned for me to set aside my almost empty bowl and I did, turning just enough as I laid it on the ground beside me to catch Rensi's eyes. Her posture was controlled, no outward sign of the turmoil I saw in her eyes. I only hoped Brym didn't look her way.

"Now, go on. Walk his time and tell me what I must do."

Harysh wasn't a difficult memory to bring to mind and I'd spent so many long hours deep inside the mountain walking time that it was nothing to push past the now paper-thin wall my body built in protest and enter the stream of time that swept me into the future.

But it wasn't Harysh's thread of time that I followed.

When I opened my eyes again, Brym was still watching me.

"Well? How shall I deal with the fool when he raises his hand against me?"

"Take him beyond the guard fires that hold back the Outlands. Stake him there for all to see and let Dragon's Nest witness his death at the hands of the Outlanders." I was good at making up futures. I'd had to do it before often enough. If you tell enough of them, the lies can slip out easier than the truth.

Brym's fingernails tapped the dirt beside her as she considered my words. I began to worry that she could see through my deception but then her smile returned, and she rubbed her hands together. "Good, my little time walker. Very good. A sacrifice to the Outlands and a reminder to all who live under me. Very good, indeed."

She started to her feet, and I took the opportunity to glance around at Rensi only to find she was no longer in the cave. I was never sure how long it took for me to walk time, but apparently it was long enough that she'd cleaned up our meal and returned to Harysh's cave for the night. Which meant I had to assume our plan was still our plan. And I had to assume that she would return after dealing with Harysh, however long that took.

That left me to deal with Brym.

Brym was already gone, disappearing into her room full of steam and warmth and her pool of water. She'd never forbidden me from following her in there, but I'd only ever gone in when she'd told me to.

Slipping the vial free from my pocket and pressing it against the sweating, shaking palm of my right hand, I started toward the entrance. Before I pushed aside the heavy animal skin that hid the opening and trapped the heat inside, I took two or three deep breaths. If either Rensi or I failed, it was over. And I could only imagine what new horrors Brym would invent as punishment for our attempt.

I stepped inside.

Heat washed over me, leaving my skin damp with steam and sweat. Brym was seated in her usual spot, her bare feet and legs dangling in the water. I guessed that her eyes were closed because it was impossible to make out such details through the dense curtain of steam that hung between us.

"Missing my company, are you?" Brym said.

"A question for a question?"

"I would have thought you'd wish to rest after walking time again this evening."

"My head hurts too badly to sleep," I said, quite honestly. It was throbbing from my brief venture into the future. But even if there'd been no pain at all, I couldn't have slept. "I'd rather be distracted."

"Very well. My question first."

"Fine." I leaned forward, brushing my fingers over the surface of the water, sending ripples across the pool.

"Who tried to steal your gift?"

"A chieftain from a plains' tribe."

Brym shook her head. "Try again. An actual answer this time."

I wasn't sure why I was reluctant to reveal the name of the man who'd tried to rob me of my gift. Perhaps it was because I'd trusted him, just briefly. Perhaps it was because I regretted, just a little, keeping silent about the attack on his camp. Perhaps because I was coming to understand that my gift meant a little more than I'd grown up thinking it did. None of those reasons mattered, though. He was dead anyway and if all went to plan, Brym would join him in death.

"Drakkus."

The smile Brym gave me told me she'd known the answer all along. "Your turn, my little time walker. What question do you have for me tonight?"

The stopper in the top of the vial came off with a soft pop that I hoped wasn't loud enough to be heard across the pool. I ran my tongue over my dried lips as I leaned forward a second time. My knuckles barely skimmed over the surface of the water in a repetition of the motion Brym was already used to seeing from me.

In the wake of my hand, drops of amber liquid spilled out and mingled with the warm water. I lifted my hand just enough to make sure I wasn't in any danger of touching the poison or the water it mixed with. My heart pounded in my throat as I withdrew my hand and leaned back, letting the empty vial roll away behind me, hidden from sight by the dense steam that swirled around us.

"What," I started, my thoughts frozen by what we were attempting. I shook my head to clear my thoughts and tried again. Rensi hadn't said how fast the poison would work. She hadn't said how long I would have to wait to see if we were successful or not. Actually, there was a lot about her plan that she hadn't said. It was too late to worry about that, though. "How long did you know Fentra?"

Brym's face darkened at once at the mention of Fentra. "I thought I'd made it quite clear that she was not to be brought into this anymore."

"That was before I knew you tried to steal her gift. You talked about her down in the cavern then."

"Because I felt like it."

I waited; my eyes drawn again to her legs soaking in the pool of water. I couldn't see anything happening. But I wasn't even sure I was supposed to see anything happening. If Harysh had lied to Rensi... If he'd betrayed us...

We might have already failed.

Beads of sweat tickled the back of my neck, soaking into the collar of my worn jerkin. I brought a hand up to rub it away and to release some of the tension that wound itself up inside me.

"Fentra was my sister." Brym's answer was spoken so softly that I almost missed it.

"What?"

"You heard me. She was my sister. The gifted one."

"She was your sister and you tried to steal her gift?" I tried to imagine either of my brothers turning on me like that, I tried to imagine them doing to me what Borssa and Drakkus had done. Missel might have teased about it and Jarris would have laughed at the joke, but both would have been appalled by the idea of actually doing such a thing.

"It ought to have been mine." I might have imagined the slight slur I heard in Brym's voice as she answered. Desperation has a way of tricking one into believing whatever will give them hope. If I'd thought the Fates would listen and care, I might have prayed to them to make the poison work. "Now it is my turn to ask a question. Why have you tried to poison me?"

I gulped and my heart gave a wild thump. Choking out my denial, I said, "What makes you think I have?"

"Just because I cannot die doesn't mean I cannot feel death when it comes to visit. And there is death in this water."

"How would I have gotten my hands on poison?" My voice sounded high in my ears.

"What do you think I saw Harysh doing that made me suspicious?"

It had to work. It had to work. I pounded the words into my head as if saying them enough times could force them to be true. It had to work, or the entire world was doomed. I shut my eyes and fought the temptation to walk Brym's time. If it did work, I needed to be present and I didn't need to add to the pain I already suffered. If it didn't...well, if it didn't, I would know soon enough and walking her time wouldn't change the outcome.

The room slowly filled with the sound of Brym's soft chuckle, the one that echoed the deep madness in Brym's mind.

"Foolish, foolish boy. To think you could cheat Fentra's curse. I cannot die until the end of the world is seen."

"Just that?" A fragile hope stuttered to life inside me. "That's what Fentra said? *'Until the end of the world is seen,'* those were her words?"

Her laughter was swelling, her mouth opened wide, gaping holes where teeth ought to have been. "Those very words, my little time walker."

She was laughing still when the first trickle of black blood crept out of the corner of her mouth and rolled down her chin. She was still laughing when a web of black started spreading up her legs and down her arms. An awful stench filled the room and still she laughed. The poison seemed to cause her no pain although the sight of its steady advance was enough to make my stomach heave.

I covered my nose and mouth with my hand and stared in horror as the poison did its work. A voice in my head whispered that I should feel some remorse or guilt. The greater part of me remembered everything Brym had done, everything she'd said, and couldn't deny that death was long overdue. Scrambling to my feet and backing toward the door, I watched as she fell back, still laughing.

"You forgot, Brym," I said, any pity I might have felt drowned out by hatred and turning me into a different creature entirely, "you can't die until the end is seen, but I've seen the end."

CHAPTER 30

SHE DIED LAUGHING.

She died believing she couldn't.

She died while I watched.

She died and within moments, three hundred years' worth of rot and decay descended on her body.

There was nothing left of Brym but a pile of dust and furs and a necklace with her periapt and key.

There was nothing left but me.

I stared at that pile of dust, trying to convince my mind that it had been a person only moments before. Trying to convince myself that the reason there was no longer a person there was because I'd killed them. The thought crossed my mind like a brilliant flash - what would my mother think of me now?

Silence echoed where her laughter had died with her.

Brym was dead.

I crept around the pool. My footsteps fell silent on the dirt. I reached the spot she'd last occupied and my hand reached for the leather thong with its periapt and key. Green and gold light shone from the periapt, coloring the white steam around it. The periapt was useless to me. I shared none of Brym's blood. Harysh could use it, though. And Harysh would use it if he could get his hands on it. I stared down at the pile of dust and then at the pool of water. The pool whose bottom I could not see. I wondered if I tossed the periapt into the water if Harysh would be able to retrieve it again or if that pool went down forever, reaching beneath the mountain.

"Kor?"

I spun around to find Rensi standing in the doorway. Only, I didn't recognize her at once. Blood splattered the front of her, a bloody handprint staining the side of her face. On her back was a large pack and tucked inside her belt were at least three knives. Her eyes were glassy and bright and unblinking. She stared at me and I at her for several long seconds.

"Is she...?"

"Dead. Gone."

"Where?" Rensi cast a glance about the steam filled room, no doubt searching for a body.

"No, gone."

"Where?"

"She just turned to dust." I could not recognize the sound of my own voice in my ears. It was a stranger's. What I'd just done was the action of a stranger, not myself.

Rensi came toward me, Harysh's keys in her hand, found the right one and unlocked the chain from my ankle. Then she spun around. "Let's go. We have to be gone by the time anyone realizes they're dead."

"Wait," I called after her as she disappeared into the front room. When she didn't seem to hear me, I followed her and caught her by the arm. "Wait. Harysh?"

"Dead. But not gone. If anyone goes in, they'll find his body. Come on." She pulled free from my hand and started for the entrance once more.

"Wait."

"What now?"

"Not that way."

I didn't take the time to explain as I looped Brym's necklace around my own neck, snatched Harysh's keys out of her hand and headed for the staircase that led deep into the mountain. Her footsteps pounded close behind me so I knew she followed as I descended those stairs for what I hoped would be the last time. At the foot of the stairs, torches burned on either side of the opening. I stopped long enough to loosen one from its mount then I hurried on to the center of the cavern where a large cage stood.

"Kor, what are you doing? This isn't what we planned," Rensi whispered in my ear.

"Isn't it? I wouldn't know, since you didn't actually tell me what the plan was. You were too busy using the tether to get me to do what you wanted. Besides, you're the one who wanted me to find a different way."

"Did you?"

I bit my lip and worked it back and forth against my teeth. What I'd found in the future wasn't clear. Nor was it promising but still..., "I don't know. But it's our best chance."

We'd reached the cage by then, with the men inside it still half asleep and unsure of what was going on. If Rensi had more she wanted to say, she bit her tongue and kept it to herself. Instead, she stole the keys back out of my hand and went to work trying to fit one of them into the lock.

"What are you doing, Ren?" It was the man I'd spoken to, the one who had told me to run and forget about them, the one who'd laid the blame of what would happen to Abirell at my feet.

"Getting you out, Edronn." A key slipped all the way into the lock and Rensi twisted it until it came undone with a click. "Kor's idea, not mine."

"Korris...," Edronn started to speak.

"Hurry," I said, cutting his protest off. "If we waste time arguing, none of us get out."

Few of the men looked strong enough to walk but I suppose the prospect of freedom and survival were all the strength they needed because they all managed to step out of the cage on their own. Rensi started to lead them back to the stairs.

"No, not that way. We'll be caught. Our only chance is through the cavern," I said.

Rensi gave me a funny look but, aside from pausing to grab a second torch, she didn't hesitate to follow me as I took the first few steps into the deep shadows that hid the rest of the cavern from our eyes.

It was a good thing we couldn't see what lay inside the shadows until we were already well on our way. After having watched Brym feed two of her prisoners to her Outlanders, we all knew that she kept the monsters caged in the dark recesses of the cavern. But that was nothing compared to what the dim, dancing light of the torches revealed as we stepped past those first two beasts. In the cage of the one, the enormous creature still paced, snarling, and gnawing on the bones of Alkan. In the second was...

...Nothing.

I stopped, Edronn almost running me over because I was so abrupt. Plague, or whatever name that monster went by, was gone. Not even the remains of the man Brym had fed to it remained. She'd already set it loose to find Abirell. Killing her hadn't happened in time to stop her from doing that. Abirell would still fall unless I could find a way to outrun a monster. I'd known that. It was seeing that empty cage with my own eyes that sent a jolt of guilt through me. Nothing else I did would change what I'd already done.

Shaking the weight of that thought away, I moved on.

And almost wished I hadn't.

Screeches, hisses, howls, and snarls surrounded us as we hurried on into the darkness. Cage upon cage, row upon row of Outland creatures greeted the light of our torches with snapping jaws and a racket loud enough to rouse a corpse.

The cavern stretched on and on, a never-ending prison. The further we went, the lower my heart sank. There were so many. So many that I could scarcely make my mind believe what my eyes were seeing.

When Brym had spoken of bringing the Outlands in, I'd thought she meant to open the gateways and let them in. I hadn't realized that she had an entire army of them already caged and waiting beneath her. How many years had she spent collecting her army? How many innocent people had she fed to them to keep them alive?

I stopped a second time, my breath coming hard both from my exertion and from the weight of realization. A knot of pain was beginning to tighten inside my head. A knot of pain that I was very familiar with but hadn't felt since I'd begun walking time on my own. As I held my torch up and took in the sight of Brym's legions, the last of my hope fled.

"Keep moving, Kor," Rensi said, giving me a shove.

"It won't matter."

"What won't?"

"Killing her. It's..."

I got no further. The vision had me in its grasp.

Screams filling the air. A roar, a howl. Teeth tearing into flesh. Outlanders ripping through the plains' tribes as they journeyed north, following the herds. The tribes were broken up, the people mingled in chaos and disorder. Some trying to fight. Others trying to flee. Children watching their parents die and parents watching their children die. Blood staining the lush green grass of the spring.

A shift.

No longer was I seeing the plains and the massacre there. I was back inside the mountain. Fire raging all around. And that voice again. Those words again. *"Free me."* No longer full of sorrow and pain and anguish. Full of hope, instead. Anticipation. Excitement even, and exultation.

Pain scorched my arm and the future wavered like shattering glass before my eyes, dissolving into a dark cavern and a group of men gathered around me in a tight circle and Rensi standing just in front of me, her hand resting on an alabaster knife.

"Stop. Doing. That." I bit each word off through gritted teeth, glaring up at her from where I sat on the floor. The pain eased off.

“Well, don’t have a vision while we’re trying to escape.”

“I can’t control them.”

She blinked. “Isn’t that what you’ve been learning to do?”

I shot her baleful glare and staggered to my feet, not deigning to give her an answer, not bothering to explain the nuances between visions and time walking. She wasn’t worth explaining anything to, not after what she’d just done to me. The Fates chose when to send their visions and they seemed to have little regard for how inconvenient their timing was in my life.

Edronn had apparently moved fast enough to pluck the torch out of my hand before I let it slip out of my grasp. He lifted it now to get a better look at my face and I couldn’t even attempt to conceal the despair in my expression.

“Killing Brym and Harysh hasn’t changed anything. Someone else here is going to set these Outlanders free on the plains. They’re still going to kill everyone.”

“How do you know that?” Rensi asked.

“Because I just saw it, right before you decided to drag me back here with that,” I gestured toward her periapt. “But I’ve only seen it once.”

“What’s that supposed to mean?”

“Once means there’s still time to change it. There’s still something we can do to change it.” At least, that’s what Brym said. I never knew whether to believe her or not.

Aside from the impatient and hungry noises coming from the beasts around us, there was not another sound. Even Rensi couldn't think of a response.

"How do you kill them?" Edronn asked at last.

"Fire," Rensi answered. "Not just any. It has to be kindled with firedust. At least, that's what Harysh said."

Edronn stepped out of our tight huddle and approached one of the cages. He dropped to one knee and ran his fingers through some black substance sprinkled on the ground.

"This is firedust?"

Rensi nodded. "Harysh said that they put it on the floors inside the cages and all around them to help keep them contained."

A look passed between the ten men, the sole survivors of Drakkus' band of almost fifty. They were no ordinary plains' men, that I was sure of. The idea had grown on me and came to fruition in that moment as I watched them. They'd fought too well, too organized. They'd endured too stoically. They'd agreed to sacrifice their lives for the sake of everyone else far too willingly.

Whoever they were, I didn't know, and I didn't understand. But I had a grudging sort of respect for them that inhabited a space inside me right next to the hatred I'd stoked for weeks. Edronn nodded once at whatever it was they communicated in that silent exchange.

"Ren," he said, turning to face her, "you and Kor are going to go. You're going to keep going until you reach the end and you're not going to wait for us."

"Edronn..."

"We'd only slow you down, anyway. None of us could get far."

"I'm not leaving all of you behind. Father wouldn't want me..."

"That was always the plan. And your father would not want you to die here."

"*Your* plan," Rensi said. She turned on me, a silent plea in her eyes. "I thought you said we could get out this way."

I said nothing. I'd given them the best chance I could find in the future. I'd given them the ability to choose. I'd given them their freedom even if it was only for an hour. It was theirs to do with what they would. I couldn't give them any more than that. No one could give them more than that.

CHAPTER 31

THERE ARE MOMENTS WHEN time itself seems to stop working. When the whole world pauses. When the sun halts its advance across the sky and the moon and stars are stayed. As if that one moment contains too much, decides too much. As if that moment is not enough for the enormity of the events held within its confines.

I knew, more than anyone else standing in that circle, what our chances of surviving that night would be. I knew what would happen when Edronn touched the flame of his torch to the first bit of firedust. I knew what was coming, both for myself and for those men. For that one, long, stretched out moment, I stared at Edronn, and I knew he knew too. Not because he'd seen it, but because he'd always known. No words passed between us, just knowledge. The knowledge that only one of us would see the rising sun.

Then the moment passed. Time ticked on as steadily as if no calamity was about to unfold itself.

The first fire was kindled with a *whoosh*.

And I ran.

Following the guiding light of Rensi's torch, I fled as the cavern behind us turned itself into an inferno with the help of Edronn and the others. Firedust erupted with a sound like thunder into flames so hot they burned blue. Heat rolled over me in waves, breathing down on my neck the way a predator will chase down its prey. The rushing sound of air being sucked into the force of the fire competed with the wild, desperate cries of the creatures trapped inside the growing furnace. The acrid scent of burning flesh seared itself forever into my memory.

In the chaos behind us, Edronn and the others set fire to one cage after another. The firedust caught and spread with amazing speed. It was scattered so thickly across parts of the floor that it carried the fire along faster than the men could move, engulfing everything in its path and turning it to ash. It was what I'd always imagined dragon fire to be like.

From somewhere beyond the roar of flames and shrieks of dying animals, shouts filtered through the air. Our escape had been discovered. Our destruction, noticed. I was too busy fleeing to give space to the small doubt that nudged its way into my mind. The firedust was so much more flammable than I'd thought. And its appetite was insatiable.

Metal, rock, and beast. All succumbed to the voracious heat of the flames.

The ground trembled beneath my racing feet. Smoke saturated the air and turned it heavy, filling my throat, my nose, my lungs. Dust and bits of broken rock rained down from the roof of the cavern as the flames licked higher, searching for more. Always searching for more.

Ahead of me, Rensi pressed on, plunging ever deeper into the darkness, past more cages, more foul beasts. On and on Brym's army of the Outlands stretched, a number innumerable. I wondered if there really was an end. I wondered if there really was a way out or if my time walking had only shown me what I wished for and not reality. Rensi's torch barely touched the darkness but behind us the light of the raging fire swept the shadows away. It was getting closer. I could feel the heat of it on my back.

Glancing over my shoulder, I tried to see if any of Drakkus' men still moved through the flames, but I could make nothing out. Against the blinding brightness of the fire, the darkness was blacker than night. The death throes of Outlanders writhing in the pain of being burned alive were silhouetted against the light of the fire. Giant forms that belonged to beasts thrashed inside their melting cages. But there were none moving that could have belonged to a man. My eyes watered with the heat that stung them and the smoke that burned them and perhaps with the realization that Edronn and the others had still died, despite my best efforts.

The distraction of looking back slowed me down. A rumble in the ground as rocks cascaded down from the crumbling ceiling threw my balance off.

“Kor,” Rensi cried out as I tripped and only just managed to stay on my feet. She reached out her hand and caught mine, dragging me along. “Faster.”

“I… don’t… know… if we… can… outrun… it,” I said between gasps.

Rensi was too out of breath to answer but the worry in her eyes told me she thought the same thing. Pain stitched up my side and I wanted to yield to it and rest, but the fire was rushing ever closer. And if the fire didn’t catch us, the avalanche of rocks falling all around threatened to crush us. I wasn’t sure how much further the cavern ran before it emptied out into the far side of the mountain. I wasn’t sure if I could make it even if it were only a few feet away. Weeks of captivity in Brym’s care, weeks spent walking time and not taking care of myself, had left me with so little strength.

“What’s… that?” Rensi's voice panted in my ear, barely audible over the flames and the thunder of the collapsing mountain.

I dragged my eyes up and followed her gaze. Cold metal gleamed in the wall of rock that rose up to confront us. Cracks splintered the rocks and as I stared, they began to shift and crumble in on themselves.

"Door." I fumbled for the necklace I'd put around my own neck before coming down to the cavern. The small key slipped through my shaking fingers several times before I managed to get a proper hold on it.

"Hurry... Kor. It's getting... too... close."

I could feel it too. My breath was coming up short, the air being sucked into the fire leaving us too little left to breathe with. The heat scorched the skin beneath my clothes as I shoved the key into the lock, silently praying to the Fates for it to work. I twisted it. No audible click could be heard over the noise that we were drowning in. But I felt it give.

"Push," I said just as a fit of coughing tore through me. I threw my own shoulder against the heavy door and beside me Rensi did the same.

It didn't budge. The rock frame around it had shifted and the door stuck fast. I let out a cry of pain and frustration as my shoulder collided with it a second time. Tears streaked down Rensi's cheeks, mingling with the blood and the ash and soot. I'm sure my face was just as bad. The fire continued its pursuit and the skin on my face tightened with the scorching heat. More rock and dirt fell. I wondered which death would be worse - being roasted alive by fire or crushed to death by the weight of a mountain.

"Kor?"

"I'm sorry." This wasn't how it was supposed to end. Fire, yes. The world ended in fire. But I wasn't the world. And I wasn't ready to die. I wasn't ready to be buried alive in a burning mountain with only Rensi beside me. Without the chance to see my father or my mother again. Without feeling the sun on my face again and without watching the wild herds of horses as they galloped free across the plains. Without ever getting the chance to see the sea. I wasn't ready to say goodbye to my life.

I shook my head. Driving the despair away. Clinging to the last bit of hope even as the fire came to claim it. Leaning back against the door, my feet braced against the dirt, I tossed my head back and yelled to the Fates that played with our lives, "Why'd you even give me a gift if you're just going to let me die?"

The Fates didn't listen to humanity. They watched us from afar and played their games with us. They used us and toyed with us. But they didn't listen to us. They never had. They never would.

But whether they listened or not, the door gave way beneath my weight, and I fell back through its mangled frame.

Cold air rushed over my burning skin, soothing it. Snow clung to my clothes as I lay on my back, staring, not at a fire, but at a star filled sky. Rensi lay beside me, equally stunned and gasping. Half sitting up, I could see the doorway that had spat us out onto the snow-covered mountainside. It was well hidden in the rocks, only visible by the faint glow in the metal. The glow I could only assume came from the fire still burning fiercely within. Whatever had opened the door had shut it once we were through, shutting us out of the monster we'd ignited.

The ground shook and bucked beneath me as I got to my feet and my eyes traveled up over the door to the rest of the mountain. A strange orange light rose from the earth of the mountain, growing stronger. Snow melted, turning to slush and then water, running down the heaving side of the mountain as the heat that was trapped inside fought its way out.

Another tremor ripped through the ground, stronger than the last.

"RUN!" I yelled at Rensi, pulling her up from where she still lay stunned on the ground.

The mountain was coming alive beneath our feet. Like a giant awakened it shifted and swelled and groaned as we ran and staggered and tripped our way down its side. I could not tell where the shaking of the ground ended and the trembling of my legs began.

The slope of that mountain gave way to the rise of the next. We pushed on, hand in hand, holding each other up and pulling each other along, all animosity between us forgotten in the primal need to escape and survive. A crack that sounded as if the earth itself had split open shattered the night air and threw us forward onto our faces.

Rolling over enough to catch a glimpse, I watched as fire spewed out of a gaping hole near the top of Dragon's Nest, cutting a brilliant orange swath out of the night sky high above our heads. It had devoured all it could in the heart of the mountain. And still it hungered.

"What have we done, Kor?" Rensi whispered in horror.

The worst of it was that I didn't know.

I hadn't looked that far into the future. All I knew was that the army of Outlanders was no more. The people of the plains, my people, were saved. I hadn't thought to look at how many others would die instead. Nor could I care in that moment. The people of Dragon's Nest would have willingly followed Brym's path of destruction so long as they ended up on top.

"That's all of Dragon's Nest," Rensi went on. "Without them..."

Without them, a gateway to the Outlands was open. "It's only this half of Dragon's Nest," I said. "The other half still stands untouched."

We stood there when we ought to have run. We stood there as ash and cinder and fire and rock rained from the sky. We stood there and watched the fall of Dragon's Nest, and I tried hard not to think of the end of the world that I'd seen so many times in my visions.

CHAPTER 32

NIGHT GAVE WAY TO DAWN.

Fire gave way to sunlight.

Ash and smoke hung heavy in the air, creating a haze that played tricks with my eyes.

Rensi and I had put many hours between us and Dragon's Nest. Many long, silent hours spent running and then walking and then running again. All fear of pursuit had vanished the moment I'd seen Dragon's Nest erupt in a spectacular vision of flame against the night sky. Even if some of the people of Dragon's Nest survived, they would be in no condition to hunt down captives. Especially since the fire had wiped out every trace of our existence there.

A fine layer of gray and white ash covered the snow, even as far away as we were. It stuck to everything. My hair, my skin, my clothes. I could taste it on my tongue and feel its grittiness in my throat every time I swallowed. I couldn't draw in a breath that wasn't tainted with the smell of smoke.

A glance at Rensi in the newfound light had me recoiling from her. The effect of ash and soot, of blood and tears combined to make her resemble some ghoulish creature. She met my eyes, her own dull with weariness and horror. Not a word had passed between us since we'd turned our backs on Dragon's Nest for the final time.

We ought to have been running still, trying to get out of the mountains and back to the plains as fast as we could. It was all I could do to put one in front of the other without crumpling to the ground in a heap of exhaustion. I'd stripped myself bare trying to outrun that fire and there wasn't enough left inside of me to be afraid or even concerned about what had to happen next. There wasn't enough left inside me to think about what had to happen next although there was the niggling reminder in my head that there was a lot I needed to think about and none of it was pleasant.

Rensi was little better off than I. She kept pace beside me, her ragged breathing sometimes the only reminder that I had of her presence. I felt her gaze on me from time to time and the few times I caught her guilt flushed her face. I'd have thought nothing of it if it weren't for the way in which she watched me, as though I had transformed into something she did not recognize overnight. Probably she blamed me for the fall of Dragon's Nest.

We didn't run. We trudged, one weary step at a time, around the side of the mountain we'd found ourselves on. There was no trail. No way of knowing exactly where we were going. We only knew that we had to get as far away as possible. The ground was rugged, rocks jutting up, hidden by the snow and waiting to trip our shuffling feet. It was uneven and resulted in a never-ending battle to balance on the slope without slipping on the slick patches of ice and snow. Spring might have been close, but in the mountains, winter wasn't ready to give up its hold just yet.

Cold air embraced us. At first, it had been a relief from the burning heat. But as it chilled the sweat that clung to my skin, I began to shiver. It made me wish that I'd thought to grab some of the furs that had lain around Brym's front cave room. Wind battered us, pushing at us hard as we fought our way through deep drifts of snow and navigated frozen streams.

To our right, the darkness of the Outlands provided our only landmark. I glanced at it often, listening to the howls that rose from the darkness that was immune to the light of the morning sun. Nightmares, Harysh had called the beasts that dwelled in the Outlands. Nightmares wasn't a strong enough word to describe them. I'd seen what they could do.

As those first faint touches of gray and pink and yellow painted the eastern sky that peeked out at us from in between the mountains, my legs buckled beneath me, and I could go no further. The pain in my head from the vision finally forced itself into the forefront of my attention. I'd pushed it off for hours, numb to it as all my thoughts were bent on escaping.

"Rensi, I have to rest," I called to her when it became clear she had no idea that I was no longer at her side.

She turned around and frowned. "Not yet, Kor. We should keep going. We have to find Mother and Otho. We have to tell them..." she trailed off with a catch in her voice. She'd spent so much of her time around me angry while at Dragon's Nest that it had been easy to forget that she'd watched her father killed and still mourned his death. Straightening, she pushed a strand of her hair back as if to push away the sadness. "Anyway, we need to get back to Mother and Otho."

"Well, I can't go any further." It occurred to me then that I'd never bothered to inform Rensi of what I'd seen when I walked Rayka's time. Since our every conversation had dissolved into an argument of one sort or another, I'd kept the knowledge to myself both out of spite and forgetfulness. Rensi still believed them to be with Borssa. At the moment, I was too tired to explain the truth.

Instead, I watched her every move with caution as she took in my refusal. She had Drakkus' periapt within easy reach and I'm sure I saw the temptation to use it flit across her face. Then her shoulders slumped forward in resigned defeat. Our run had left her as tired as I was, although she didn't suffer from the same headache as I did. She let the heavy pack she'd been carrying all night drop to the ground and sank down beside it, facing me. One hand pressed to the ground, she furrowed her blood and ash covered brow in concentration.

"There's no one following us so I guess we can rest for a bit."

"How do you know?"

She gave me a quizzical look. "I'm a tracker, Kor. I can feel if something is coming. I know I've said that before."

She had. It had just never been at a time when I could give her words much thought.

"So, you're gifted too?"

"Obviously. But," she scowled down at the ground, "it's not like yours. Every tribe has at least one tracker." That was true. Jarris was one of ours. It made him invaluable when searching for the herds. "And it doesn't hurt me."

"Like my gift does me."

She nodded. "I've never met any gifted that were hurt so much by their gift."

"Almost makes it seem like it's not a gift," I mumbled, giving voice to a thought I'd had many times in my fourteen years. Fifteen years, I corrected myself. If we were really so close to spring, then I'd passed my fifteenth winter. If I'd been home with my family and tribe, there would have been a celebration. A rite of passage into manhood. Instead, I'd spent it chained inside a bleak cavern, surrounded by monsters, both human and beast, so lost in the future that I hadn't even known how much time was passing. Sadness filled me at that realization.

Rensi shifted enough to reach into the pack she'd brought. The moment she brought a round golden colored loaf of bread out of it, my stomach remembered itself and growled with hungry anticipation. Rensi broke the bread in two and tossed one part of it to me.

I was only halfway through my portion when Rensi brushed the crumbs from her mouth with the back of her hand and looked out over the mountains that remained between us and the plains, her face turned away from me.

"Do you think there's any chance the others... you know... made it out?" Her voice was soft when she spoke.

I wanted to tell her there was. Usually, I could lie with ease. Usually, I could tell someone whatever it was that they wanted to hear and I knew she wanted to hear that there was hope.

"No," I said. The lie wouldn't come.

"You could," she paused and shrugged, still turned away from me, "you could walk their time, see if they made it out."

"Rensi." I didn't want to refuse her. But more than that, I didn't want to go back and walk the time of men as they died. I didn't want to witness any more death. I'd had my fill of it. Besides, there was only one time I was planning on walking still, just as soon as I worked up both the strength and courage, and that would be the last time I did it. I'd decided that in the long hours of the night that we'd spent running. Brym had taught me to do it and I wasn't taking any part of Brym with me except for the necklace I still wore around my neck. "I..."

"I know. Don't bother."

We slept then, too exhausted to even argue. Too exhausted to keep watch. Any other mountain dweller might have been on the hunt for us and we would not have known until they were dragging us out of our sleep. I suppose that ought to have been a little frightening, but I didn't see how anyone could be worse than Brym, so I slept without any nagging fear.

~ ~ ~

Rensi must have spent weeks planning our escape, although she hadn't bothered to tell me about it. The pack she carried was laden with enough bread and dried fruits, vegetables, and meats to keep us from starving right away. The knives that she must have stolen from Harysh, she split between us, giving me two of the stolen blades to me while keeping one and her father's periapt for herself.

A knife isn't the best weapon to go hunting with. Most animals would never let you get close enough to them to use it. But having at least that scant means of defending myself brought my spirits up.

It wasn't until our second day, when we were finally out of the haze of smoke that emanated from Dragon's Nest, that I decided it was time. I caught up to Rensi as she took the lead and fell in step beside her. She gave me the same look that she'd been giving me since we'd run. A look that said she had found a new piece of me, and she couldn't figure out where it fit.

Considering how much she'd had to say every time we'd seen each other in Dragon's Nest, she'd been almost silent in the last two days. Her silence was worrisome. But not worrisome enough to prevent me from holding my right arm out in front of her as we hiked up a steep incline.

"You can take it off now," I said.

She gave me a blank look and then her eyes widened with understanding. Her gaze skimmed away from me. "Kor, I..."

"Don't. Don't give me another excuse about why you have to keep it on. I've belonged to one person or another long enough. I want it off. I want to be free."

There was that look in her eyes again, troubled and doubtful. Something about me disturbed her and had since we'd escaped Dragon's Nest. "It's not an excuse. But maybe it's better if I leave it on for now."

"What?" I stopped.

"I just mean... Come on, Kor, right now we just need to get back to Mother and Otho. I'll take it off then."

She kept walking, not noticing that I'd not moved. "I don't want to go back to them. Besides, they aren't even with Borssa anymore."

"I know you don't, Kor. I know that. But...," she sighed, throwing her hands up in the air and stopped finally, turning to face me.

Her decision wavered and I pressed. "Rensi, just take it off. I'm tired of being a prisoner. I want to..."

"Wait. You said they're not with Borssa anymore. How do you know that? And where are they?"

"Take it off and I'll tell you."

Her hand hovered close by the hilt of the periapt blade and I took another step back, bracing myself for the pain and the compulsion, hating that she had that power over me. Hating how willing she was to use it. Drakkus wasn't blameless, but at least he had only used the periapt's compulsion once. He'd allowed me to refuse him.

With another, heavier sigh, she turned around and started walking again. "If they left Borssa, they'll have gone back to Uncle Mitkas. That's where we'll find them."

I didn't move. It wasn't until she'd gone far enough for the tether to send its pain up my arm and force me forward that I took my first step after her. As the day went by, I got no closer to her, maintaining that distance no matter how it hurt my arm. The pain made me furious, and I wanted to be furious with Rensi. She tried to slow down, tried to walk back toward me, but I either stopped or backed away until she finally gave it up.

~ ~ ~

"If we can get to my uncle," Rensi said, breaking the days-long silence between us, "I'm sure he'll give us shelter."

Suspicion gnawed at me as I twisted the tethering band around on my wrist. For six days, we'd trekked our way through the mountains, getting nearer to the plains with every step. For six days, I'd stayed as far from her as the tether allowed me while we walked. At night, it was impossible to maintain the distance. The threat of wild animals and other mountain people demanded that one of us stay awake at all times. I'd taken to just ignoring her efforts to speak to me then. But, after six days, the plains were within sight, and I was desperate enough to try asking her again and that meant speaking to her again.

Rensi was watching me, trying not to look anxious for me to respond, to say something. She was like Drakkus in that way, pretending that the hurt was worse for her than me. Pretending that my anger at the tethering was undeserved.

Still, after I'd waited long enough to make her shoulders sag, I answered her. "And your uncle is in the south with the other tribes?"

She gave me a funny look then, as if I'd said something rather unintelligent. "No. He's in Ludys."

Ludys. The city Drakkus knew just from my description. The eastern gateway to the Outlands.

"I don't understand. Why isn't he with a tribe?"

She stopped and turned to face me, shaking her head slowly. "Kor, we're not plains' people. Did you really think we were?"

Fragments of a conversation, whispered in the mouth of Borssa's cave, came back to me. Words spoken for ears other than my own. My head spun with them. Something about a brother stealing a crown. Drakkus' crown. Threads wove together, forming a picture I'd been too caught up in troubles to see. Blood of a king or blood of a future king. Rayka married a king. Otho was the son of a king.

"Kor?"

"You're not plains' people," I said, restating her words in a stunned voice. "You're not plains' people, you're city dwellers. Your father was king of Ludys. Your uncle stole his throne."

Rensi sighed and raised an eyebrow. "You just figured all that out? And anyway, Uncle Mitkas didn't exactly steal the throne. He just wore the crown better than Father did. At least, that's what Mother said."

"I can't go to Ludys. I have to get back to my own family. It's been months since I've seen them." I held my arm out to her a second time. “Please, Ren, just take it off.”

She didn’t respond right away. Instead, she stared at my outstretched arm and chewed her lip between her teeth and twisted a loose strand of hair around her finger.

“Kor, I still need you. If I take you back to Uncle Mitkas with me, he’ll listen to me. He can protect you, Kor. We can stay there while he sends someone to warn Abirell about what Brym sent. And I can ask him to send word to your family, too. We can just wait there until Mother and Otho make their way back. It’s what Mother said to do if we got separated. We were to go back to Ludys. And if I bring you with me...”

“I’m not yours, Rensi,” I cried out, furious at her words. I wanted to reach out and shake her until I could make her see my side. “I’m not yours to just drag around wherever you want. You said the only reason you kept this on was so that you would survive. Well, you don’t need that anymore. Take it off.”

I looked up and was surprised to find tears fighting to spill out of her eyes. “If I let you go, you’ll run. You’ll leave me here alone.”

“I won’t. But that should be my choice. Not yours.”

“You’re the only friend I have right now, Kor.”

I shook my head in disbelief and stepped away from her. “This,” I held up my arm, “isn’t friendship and you know it.”

She didn't move when I walked away. I went as far as the tether would let me and then a little farther. The pain was subtle, just enough to keep me seething as I sat down and settled against a rock.

The sun was setting and with the coming darkness it was dangerous to be so separated but I didn't care. I didn't care about anything except that Rensi was holding me captive still.

She would let me go, I told myself. She had to let me go. As much as she missed her family, she had to understand my longing for mine.

~ ~ ~

Left to myself for the night, I finally set my mind to the task I'd been avoiding. Since I'd learned to walk time, I'd put off walking any of my family's. Fear always outweighed desire and I'd been helpless to do anything about what I saw anyway, trapped first by the tether and then by Brym and her schemes.

I was still helpless, still trapped by the tether, but curiosity was winning, and I had to know. I had to know if my family had survived the winter or not and where I would find them if I could just persuade Rensi to free me.

It would be the last time I walked time.

The last thread I followed.

The last future I chased.

Reaching back into the recesses of my memory, I found my mother's thread and, trepidation gnawing at me, I followed it.

~ ~ ~

A soft murmur and a warm touch against my hand woke me many hours later, jolting me out of a deep sleep. Rensi knelt in the snow in front of me, tears running silent streams down her face, cleaning away some of the ash and grime. In her hand was the alabaster knife. Her other hand rested on my wrist, a single finger running across the markings of the band as she whispered her words too softly for me to make them out.

I stared at the band as it came apart and dropped away from my wrist. It hit the dirt with a soft thud. In gentle, cleansing waves, the binding of the tether rolled off of me. Its release was quiet, the absence of nudge, a touch. Its presence, that I'd grown so accustomed to in the months since Drakkus put it on me, was gone. My mind and body were fully my own once more.

I was free.

I couldn't stop the smile that spread across my face. I almost couldn't stop the exultant laughter that rose up inside of me. I was free. For the first time in so many months I was on my own again.

Rensi turned away, brushing away the tears that betrayed how difficult her decision had been. "Don't tell me you won't run and leave me because I know you will."

There was nothing harsh in her tone, only sorrow. But she was right. Telling her I would stay would have been a lie. So, instead, I asked her, "Why?"

"You were right. Why do you always have to be right?" She swiped an angry hand across her eyes. "This," she picked the band up from where it had fallen, "isn't friendship. And I've no right to force you to come with me."

"Thank you." You shouldn't have to thank your captor for setting you free, but the words slipped out anyway.

Rensi let out a soft huff of breath, almost a laugh but not quite. "Don't pretend you don't still hate me."

Since it was true, I didn't bother to respond. I rubbed the spot where the tethering band had sat for so many months. The skin underneath was completely white and soft, untouched by the sun or wind. Free of it, I started to consider my own future; unseen, I had no way of knowing the outcome of any of my own choices but at least I was free now to make my own choices. It was like a breath of fresh air after so many months of captivity.

"Kor," Rensi said, breaking into my thoughts, "when you go, be careful."

"I know. I'm not going to be anyone else's prisoner. Not ever again."

"No. I mean, be careful what you choose to do."

"What do you mean?"

Rensi bit down on her lip hard enough to make the skin around it go white. "I mean that I think we were wrong. I think we thought the curse was a thing. And we thought we could break it. But I don't think it is a thing. I think you're it. You're the reason my family was torn apart. You're the reason Dragon's Nest fell. You're the reason Brym's death was even possible. I think," she paused, weighing her words out carefully, "I think you are Fentra's curse."

Chapter 33

I WAS GONE BEFORE THE sun rose.

Free to follow my own course at last.

With the weight of captivity gone, I felt as if I could soar.

By the time it reached its zenith in the sky, the windswept plains spread out like an ocean of grass before my feet. On my back was a portion of the remaining food Rensi had packed. She'd left it sitting beside me, bundled in an animal skin, waiting for my inevitable departure. I had waited until she appeared to be asleep, although I'm sure she wasn't. It was easier that way, for both of us.

In my mind, I recalled the future I'd walked the night before, the last I ever planned to walk, and smiled. My family still lived. They were safe. They would be safe for some time. Whatever danger threatened them from the Iron Towers no longer existed.

My steps carried me south, into the heart of the plains, the call of home and family too strong to ignore. It would take me weeks. They would be long, lonely weeks. But with Drakkus and his ritual, Brym and her demands, behind me, the daunting task of crossing the plains alone was less frightening than it would have been months before.

Other titles by S. T. Hobbs

The Divalian Chronicles –

Prequel ~ The Thief and the Slave

Book 1 ~ The Traitor's Alliance

Book 2 ~ The Last Chief

Book 3 ~ The Courier's Apprentice

Book 4 ~ The King's Successor

www.ingramcontent.com/pod-product-compliance
Lightning Source LLC
Chambersburg PA
CBHW031437240626
47154CB00001B/301

* 9 7 9 8 9 8 5 7 2 1 7 6 8 *